BLUEBLOOD

BY THE AUTHOR

Crime Fiction

{The Marty Singer Mysteries}

A Reason to Live

Blueblood

One Right Thing

The Spike

The Wicked Flee

{Standalone}

Stealing Sweetwater

{Short story collection}

one bad twelve

Psychological Suspense

The Kindness of Neighbors

Fantasy & Science Fiction

{Short stories}

"Sword of Kings"

"Assassin"

"Seven Into the Bleak"

"Trial By Fire" (anthologized in *Walk the Fire #2*)

BLUEBLOOD

A Marty Singer Mystery

MATTHEW IDEN

Text copyright © 2012 Matthew Iden
All rights reserved.

Published by Thomas & Mercer, Seattle
www.apub.com

Amazon, the Amazon logo, and Thomas & Mercer are trademarks of Amazon.com, Inc., or its affiliates.

ISBN-13: 9781477829424
ISBN-10: 1477829423

Printed in the United States of America

For Renee, who continues to make the whole thing possible.
For my family.
For my friends.

In valor there is hope.
—*Tacitus*

CHAPTER ONE

My hands are behind my back. The thumbs have been lashed together with a short length of zip tie, the kind of stuff that gets tighter the more you pull at it, and right now the short strips holding my thumbs and pinkies are so tight that the tips of my fingers feel like they're going to burst like hot grapes. It must be bad, since I lost feeling in the rest of my hands hours ago.

Blood is rolling down my hairline, making a half circuit along the side of my face like a scarlet moon before cutting in and dribbling over a cheek and into one swollen eye. The blood comes from a six-inch trench going from the top of my scalp to just north of my forehead. Someone put it there with a two-foot length of rebar wrapped in electrical tape. The tape wasn't there to soften the blow; it was to give him a better grip. The deep, diamond-shaped cross-hatching that gives rebar a better bond with cement is what laid my scalp open, but it was the force of the blow that cracked my skull. I'm nauseous and can smell my own vomit, which is puddled in front of me. That probably means I'm lying on the floor. I can't tell since my good eye is closest to the ground and any time I move my head, I scream.

The pain doesn't stop at my face. My ribs feel gone, too, half of them snapped like plastic straws. It's hard to breathe, though that may be from the blood running down my throat. The bruises up and down both arms aren't worth mentioning, but my gut is aching and my testicles have ballooned to the size of tennis balls, which is what happens when they've been kicked repeatedly.

The beating, as brutal as it was, wasn't systematic. For what it's worth, this was done in a frenzy; it wasn't an interrogation and it wasn't about payback. Nobody asked questions or took time to gloat. They just wanted to hurt. Small consolation, but the guy with the rebar hadn't done anything a hospital couldn't put back together with enough time and health insurance. No one had lopped off a finger or spooned out an eye. It might take weeks or months or years, even, to heal. But as long as I have a pulse, I have a chance.

I'm still thinking that when he comes back. Quietly this time, maybe to watch me struggling to take a breath. I don't hear him at first. Blood has pooled in my ear and my pulse is loud. Then a shoe scuffs a wall or a doorframe or a piece of furniture and I turn my head toward the sound instinctively. But a small click, like a gear falling into place, tells me my chance is done, and I want to yell, to tell them, no, I need to see my boy and my wife and—

◆　◆　◆

"You see it?"

"I see it," I said, putting the last of the crime scene photos down. I was happy to get them out of my hands. A year ago, they would've been nothing special for Marty Singer, homicide cop, especially after thirty years in Washington, DC's police force, the MPDC, but time had given me some distance from that life and I realized I didn't have quite the same perspective on things now that I did then. "This is bad."

"It is," Sam Bloch said. He was a lieutenant with the MPDC Major Narcotics Branch, the catchall division that did most of the city's drug enforcement. Bloch was a slim, tall man with a pinched face and a small, pencil-thin mustache. With his black hair and dark eyes, he could've been Clark Gable's twin, but with a nose so broken that the tip almost touched one cheek, he would've had to have settled for being the stunt double.

"Who was he again?"

"Danny Garcia," Bloch said. He picked up the photos and slipped them back into a manila envelope, conscious of the people passing our table at the Java Hut. We had a nook in one of the duskier corners of the coffeehouse, but still, no sense risking someone tossing their biscotti just because they happened to see a stack of eight-by-ten glossies of a mutilated body.

"Danny was one of our best undercover guys," Bloch continued. "Hispanic, obviously, so he was a huge help with the Latino gangs, but it was more than that. He was good because he fit in anywhere. Fast talker, knew the street, great instincts on when to step it up or back off. He could put together a buy over in Southeast where even the black cops won't go, for Christ's sake, and the next day be out in Hicksville, picking up a John Deere full of weed from some good old boys spitting Skoal between their last two teeth."

I took a sip of coffee. It picked a fight with the bile Bloch's pictures had brought forth. "Looks like somebody wasn't buying that night."

Bloch lifted the cover of the folder, glanced at the top picture again, then let it fall back shut. "I couldn't believe this when I saw it. We get our share of outrageous shit—more than our share—but Danny was good and this kind of . . . butchery doesn't happen every day. Not anymore. Maybe in a gang war or when people are sending a message about who's boss, but no one was going to mistake Danny for a *chavala*."

I frowned.

"A rival gang leader," Bloch explained. "Danny was going on fifty. The only gangsters that old are either in maximum lockup or dead. Most of today's honchos are in their twenties."

"Maybe someone just made him." I gestured at the folder. "This was vicious enough to be driven by cop hate."

Bloch shrugged, a short roll of the shoulders. "It's possible. Anything is. But, like I said, he was good at what he did. Too good for me to believe he just happened to slip up."

"When he was on a case, did he pose as a junkie? Or a buyer?"

"A little of both," Bloch said, picking up a sugar packet and turning it rhythmically in his hands, corner to corner. I had smelled the cigarette smoke on him when we'd met. Judging by the urgency with which he was spinning that packet, it must've been a while since his last puff. "He'd break in as a user, see who was dealing. Then he'd graduate to hand-to-hand deals. Penny-ante shit, but it gave him an idea on who was willing to play ball. Final stop might be to set up a mid-level buy for a small cut or to get two dealers together, see if they would do business."

"Why such small beans?" I asked. "He was a twenty-year pro."

"For just that reason. If we used Danny once on a big bust, he was burnt. He'd have to sit at a desk for two years before he could go back on the street. Instead, I kept him simmering somewhere in the middle, which worked. We set up three major busts a year without compromising him."

"How'd he like that?"

"Not much," Bloch admitted. "It was blue-collar work. No glory, none of that lining up millions on a kitchen table with a dozen AK-47s and getting on the evening news. He wasn't happy about it, but he knew he was doing good work."

I wondered about that. Cops are people, too, and it can be hard to see the light at the end of the tunnel if you're asked to turn the crank on the same wheel day in, day out. But I kept that to myself. "What was he working on when this happened?"

"I don't know."

I raised my eyebrows.

"Danny demanded a lot of rope," Bloch said. "He kept his own list of snitches, dealers, leads. I got him to agree to weekly updates, but he missed them all the time and even when we did connect, he was cagey about everything."

"So you don't know if this was part of a case or not."

Bloch nodded. "There's no reason to think that it wasn't, but which one? New or old? Was he just fishing, or was this the next-to-last meet before he set up a bust? He left us crap for notes. I've gone over all of them and don't have a clue."

I spun my coffee cup around by the handle. Bloch's fidgeting was contagious. "When you called, you said you had something that made you nervous, something you wanted to talk over. Garcia's killing is bad, really bad, but—no disrespect—it's something you should take up with Homicide."

"They're on it. In their own way."

"So why me?"

"What do you know about HIDTA?" He pronounced it *hide-uh*.

"High Intensity Drug Trafficking Area," I said. "A task force. Feds and locals from all the Metro jurisdictions get together to compare notes on drug traffic, trying to keep the left hand in touch with the right."

"Right. Crack dealers don't pay attention to county and state lines. Dope that winds up in DC didn't magically sprout there, it had to come through Virginia or Maryland. And it didn't start there, either, of course; those are just distribution points along the chain."

"Every city with a population of two or more's got that problem."

"Sure, but we've got two states, a city, and a federal jurisdiction in a ten-mile radius. Dealers know what a headache it is for a DC cop to try and get a warrant in Maryland or set up a wiretap in Virginia. And if they decide to go up to a sunset overlook on the George Washington Parkway to do a deal, well, that's a national park, right? All of a sudden it's a federal case. Then the DEA and Park Service police are in charge, even if every ounce of the dope from that deal winds up on K Street in the District."

"Enter HIDTA," I said.

He nodded. "Virginia cooperates with Maryland cops who work with MPDC who partners up with the DEA. Jurisdictions melt away, everybody shares the work and the glory, bad guys have nowhere to hide."

The wood of the booth popped and creaked as I leaned back. "Must look good on a poster."

"It works better than you'd think. There are a lot of egos, sure, and the higher up you go, the crustier everyone gets. At the soldier level, though, everybody's on the same side."

"It sounds beautiful," I said. "Before I tear up, though, what does this have to do with me?"

"I'm mid-level at HIDTA. Danny worked directly for me. The important point is that, while I might be a DC cop, I'm also dialed in to all the other players. I hear things, I see things I might not get to if I was buried all by myself in Major Narcotics."

"Okay."

Bloch reached into a briefcase resting on the floor and pulled out a thick handful of manila folders identical to the one he'd produced on Danny Garcia. He pushed them across to me.

Inside the top folder was a single photo of another crime scene, another murder. It was a black man in his boxers and a T-shirt. He had a belly and soft, unmuscular arms and legs. Salt-and-pepper hair cropped close. He'd been beaten badly—the bones of his arms and hands were broken and bent out of shape—and shot in the back of the head, apparently with a small-caliber round since there wasn't much of an exit wound to speak of. Blood and probably urine had puddled around the body. It resembled a lot of other scenes I'd seen over the years.

I flipped the photo over, revealing another. A white guy in a tank top and shorts, young and in good shape. Red hair. Pale. Freckles.

Or maybe it was blood. Superman tattoo on his left deltoid—a little ironic. Like the first body, he looked like he'd gone through a thresher, with arms out of joint and a lot of bloodletting. The photo had been taken from near his feet, so I couldn't make out details, but two small, quarter-sized black dots in the side of his head testified to more gunshot wounds. His fingers were broken and mangled.

I turned that one over. Beneath, a third scene, a third body. Or fourth, counting Danny Garcia. Like the first, this was a black man, sprawled on a blacktop parking lot or road. There wasn't much context, but comparing him to a nearby car door, he was enormous, maybe six and a half feet tall. Two-seventy, two-eighty? He was fully dressed, sporting jeans and a University of Maryland polo shirt. Blood was hard to discern against his ink-black skin and the asphalt. Unlike the others, he hadn't been beaten. I couldn't see evidence of a gunshot, but on a body that big, it could be anywhere.

"Bloch, I don't want to look at this," I said. But I cycled through the pictures again. I could feel Bloch's eyes on me as I peered at the glossies, closer this time. Not surprisingly, I'd focused on details at first glance. Looking for setting, characteristics, gunshot wounds. I shuffled back and forth between the three photos several times, then added Danny's, checked, and glanced up. "The beatings. They're crazy. Vicious. Faces broken apart. Arms and hands and feet twisted, pulled."

Bloch nodded.

"Except for that last one," I said. "That one's odd man out."

"Maybe. But for the rest, they're the same. It's the beatings. They were all pre- and postmortem, or so the coroners tell me."

"Coroners? Plural?"

He reached across the table and flipped the stack over so that I was looking at the first body again. "Terrence Witherspoon. MPDC beat cop, First District."

"PSA?"

"One-oh-six."

I grimaced. One of the worst in Southeast DC. "Okay."

He flipped to the next photo. "Brady Torres, Arlington PD." Flip. "Isaac Okonjo. Montgomery County Sheriff's Department, Maryland."

I felt a twist in my gut that had nothing to do with the coffee. "Danny Garcia. MPDC Major Narcotics Branch."

Bloch nodded, looking at me with eyes like twin lumps of coal. "You see it?"

"I see it," I said, but not liking it. "Someone's killing cops."

We were both quiet for a minute, looking down at the photos. The noise swelled around us as a small group of businessmen and -women swept in to get an afternoon latte, bringing a wash of spring air in with them that seemed out of synch with what Bloch and I were talking about. The scenes of death seemed more appropriate for the moldering back of the coffee shop than the scent of flowers from a late May morning. The group chatted and laughed about some dustup at the office, then left in a swirl of coffee and perfume.

"You heard about these through HIDTA?" I asked, once the noise had subsided to a more comfortable murmur.

"More or less," he said. "When Danny was killed, I couldn't find what he was working on, like I told you. But his killing wasn't random. No one does that kind of damage over a mugging. So I started to ask around through my connections with HIDTA. Anyone heard about random killings, especially with an MO like this?"

"And these came back?"

"Not at first," Bloch said. "I wasn't looking for cop killings, I was just working backwards from the MO. The beating, the weapons, ballistics. But nothing came up. Eventually, these did, but I didn't really look too close at first. No pattern. Only one cop was MPDC and none of them worked Vice. Only Torres was even close."

"What was he?"

"Arlington gang detail. MLA, La Eme, Aryan Brotherhood."

"Then what?"

"I asked for the files on Witherspoon and Torres and that's all I needed to see. Okonjo's rolled in after that, but it was just icing on the cake. I already knew I was dealing with a multiple."

I rubbed my eyes. "Besides the beatings, do you have any other connections? What did ballistics get you?"

"A .22 for Witherspoon and Torres. The slugs weren't recoverable for Garcia or Okonjo, though they were small caliber."

"Match on the .22?"

He nodded. "Same gun. Registration went nowhere."

"What about the beatings?"

"Done with whatever was at hand. The rebar, a chair, a trophy. No other connections. None of these cops worked together or knew each other as far as I can tell."

I closed the manila folder and squared it with the edge of the table. "As far as you can tell? Isn't MPDC or Arlington or someone all over this?"

Bloch's shoulders slumped and I saw for the first time how tired he was. "Someone? Like who? Who looks into multijurisdictional cop killings?"

"The FBI, for one."

"And big-foot each jurisdiction's own Homicide Department? Piss off half a dozen local chiefs? Not on your life."

"I thought you said HIDTA meant everyone played nice-nice."

"Sure, for drug busts. Multiple unrelated homicides that, if proven to be related, would indicate that no one's been aware of a serial killer who's been on the loose for a couple months? Not so much."

"Really?"

He sighed. "I went there, Singer. Really, I did. I went down to the Bureau office, laid out the pictures just like I did for you."

"And?"

"And they told me to get back to them when I had more evidence. Wasn't a serial. Their profilers took a look and said these were vanilla, on-the-job 'events.'"

"And the victims' departments?"

He shrugged. "They'll take the info I give them and they'll cooperate if it's in the best interests of *their* case, but no one wants to take on all of these murdered cops at once. They'll spare no expense to track down the guy who killed their own. But work overtime for another department? Sure, if they get to it."

"Are you telling me you've been doing this on your own?" I asked, incredulous.

"You got it," Bloch said. "Funny, huh? You and I can see it, plain as day. And maybe they can, too. But no one else wants to touch it."

"So, they're all handling just their own department's murder? But nothing else?"

"While there's a guy out there, offing cops," Bloch said, nodding. "And he's got his pick of ten or twelve different districts to do it in. None of which will cooperate with each other."

I blew out a breath. "I think I see where I come in."

Bloch gave me a weary smile. "I figured you would. Once I caught on I was being stonewalled everywhere, I started asking around, seeing if anyone would take this up as a hobby, do the legwork for me. I can't do this thing by myself."

"Any takers?"

"What do you think? But I got a couple of nods about you from some guys I know in Homicide. Great track record, a good cop. They said you retired, but still had a hand in."

"Ah," I said. "That thing last year was kind of foisted on me, Bloch. I didn't ask for it."

"I get that. I didn't ask for this, either, you know? But sometimes things come looking for you. What am I supposed to do with this—walk away, act like everyone else? What happens next week or next month or next year when I hear about another cop getting shot and tortured? Send a memo? I owe Danny more than that. I owe these other cops more than that."

I looked at Bloch. I didn't need the rah-rah, brothers-in-arms spiel. But he had a point. When you see something's broken, you fix it. Just because it isn't any of your business doesn't mean it's less wrong. Or any less your responsibility to do what you can to help. Even if I didn't already have debts to pay in that regard, I knew about this now. And that meant I should do something about it.

I held out a hand. "Let's see those files."

CHAPTER TWO

If the Charles E. Smith auditorium seemed like a university basketball arena converted into a semi-respectable graduation hall, it's because that's exactly what it was. The George Washington University staff had made a valiant effort to make the place exude the kind of storied tradition that universities are supposed to have on graduation day. They'd draped flowing royal-blue sashes over everything and portraits of the Father of Our Country gazed serenely down on us, but I was still sitting in a fold-down bleacher seat with my knees touching the back of the row in front of me and bumping elbows with my neighbors on either side. At six three, I'm not exactly NBA material but I would've had to saw my legs off mid-calf to fit. I wondered for maybe the thousandth time why makers of auditoriums gave each seat just one armrest, as if every person in the place only wanted to be comfortable half the time.

"Which one is yours?" asked the woman to my left. Our elbows had been fencing over our shared armrest for the last twenty minutes. She was stout, about fifty years old, with short, burnt-orange hair the color of nothing found in nature. A chunky man I took to be her husband sat on her other side. He was scowling and his arms were crossed so tightly that his hands were jammed into his armpits. His suit strained over his chest and belly like he'd been blown up by a tire pump.

"Uh, mine is the black speck in the . . . seventh row. In section H," I said, trying not to squint. "That's her, there."

"Oh, she's in Arts and Sciences?"

"They're all in Arts and Sciences, Marie," the man said without looking at her. "That's what this is, the graduate school of Arts and Sciences."

Marie smiled, undeterred by her husband's scorn. "Our Kenny is graduating with a master's degree in English."

"That's swell," I said.

"He'll be living at home until he's forty," the man groused.

"And yours? Is she getting her master's degree, too?"

"Yes, ma'am," I said. "In gender studies."

"Oh, that's wonderful," Marie said. "What will she do with that?"

"Beg pardon?"

"What kind of job can she get with that? With a degree in gender studies?"

I considered. "She's leaning towards counseling, law, social work, I think. The world is her oyster."

The man snorted. "Kids pull their careers out of a hat, don't even know what the hell they want to do."

I gazed out over the mass of black gowns. "Her mother was murdered by a stalker when she was a little girl. She was sleeping next door at the time. The same guy kidnapped and almost killed her twelve years later. That's probably what prompted her decision to help other women."

The armrest was mine for the remainder of the afternoon.

I caught up with Amanda two hours later, after listening to the commencement speaker, the Big Cheese of some Big Corporation. He droned on about the Big Profits his company had earned and the Big Decisions he'd made before he remembered he was speaking at a commencement and should probably give the graduates some value. He wrapped up with ten tips for success. In my head, I named them the Ten Big Cheese Tips, which made me smile and got me through the rest of the ceremony with my sanity intact. We all clapped politely, suffered through five more speakers, and then the graduates crossed the stage. Some sleepwalked, others sprinted, but every one of their faces were split wide with smiles. We clapped some more and then all five thousand of us stood and tried to find each other on the basketball court at the same time.

I'm a trained investigator, so it only took me the better part of an hour to find the object of my search in a corner of the auditorium. Amanda was chatting with a half-dozen other student types. Two, like her, wore graduation gowns. The others were dressed in street clothes. One, Jay, I'd met before and waved as I walked up. Amanda turned around.

"Marty!" she said and gave me a hug like she was trying to squeeze me in two. She was slim, but I'd seen her carry a backpack that would've bent me over double. In heels she could almost look me in the eye. I hugged back and smiled.

"Congrats, kid. You made it."

Her face was radiant. "Thanks, Marty. Some days I didn't think it was going to happen. And this is the easy one. Tack on five more years for a PhD."

"Then you teach for a year and you're old enough to retire?" I asked.

"Hey," Jay said. "I'll only be twenty-eight when I get my doctorate."

"You say that now," Amanda said. "Wait until it's just you and your dissertation staring you in the face. You'll find all kinds of reasons to put it off."

"I'll knock that sucka out in six months," Jay said, doing a flabby one-two combination into the air. The group, almost as one, burst into laughter. He looked equal parts surprised and offended. "What?"

"Jay," a short girl with a butch haircut said. "You haven't finished a paper on time since grade school. You'll probably be ABD until you die."

I quirked an eyebrow at Amanda. "ABD?"

"All but dissertation," she said. "Your required classes are done and only the writing is left, but fewer than half finish. It's the most dreaded acronym in higher education."

"Ah," I said. "Kind of like DOA?"

"Yes," she said, then tilted her head. "Exactly like that, actually."

I nodded. "Say, I've been wondering. If a guy gets a master of arts degree, does this make you a mistress of arts?"

"God," one of the girls in a graduation gown said, rolling her eyes.

"It's okay, Miranda," Amanda said. "He's just trying to get my goat. His macho male id reacts instinctively against the thought of someone getting an advanced degree in gender studies, so he pokes fun at it, trying to diminish the importance of the degree in order to bolster his own frail ego. Childish, really."

"Marty sees button, Marty pushes button," I said. "What are you crazy kids up to now?"

"There's a lunch and reception, then a happy hour, then a party at the dean's house."

"Followed by parties at everyone else's houses?"

"Pretty much," she said. "Are you up for it?"

I shook my head. "I can't. I've got some work to do for a friend. But pick a night sometime this week. I want to take you out to dinner. Bring Jay or whoever, too. If they're not DOA."

"ABD."

"Whatever," I said. "I want to celebrate. You deserve it. Hell, I deserve it."

Her eyes were shiny. "Thank you, Marty. I couldn't have done it without you."

I smiled and squeezed her arm. "No sweat, kid. I could say the same."

CHAPTER THREE

By four the next morning, the sleep thing wasn't working. Predawn hours weren't anything new to me, of course; as a homicide cop, rising early was practically a job requirement. But most cops look forward to retirement as a chance to get some real sleep and learn how to wake up at more human hours. And I probably could've trained myself out of getting out of bed before the sun with a few months of late-night TV and beer. But last year I'd received news that would keep anyone awake at night.

Stage two colorectal cancer.

I'd like to say I handled the news well, but I'd be lying if I said it didn't rock me. I thought my life was over. There was the basic issue of staying alive, of course, but then all the things that made life worth living seemed like they were being taken away, too. Like being a cop. Doctors told me I didn't have to retire, that plenty of people worked through their disease, but it wasn't like I answered phones for a living. I was a cop. I couldn't afford to fall down—literally—on the job. So I quit rather than let anyone down.

Doing the right thing didn't make it more palatable, though. It was a retirement that I hadn't wanted or planned for. I was angry and scared and sick. A few things kept me distracted—like helping keep Amanda alive while she was being stalked by her mother's killer, for instance— but a poor night's sleep became a constant. When the disease didn't have me up, pacing the floor, anxiety did.

Hopefully, though, it wouldn't be long before I had some news. Round one of chemo was over and I was due to go to my oncologist's for a checkup soon. I had no idea if the news would be good or bad. Amanda had been a rock through the months of chemo, coaching me to think positive, look for silver linings.

But silver linings and wishes weren't always enough to keep the fear and the anxiety and tension away.

So it was still dark out when I grabbed a bowl of plain oatmeal, sat at my kitchen table with the overhead light on, and put Bloch's files in front of me. I started to read. And read. And read some more. By the time the sun peeked over the trees in my backyard, I'd already been through his files twice and was going back to recheck some of the facts. I'd made my own notes, a list of questions, and a rough time line. The question was how to proceed.

Terrence Witherspoon was a twenty-six-year veteran of the MPDC, never making it past Master Patrol Officer. In the army, he would've been a corporal. Some guys are just cut out for the beat. They don't want to or can't do anything else. Which is fine; we need all the cops we can get and there were plenty of times when a patrol officer coming through with a tip was better than what the guys on my own Homicide squad could do.

Witherspoon had worked the First District, which put him solidly in Southeast, the roughest part of DC and where the city's most spectac-ular violent crime went down. That alone was a feather in Witherspoon's cap, but adding to that was the fact that he worked Police Service Area 106, which had a reputation for violence and drugs even in Southeast.

The demographic was solidly black. Hispanic and Asian gangs generally stayed out or sourced drugs, guns, or prostitutes to the black gangs. What surprised me the most, though, was that Witherspoon actually lived in his PSA. It's something the chief always wanted his troops to do—it made for good press, our DC cops are vigilant and caring enough to live in the place where they work, yadda yadda—but most cops wouldn't even consider it. There were bennies, like having 90 percent of your rent knocked off if you parked your cruiser in front of the apartment building, but you weren't going to get any love if you took a run at the local crack dealer . . . and he happened to be your landlady's nephew. Or supplier.

Witherspoon had been killed in early March. He was the first victim in what Bloch was lumping together as a serial murder, but I refrained from thinking of him as "the first" of anything. I had to keep an open mind. There might not be a serial killer, or Witherspoon might be the third and we didn't know about the first two yet.

I flipped open a new file. Brady Torres lived a completely different life from Witherspoon. Young, just six years out of the police academy, already off the beat, working the gang detail. It was a dangerous specialty, but fast-track stuff that would get him noticed and promoted to detective inside of three years if he didn't get shot or start to love the work so much that he never left. Gangs were serious business in the whole Metro area, but they seemed to really gravitate to Arlington, where Torres had worked. Maybe it was the easy access to highways, or the strip malls, or the cheap housing. Whatever the reason, Torres had made a number of good busts against the white supremacists and had just started making inroads with the Latino gangs when he was killed in his own apartment on Columbia Pike. He'd been single, with a reputation for partying off duty, so no one paid much attention to the noises coming from his two-bedroom pad on a Friday night. A buddy coming over for a Sunday afternoon hockey game had found the body. It had been in March, too. In fact—I flipped back to Witherspoon's file—it had been four days after the DC beat cop had been killed.

The body of Danny Garcia had been found in the back of an abandoned auto repair shop in Southeast. Not Witherspoon's beat, but not far away, either. Date of death was a shot in the dark. A small-time chop-shop crook had broken in looking for something to rip off, found a whole different set of "parts" than he'd bargained for, and called it in. Garcia's body had been there for some time, which made pinning down a time of death problematic. The coroner had put it somewhere in the last week of March, but in the notes had allowed himself a lot of leeway.

Isaac Okonjo had been with the Montgomery County Sheriff's Department just seven months when he'd been killed, off duty, in the parking lot of a bar in Rockville, Maryland, just steps away from his cruiser. Like Witherspoon, he was a patrolman, but assigned to Bethesda and Chevy Chase, more affluent areas than Witherspoon had ever seen. Okonjo was the son of Nigerian immigrants, had attended high school in Rockville, and had graduated from the Maryland Police Academy, finishing unspectacularly in the middle of his class. He'd been killed mid-April, several weeks after Witherspoon, though potentially only ten days after Garcia.

Since Okonjo's body hadn't been beaten, his case was obviously different from the others. The fact that he'd been killed in the parking lot of a bar suggested a rushed or botched attempt. Either something had gone wrong and the murderer had been kept from going through with his gruesome routine . . . or Okonjo's murder simply wasn't connected. The discrepancies bothered me. Only the damning fact that he'd been shot with a small-caliber bullet, like the others—and so close in time—kept me from pulling out all the references to his murder and putting it in a "not the same" box.

I squinted at the clock on my microwave, then at the golden rays filtering in my kitchen window. It was just before seven. I picked up my cell phone and called Bloch, betting that he was an early bird. He picked up on the second ring.

"Bloch."

"It's Singer. You told me to give you a ring when I was ready."

"Yeah."

"Okay, so I'm going to have to interview some people," I said. "I saw some next of kin stuff in some of the files, but I wanted to get your thoughts on who else I should approach."

"Got something to write with?"

"Yep. Shoot."

I heard him drum his fingers on something hard and hollow. "Witherspoon left a widow, Florence. They got one kid. They still live in Southeast. Same one as his beat, by the way."

"I saw that," I said.

"Torres, there's not much to go on. Single, hotshot guy in his twenties. There's the friend who found the body. I'll have to get back to you on a name. Maybe some guys in his squad. But Gangs is a tight group. They might get uppity that a civilian is poking around."

"Something you could smooth out for me?"

"I can try," he said, but his voice wasn't brimming with confidence.

"While we're on the subject," I said. "What exactly is my status on this? Interested bystander? Concerned taxpayer? Nosy S-O-B?"

"I can get you put on the HIDTA payroll as a 'valued informant.' Doesn't give you much status, but at least people can call me if they want some kind of official confirmation."

"Great. I'm in the same class as your snitches?" I asked.

"More like an expert witness. Anybody gives you a hard time, steer them my way," he said, then cleared his throat. "Don't take this the wrong way, but try not to, uh, stick your nose in too far, get me? If you piss off a half-dozen chiefs around the Metro area, our case'll get shitcanned for sure. It'll be over before it's started."

"I smell what you're cooking," I said. "Now, what about the others?"

"Danny's got a wife and son. Libney and Paul Garcia. Paul was just about to start up at the academy when Danny went missing. He's put it off indefinitely. I don't know anything about the wife."

I scribbled down the address and a phone number that Bloch gave me. "Garcia was found in Southeast. I know the neighborhood, but not the exact address. Anything you can tell me?"

"The auto shop turned out to be a sometime crack house. It was cleared out before anything went down. Junkies aren't talking."

"Big surprise. Whose turf is it?"

"Black gang. The Chosen."

"I know them," I said. I flipped some pages, frowning. "Isn't there anybody Garcia was working with? Even his last case or something? Talking to the family's going to help, but I doubt it'll get me any closer to whoever's killing these guys."

Bloch grunted, then I heard the unmistakable *whump* of a stack of folders being moved from one large pile to another on a desk. "Maybe. Write this down. Bob Caldwell. He's an old pro with the DC office of the DEA. He and Danny collaborated on a number of cases over the years. Nothing recent, unfortunately, but Danny was such a lone wolf that there isn't anybody at HIDTA he was close to and I doubt anybody in MPDC could give you much, either."

"That'll help," I said. "Where's he?"

"He's kind of a crank," Bloch said. "Lives on a sailboat on the DC waterfront, working off a disability."

"What's the name of his boat?"

"*The Loophole.*"

I snorted. "What about Okonjo?"

"Young. Single. Popular, I gather, judging by the rumblings I'm hearing over at the Montgomery sheriff's office. You might get too much cooperation when you go over there, if you know what I mean," Bloch said. A voice in the background intruded. After a muffled exchange,

Bloch came back on the line. "Singer, I gotta go. You have enough to get started?"

"Yeah," I said. Life went on, even for worried HIDTA lieutenants. "Can I give you a buzz later if I need to?"

"Sure. Wait, use this," he said, giving me another number. "That's my cell. Use it instead of the office phone. It'll be easier."

"And no one at the office will know about our little side investigation."

"That, too," he said, without embarrassment. "It might be a side-show, but I'm not taking any chances. I don't want anyone coming in and scooping this. Or, worse, telling us to walk away from the whole thing."

"Fat chance," I said. "I'm a retired cop with too much time on my hands and no supervision. I'd do this for free."

"Who's paying?" he asked and hung up.

CHAPTER FOUR

After my call with Bloch, I hopped in the car and headed west to the Garcias' house in Chantilly. I'd debated with myself if I should start the murders chronologically. Beginning with Terrence Witherspoon would've made more sense, probably, and would've helped me straighten the corners on the investigation, so to speak, by following the killings in order. Being methodical can be its own reward, and produce results you might not have gotten by winging it. But the reverse is true, too: it was Garcia's murder that felt the most charged, the most at risk, and of course had been the one drop-kicked into Bloch's lap. Something felt right about beginning there instead of at the starting line. And how much time did I have before another cop died? "Methodical" didn't seem to be the right approach to use in this case.

The neighborhood was a suburban plan made up of nearly identical split-level homes, all of them with funny, canted roofs that, on one side, went from the peak of the house down to almost ground level so the extension became the roof of an attached carport. The effect was to make the houses seem lopsided, as though they were about to tip over. It was a silly, house-of-the-future design that only the sixties could've spawned. Plenty of homeowners seemed to agree. There were extra walls, doors, porches, brick faces, siding, and landscaping, all added in an effort to differentiate one home from the other and soften the effect of the architecture. Unfortunately, none of these superficial changes could take away the rakishly tipped roofs, so the homes all seemed like kids trying on their parents' clothes. But they still looked like kids.

I found the Garcias' house and parked on the street. They had converted their carport into a garage and done some nice things to the porch, but it was still obviously part of the overall community plan. One car, a burgundy Corolla, sat in the short driveway leading up to the garage. I watched the house for a minute. At ten o'clock on a Sunday, I might strike out if they were at church, but failing that, I was hoping this was the best time to visit. I could've called, but it's easy to say no over the phone. I got out and went to the door and knocked.

There was no immediate answer, so I had time to admire the newly mown grass, the clean windows, the swept front porch. My expectations tapered off as I waited some more. The third knock was a formality, just to say I tried, and I was already half turning to leave when the door opened. Good things happen in threes.

A petite Hispanic woman answered the door. She was a well-kept forty-five or forty-six, with poker-straight brown hair down to her shoulders and a hint of makeup, but her eyes were hollow and hovering at half-mast, like she might fall asleep where she stood. She wore a pink polo shirt with the collar turned up, like kids did in the eighties. She spoke to me through the screen, holding on to the inner door for support.

"Yes?" She said it like *Jes*.

"Mrs. Garcia? Libney Garcia?"

"Yes?"

I introduced myself and gave her a brief and heavily sanitized version of what Bloch had asked me to do. The drive over had given me time to think through how I wanted to position myself to the people

I'd have to talk to. Almost all of them would be cops, or related to cops, and they weren't going to be awed or blown away by the words "police investigation" like John Q. Public might be. They'd ask hard questions and want straight answers. I had to give them most of the truth without actually letting the cat out of the bag or having the door shut in my face.

"You are with the police?" she asked.

"Not anymore, Ms. Garcia," I said. "But Danny's supervisor asked me to look into his death personally. I'm happy to have him call you, if you'd like confirmation."

She shook her head, too weary to question it. "What is it you want?"

"Just a couple minutes of your time," I said. "I know it must be hard to talk about your husband so soon after his death. But any little bit might help catch whoever killed him. You never know what might be useful."

She waved her hand in a languid sweep, as if to say she didn't care, but opened the screen door. I went into the house. She shut the door and led me to the living room. The furniture was of the Swedish outlet, put-it-together-yourself variety, but still clean and smart-looking. The floor was hardwood and half of it had been sanded down, giving the room a two-tone cast. Pictures in little easel frames crowded together on top of a TV cabinet. A couch with a plaid throw bunched up at one end held down one corner of the room. I sat in a chair with rounded plywood arms that looked a lot more comfortable than it was.

"You want coffee?" she asked.

I hesitated, then said yes. She left the room and came back five minutes later with two steaming cups.

"I'm sorry. Is instant," she said, handing me the mug. It said "World's Greatest Dad" on the side. I cupped my hand around the lettering to cover it. She sat on the couch across from me, absentmindedly straightening the throw as she did so.

"This is fine," I said, taking a sip. It tasted like burnt cardboard water. I took a deep breath.

"Thank you. You want to know about Danny?"

"Yes."

She hesitated. "I don't know about his police work. He never want to talk about it."

"That's all right. Just tell me about him. As a person."

She was quiet. I thought I'd said exactly the wrong thing, but she was only getting her thoughts together. "He was a beautiful man, very passionate. He never did nothing partway. When we first met, he wouldn't stop calling me. Call me every night 'til my mother took the phone away. He would say poetry to my window, throw flowers on the front porch. Like in a song. My father threatened to shoot him, he caught him, but Danny would sneak into the yard anyway and whisper to me through the window. We got married a year after we met, but is like he never stop trying to . . . to . . ."

"Court you?"

She smiled. "Yes, to court me. He go after everything the same. No halfway."

"Was he born here?"

"In the States? No. He was born in Oaxaca. Come up across the border when he was fourteen, fifteen. Had cousins near here, in Woodbridge. They raised him. He learn English, graduate, went straight to the academy."

"He wanted to be a cop?"

"Always," she said. "He saw many things in Oaxaca, many things crossing the border that made him angry."

"He talk about them?"

She shook her head. "He got here, thinking, you know, the worst is over. But crime is everywhere, yes? There were gangs in Woodbridge where he grew up. He hated them, wanted to do something."

"He wanted to fix the broken things?"

"Yes," she said, then considered. "And no. He get very, very angry when he see something wrong, something bad. He tell me, Libney, sometimes you can't fix. Sometimes you have to punish."

"Like what?"

"We had a neighbor once, beat his dog. We hear it crying at night. Danny let it go three days. Then he talk to the man. Very quiet, on his porch. He never touch him, never make a move to him. But the man move out the next month."

"What happened to the dog?"

She smiled again. "We took him. Spoil rotten for ten years."

"Do you have a picture of Danny?"

She got up from the couch, shuffled to the TV, and picked up one of the large pictures. She traced the face of it with a finger, then walked back and handed it to me. It was one of those canned studio portraits you get at a department store, with the weird gray clouds in the background. There were three people in the picture: Libney and a man I assumed was Danny were seated, holding hands. Danny was dark and whip-thin, with medium-length hair and cocoa-brown eyes. He had that sparse mustache that some Latino men can never seem to grow in completely but insist on wearing anyway. He was smiling, but his strong white teeth had a predatory gleam. The hint of a tattoo peeked out from under the cuff of one sleeve. Behind them stood a stocky younger man with a buzz cut so close the skin of his scalp gleamed through. He was smiling, with an arm around each of them. He wore a dress shirt that, despite the generous cut, couldn't hide a wide set of shoulders.

"Danny looks . . . fierce," I said, handing the photo back.

She smiled again. "Yes. I tol' you, no halfway with Danny."

"Is that your son in the picture, as well?"

"Yes," she said, putting the frame back on the TV. She adjusted it carefully before sitting down. "Paul."

"Is he home?"

She shook her head. "No. He run all my errands since . . ." She trailed off. She seemed not so much occupied by grief as sinking into it. Sadness rolled off her in waves.

I gave her a moment, though it wasn't easy. Time was running away from me, or at least that was how it felt. This interview was necessary, critical even, but it already seemed like I'd spent too long here. I took a deep breath. A car that needed muffler work burbled on the road outside, faded away. I waited until her eyes rose to meet mine.

I asked, "Is Paul in the military?"

"Was. Iraq. Afghanistan."

"He came back recently?"

"Las' year. He was going to go into the academy like his father, this fall. He dropped out when Danny was . . ." She turned her head.

I nodded. "I know this is hard, but did Danny say anything about his work? Anything recent?"

"Never. He want them to be very separate." She made a chopping motion with her hand. "We don't even go to picnics, parties. All our friends are here. He get very mad when I ask him anything."

"Do you know what kind of work he did?"

"No. He was gone for days sometimes. He'd let me know when, how long. He come back very tired. Smelled like cigarettes an' beer. But happy."

"Did he have any friends on the force? In law enforcement?"

She shrugged. "I don't know."

I raised my eyebrows. "What were you supposed to do if something happened to him? To you?"

"I have his office number. He tell me to call that if I don't hear from him in a week or if I have a problem."

I asked a dozen more questions while my coffee grew cold, but the answers were generally the same and all unhelpful. Whatever else he had done, Danny Garcia had shielded his wife from his work. He could've been an astronaut for all she knew. I don't know if it was part of the Latin culture, or just an ironclad policy Danny had made for his own family, but there seemed to have been no questioning the issue. No friends on the force, no favorite cop bars, no other cops' wives to share the burden and the anxiety with. No diaries, no shaky midnight pillow talk, no marital blowups about the life of the law enforcement family, like the one that had ended my own marriage. There was Danny Garcia, undercover narc, and Danny Garcia, devoted husband and father, and never the twain did meet.

I thanked her and put my mug down on an end table. "Would you mind if I came back and talked to Paul?"

She shrugged and seemed more likely than ever to go to sleep on me. I had the impression she would probably crawl back onto the couch after I left. Some of the memories had been kind to her—she had smiled once or twice—but overall, the grief had robbed her of her essence. I hated to call it the will to live, but that's what it felt like. I jotted my number on the back of an old MPDC card, handed it to her, then stood. She walked me to the door, where I shook her hand.

I said, "I know this is very hard. There might not be anything harder in the world. I've been through this before. If you need anything, please call."

She nodded, but said nothing, and quietly closed the door.

CHAPTER FIVE

I was at Restaurant Nora on Florida Avenue, trapped in a tipsy debate between Amanda on one side and Jay on the other with their friend Zenny chiming in whenever she felt like it. The topic, not unexpectedly, was the state of career options for postgraduates in gender studies. I had less to contribute to the discussion than if I'd been asked to describe the inner workings of the digestive organs of a Maryland blue crab. Then again, that's what was on my plate with a side of wild mushroom risotto, so I could probably have gotten somewhere on that question by poking around with my fork. I felt a small twinge of guilt that I wasn't out there, chasing down more leads for Bloch, but I'd done what I could to this point and I told myself I had to eat sometime.

"But what I'm saying is, there are real needs right now in community centers and shelters and counseling practices," Amanda said. "It's fine to talk about higher academics and pushing the borders of the field, but there are practical applications to what we've studied. You can't say that about all liberal arts."

"None of them, actually," Zenny quipped. She was a tall, slim brunette model masquerading as a graduate student. She slung back half her glass of Riesling.

"Sure, but that's stuff that can be handled by people with a certificate from a community college," Jay said. "You just walked out with a master's degree from one of the most prestigious non-Ivies in the country. You could do more with it, is all."

"Don't qualify GW like that just because you went to Princeton for undergrad," Amanda said, picking up her fork and jabbing it at Jay with each word. He flinched as though she might stab him. "And don't belittle my degree just because you're in for the whole ball of wax and are scared you won't get tenure somewhere."

"I'm *not* belittling your degree," he said, a little desperately. "I'm lauding it." He turned to me for support.

"Speaking of lauding, how's everyone's moderately expensive dinner?" I asked.

Since I was talking to three graduate students who had subsisted primarily on boxed macaroni and cheese for several years and since we were at one of the best restaurants in DC and—most important— because I was paying, my question deftly steered the discussion to less dangerous ground. The three tucked in like they hadn't eaten since freshman year.

The relative quiet allowed me to take a gander around the place. I hadn't gotten out much in the last year. Hell, in the past ten. Before cancer, I'd rarely raised my head from my plate. Now, I valued the times that I could visit a swank place like Nora's and I noticed small things I wouldn't have before. The high walls were painted sage green. The woodwork was well done, ornate without being gaudy. Instead of paintings, spaced evenly around the walls were colorful and nonlinear quilts that were less like your grandmother's bedspread and more like something Chagall would've done if he'd been handy with a needle and thread. The lighting was just right and the tables far enough apart that diners felt privacy, but not isolation.

The grads mopped their plates and sat back, content. They waxed poetic and effusive in their thanks, which I encouraged with an "aw shucks" look on my face. I basked in it for a while, then ordered a third bottle of the Alsatian Riesling we'd been drinking, which was probably the real reason they piled on the compliments.

We enjoyed that for a while, then Jay and Zenny started comparing notes on the dessert menu. I turned to Amanda. "Without opening the can of worms again, what *are* the job realities for you? I'm not trying to be an ass. I really don't know."

She played with her silverware and sighed. "I want to do counseling, but I'm not qualified. I don't have the education, believe it or not. That's the hands-on work I want to do, but it takes a psych degree and certification."

"And a willingness to live like a refugee," Jay said, still looking at the dessert menu. He glanced up to receive glares from the two girls. "Sorry."

"So, there are definitely shelters that would be ecstatic to get an educated helping hand on staff," Amanda continued, turning her gaze from Jay to me. "But they can only afford to pay one or two of them. Seventeen of us just graduated from the program. I could volunteer somewhere with an eye towards becoming full-time staff, but how long can I afford to do that?"

"So what's the answer?" I asked, but I'd already guessed. I tried to ignore the tightening in my stomach.

"Follow the money," Zenny said.

Amanda nodded. "Wherever there's a position. San Francisco, Austin, Chicago. Whoever got the last big grant will be looking to staff, so I've got to be in line when they start looking."

I didn't say anything to that and the discussion took a sharp right turn into DC politics, veered off into Capitol Hill scandals, and crashed headlong into a critique of the latest reality TV shows.

I smiled and nodded at all the right places, but I wasn't hearing much. The news that Amanda might be leaving shouldn't have been unexpected, but we hide the most obvious truths from ourselves. Over the past half year, Amanda had become like a daughter to me. Besides my ex-partner Dods and his wife, I'd managed to acquire a lot of acquaintances but not a lot of friends in my fifty-three years, and had no family to speak of. I'd only had one near relationship in the past year and that had ended badly, though it was probably as much my own fault as hers. I'd have to deal with the way I'd handled Julie Atwater and what I'd seen at the time as her betrayal . . . but lately as simply her only way out of a no-win situation.

I shook my head. Now wasn't the moment to face those issues but, unfortunately, thoughts of Julie made me think of another ex-partner, Jim Kransky, who was dead and gone, thanks to a lunatic's bullet. A faltering friendship that would, now, never be fully healed.

Which left Amanda, who had made an emergency landing in my life with her own problems not long ago, but now it seemed like she'd always been there. And at some of the lowest points of dealing with my cancer she'd given me something to think about besides myself, which was exactly what I'd needed. If she left, it wasn't just a matter of loss for me, it was a matter of survival.

"Marty, are you feeling okay?" she said, as if on cue. Both my disease and chemo had made me queasy in the past and she'd seen the effects firsthand.

I forced a smile. "I'm great. Who's up for a bottle of champagne?"

CHAPTER SIX

Wealth, ethnicity, age, and function divide most cities into distinct neighborhoods, giving them their own particular character and sense of difference. But a lack of industry in DC brought the common divisions of race and financial status into starker relief than almost anywhere else. Without factories or docks or rail yards, the only thing that separated people from each other was themselves.

As a result, DC has always been two cities in one, split down the north–south axis. White middle- and upper-class residents lived almost without fail in the northwest and southwest. Southeast and northeast DC were black and usually poor. The only exceptions were a few blocks around Capitol Hill where the old brownstones of the late Victorian period had become gentrified by virtue of the ever-increasing real estate prices and the encroaching stony gray buildings of government that were, in effect, a no-man's-land.

The section of Southeast that Terrence and Florence Witherspoon called home was Barry Farm, a neighborhood that—though located across the Anacostia River—was still technically part of DC. It was an area synonymous with crack dealing, shoot-outs, and carjackings.

I got depressed thinking about it. I remembered the area before crack poked its ugly head in the door back in the eighties. It hadn't been a playground of delights back then, either, but when crack hit the streets, it was as if violent crime found an extra gear that it didn't know it had. There were nights we'd just hang around a murder scene after things wrapped up, since we knew we'd have to turn around and come back in an hour anyway. Crack became a way of life after a while, but unfortunately so did the level of violence and now no one really remembers it any other way. There were kids who thought it perfectly normal that there were five murders a night. You could get shot, stabbed, or mugged in the northwest part of DC, too, but at least the odds seemed to be on your side. In Southeast, there were no odds. It was a sure thing.

But it was time to talk to Terrence Witherspoon's widow. I broke my rule about calling first—I realized I'd be doing a lot of driving if I was going to chase down the leads in four different murders. I'd gotten lucky that Libney Garcia had been home and willing to talk and I might not get that lucky again. Besides, I had no idea when people were awake, asleep, or at work anymore. I remembered a time when you knew within a couple of minutes when people were at their desks, at lunch, or at home watching the tube. With the Internet making all things possible in all places, I didn't know if I was catching someone as they were waking up, going to bed, or sitting at work.

But if I didn't call, I'd never know. So, I picked up the phone and dialed Florence Witherspoon's number. It rang ten or twelve times before someone answered.

"'Lo?" The voice was a man's, sleepy and deep.

"Could I speak to Florence Witherspoon, please?"

"Who this?"

"Marty Singer. I'm a friend of Sam Bloch's with the DC police department," I said, framing it in such a way that I neither alleged nor denied that I was a cop.

"Who?"

"Marty Singer."

"Who you with?"

"DC Police," I said, dropping the sham. "Florence Witherspoon there?"

But he was already not listening, talking to someone else. I couldn't make out what the other voice said, but then my surly friend said, "He say he with the police." Then, "I don't *know*. He didn't say he an insurance man."

The phone was dropped, then picked up again. A woman's voice came on the line. Soft, worn, like a cotton shirt that had been washed too much. "Hello, this is Florence Witherspoon. Who's this, please?"

"Marty Singer, Mrs. Witherspoon. I'm sorry about calling like this, but I was hoping to talk to you regarding your husband's death."

"You said you worked with my husband?"

"Um," I said, thinking maybe I shouldn't have left the sham behind so quickly. "Not exactly. I used to be with the MPDC but since I was in Homicide, I never knew your husband personally. I'm working with another department that's investigating your husband's case as well as that of several other officers."

"'Another department'?" she asked. I could hear the frown in her voice. "'Used to be'? This doesn't have the ring of something official."

"It's not," I said, feeling the fragility of the conversation and trying not to misstep. "A colleague still with the force noticed that your husband's death wasn't being investigated as . . . thoroughly . . . as it should be and asked me to look into it. There's no official connection to the MPDC or any investigation they're doing right now."

"You don't think the department is doing its job?" she asked.

"I didn't say that. I think they'll do their best on your husband's case. It's more a problem at the top."

She paused, then said, "This is all sounding very mysterious, Mr. Singer."

"It would be easier to explain in person, I think. Could I swing by sometime today, perhaps, and talk to you about it?"

"Don't you work?" she asked, sounding amused and a little less worn out.

"I'm retired, ma'am," I said. "My time is my own."

"Well, you're in luck. It's spring break at my school and so is mine. For this week, at least. Do you know where we live?"

I dressed casually but with an eye toward professional neatness: black slacks, blue shirt, black blazer. Fashion wasn't a strength of mine, so I scanned the shoes stacked in the back of my closet like they were suspects in a felony lineup. Loafers? Cowboy boots? Did I want to look casual or like I was there to kick ass? I was a white cop—or the closest thing to one—going into a predominantly black neighborhood looking for information I wasn't actually entitled to. Snakeskin cowboy boots probably weren't what I was looking for. I went with the loafers.

I might've ditched the blazer to tone down the image even more, but it gave me an air of respectability. Besides, that's where the gun went, a SIG Sauer P220 Compact in a shoulder rig, an identical replacement to the one I'd lost while saving Amanda from a lunatic the year before. I grabbed my keys and headed out early. I knew Southeast as well as most, having spent plenty of time there in my role with Homicide, but it wouldn't hurt to look the place over before I actually knocked on the Witherspoons' door. I rolled the windows down, cracked the sunroof, and headed for town.

The Fourteenth Street Bridge took me from Virginia and into the District by way of the lunatic's plaything that is the combination of Route 1 and Interstate 395. Ten lanes of vehicular madness, all gunning at about seventy-five not half a mile from the White House. Staying alive took precedence over sightseeing, but in my mind's eye, I could see the Jefferson Memorial resting along the waters of the Tidal Basin to my left, an elegant, white bump along the flat, serene banks of the Potomac. After a minute, the highway curved to the east and I could almost feel the thrum of DC to the north. Ninety percent of the city was on my left. But I was headed across the Anacostia River, the murkier, less-loved sister to the Potomac, and on to Barry Farm.

The off-ramp gave me my first taste of Southeast in nearly a year. Soiled, discarded clothes and plastic bottles of all shapes, sizes, and colors littered the sides of the road like it was the high-tide mark after a hurricane. Shattered glass had been swept to the shoulder, but not removed, marking the sites of at least three separate accidents. Chain-link fencing—leaning to one side or another, but never straight—lined the ramp, trapping plastic bags, newspapers, and fast-food wrappers like a fisherman's net, piling the catch as high as my knee in places.

As I drove toward the Witherspoons', the streets got slightly cleaner and a little less depressed-looking than the entry into the neighborhood. I shouldn't have judged the whole place from the state of its off-ramp. But still, just an hour past noon, the place had too many people hanging around on the corners, too many zombies plodding aimlessly up streets or passed out on steps, too many guys laughing and kidding each other but looking in three or four directions at once. The few storefronts that didn't have "For Lease" signs on the front had bars across every window. A couple only had cashier-style windows with a small drawer to take cash in and slip goods through. Graffiti covered most open spaces on businesses and some homes. The sides of many buildings sported efforts to sandblast or paint the vandalism away . . . but the attempts were usually covered by a half-dozen new tags.

The Witherspoons lived on a street called Douglas Place on the very edge of Barry Farm. I was pleasantly surprised as I drove past the house and apartment complexes; the area was greener than what I'd passed through to get here. There were actual lawns and the houses were small, real small, but maintained. No broken windows, no trash in the yards, no tire-less junkers parked out front. The cars were still ten years old, but the block gave off a feel of community instead of desperation.

I parked and got out. A waist-high chain-link fence surrounded the property, so I stopped at the gate and looked the place over from the sidewalk. The Witherspoons' was one of the neatest homes on the block, a prim, single-family house with vinyl siding and a black, wrought-iron railing going up a simple cement set of steps. The walkway leading to the front step from the sidewalk was cement slab, but the grass was so neatly trimmed it appeared to have been edged by hand with a pair of scissors. Open windows, framed with shutters, flanked the door. Through them, I could see filmy curtains rising and falling with the breeze.

A woman wearing a broad-brimmed hat was on her hands and knees gardening underneath one of the windows, patiently turning up the earth and sifting through the dirt, looking for pebbles and stones that she tossed into a growing pile by the porch. She wore jeans and a pink warm-up jacket. She was slim, with a good figure.

"Mrs. Witherspoon?"

She straightened and turned around. She plucked off a pair of gardening gloves, a finger at a time, and dropped them on the ground next to the trowel she'd been using. She kept the hat on, though, and the edges bounced and waggled as she approached me from across the shallow lawn.

"Mr. Singer," she said as she came near. She was about five and a half feet tall and had a slow, graceful swing to her walk. She seemed to be one of those women who kept her bearing no matter what she had on. The way she moved across the grass, she could've been gardening in a ball gown. Her face was a cocoa brown, with dark circles under her green eyes. Her nose was graced with a spray of freckles and was small but wide, giving her an almost feline appearance.

"Yes, ma'am," I said.

She gave me a low-wattage smile. "No ma'ams, please. I get that at school all fall, all spring, and sometimes all summer, too. Flo is fine."

"Marty, then," I said.

"Marty," she said, holding out a hand. I shook it, feeling how thin and light her hand was. The fingers were hot on the outside, damp and cool on the palm from her gardening. "Why don't you come inside and we can talk. This doesn't sound like something we can solve standing on the sidewalk."

I opened the gate and she led the way down the walk and inside, taking her hat off as she went. Her hair was pinned up. The door led directly into a small but tidy living room: a couch, two chairs, a modest TV. Sprawled on the couch, paying a lot of attention to the screen in front of him, was a young black kid, maybe fifteen or sixteen, in a white tank top, satin basketball shorts, and white Nikes. He held some kind of video game controller in both hands. Bleeps and bloops and bloodcurdling screams were coming out of the speakers of the TV like it was Armageddon. A glance at the screen showed me that I was right. As we came into the room, we had to pass through his field of vision, but rather than look up, he did a bob-and-weave around us so he wouldn't lose eye contact with the action. In the middle of everything, his cell phone—which was on his lap—rang with some hip-hop ringtone. With the flair of someone much-practiced, he paused the game and answered. Whoever it was must not have rated, since he pinned the phone to his shoulder, unpaused the game, and went back to saving the universe while he talked.

"Come on, let's go back to the kitchen," Flo said. "There's no use trying to get him away from that thing. With weather like we're having, I might be tempted to force him to get outside but since his father died, I don't have the heart."

I trailed her through a modest dining room filled with knobby-looking oak furniture I remember had been popular in the seventies. Decorative plates of hunting scenes hung in a column on one wall and a large painting of the Washington Monument took up space across from them. On a sideboard in a tasteful gold frame was a hinged triptych of Martin Luther King Jr., Malcolm X, and Medgar Evers. There were knickknacks—a tiny glass vase, a paperweight, a bouquet of silk flowers—on the tables and sideboard.

Flo took me through to the kitchen, which had a small table and two chairs. The window above the sink was open and a lace curtain pressed against the screen, then dropped as the wind sighed in and out of the house. Music from a neighbor's filtered in through the open back door, too soft to be annoying.

She motioned me to one of the chairs while she reached into the fridge. "Iced tea?"

"That would be fine," I said.

She poured two tall glasses and set them down as she sat across from me. She smiled when she saw my reaction to the first sip. It was so sweet I thought my teeth would crack. "T was from Alabama. He always complained that people in the North never knew where to put their sugar. He said they took it out of the tea and put it in the cornbread."

"That's, um, sweet," I said as tactfully as I could. "I'm used to something a little less . . . diabetic."

"Can I get you something else?"

"No, no, I'll be fine," I said.

She took a sip of her own and put the glass back on the table. "So what do you want to know, Marty?"

I took a deep breath. "Your husband's death was the first in a series of murders that all have some superficial similarities. At least, on the surface. But my colleague and I feel there might be something more linking them together. If there is a connection, I need to find out what that is. Once we have it, we're hoping it will tell us something about who the killer or killers are."

"How many officers have been killed?"

"Four, we think."

"My God," she said, shocked. "What's going on?"

I explained how far afield the killings were and when they were committed. I pulled out a sheet with the men's names and asked her to look at them, one by one, to see if she recognized any of them.

She shook her head. "I'm sorry. None of those ring even a faint bell. And T had been in the force for a long time. He knew a lot of policemen."

"Always with MPDC? No other departments? No moonlighting?"

She shook her head again.

"What was Terrence's career like?" I asked. "He was a Master Patrol Officer for nearly fifteen years. And the fact that he lived in his own patrol area is . . ."

"Unusual?"

"Yeah."

She drummed her fingers on the table for a moment, staring out the window. "Terrence and I met just out of school, both of us young and on fire, ready to make a difference. We had plenty of options on where to live, but we believed we had to go where the need was greatest."

I said nothing.

"Southeast has never been a treat, but we didn't choose to live here because it was easy. The idea was to change people's lives. The school I teach in is down the street. Half the staff are former students of mine. Most of the kids in the neighborhood grew up knowing T. That's the kind of career he had. Could he have worked his way up the ladder? Of course. But that's not why he got into it."

"People here knew him," I said.

"Six hundred people came to the funeral."

I ran my finger up the side of the glass, pooling the condensation. "A cop who lives in his own beat could be a local hero or public enemy number one. Were there any run-ins with particular locals? Gangs that might want him to stop busting them?"

"Naturally, he had problems with the local element. Some of it came home to roost. We've had our windows broken. Someone painted some lovely things on the front door. My room at school was trashed. But it's so hard to think one person here would want to . . . to . . ."

She stopped and put her hand over her mouth. Her shoulders heaved up and down, but not a sound came from her. I sat very still. She pulled herself together after a moment, then stood up and plucked a tissue from a box on a counter. "I'm sorry. I thought I had things under control."

"Don't be sorry," I said. "It's never easy."

She blew her nose and sat back down, closing her eyes briefly, then opening them and looking straight at me. "What else?"

"Did Terrence share his work with you?"

"Well, yes. Can you be more specific?"

"Did you know the men in his department?"

"You mean is it possible that I didn't know everyone he worked with?"

"Something like that," I said.

She shrugged. "Of course, it's possible. But T liked to tell me every little thing. Not just husband and wife stuff. It goes back to why we were here in the first place: to make a difference. He knew I'd want to hear what he was up to, what was changing in the neighborhood. I told him about the kids who were growing up, who might turn into a problem next year, kids he might be able to help before it was too late."

"You don't think he glossed over the worst parts, maybe to protect you?"

She sighed and hugged her arms to her chest. "I'm sure he spared me the worst details. It was enough to know someone was shot at the apartments next to the school or there was another stabbing on MLK."

"Any crime spree he helped stop? Backstreet gambling? Drugs?"

She opened her mouth, probably to say no, then stopped herself, thinking. "There might've been one thing. Right before school started, back in August, we had a teachers' in-service day about a rash of drug sales and drug-related violence on the street. When I mentioned it to T, he said he'd been put on alert about it. He told me—this sounds stupid—that the concern was because the drugs were coming from outside the neighborhood. Drugs aren't anything new, but we all know, or mostly know, who deals around here, who to avoid, what buildings to stay away from."

"The known quantity," I said.

She nodded. "But what had everyone up in arms was that no one knew where these drugs were coming from. And the drugs were bad enough, but you add the fact that the local dealers don't like the competition and the fear was that we might have a full-on war on the street."

"Any drugs in particular?"

"I don't know," she said.

"Was Terrence involved in the investigation?"

"I don't think so, but it's odd now that you mention it that we never talked much more about it after the one conversation. School picked up and the administration let it drop. The drug war never happened and no news is good news, I guess."

"Did Terrence work any late nights, extra shifts?"

"That describes most of his career."

I smiled. "You're right. Dumb question."

She smiled back, but the look was tired. Genuine, but without any real oomph behind it. "I haven't been much help, have I?"

"I don't know yet, Flo," I said truthfully. "Like I said, it's the spaces in between that I have to fill in. The things you've told me might be just what I need or not at all. I have to talk to a lot more people before I'll know where the lines connect."

We were quiet again. The music continued to trickle in, maddeningly unidentifiable. I watched as the ice in my glass melted, the cubes slipping past each other and down, then bobbing back to the surface.

Someone was baking cookies and the sweet smell came in on the same breeze as the music.

"It's been so hard," she said finally, her voice warbling as she started to lose control, then regained it. "So hard. His death, of course. And how it happened, how brutal. How terrible. But what hurts most of all is the idea that it might be someone from around here. A boy I might've taught or someone T gave a ride to after a basketball game. We've been trying to help this community for twenty years and someone three doors down might've killed my husband. When I walk down the street, people look at me and they say they're sorry, but maybe they're the ones that did it or know who did or are happy that it happened."

This time I reached out and grabbed her hand and squeezed. I didn't have any better answer for her.

CHAPTER SEVEN

The black bronze of the lion's head was hot as a branding iron in the late May sunshine, and it hurt, but I kept my hand on its mane anyway. Frozen in its protective crouch, the life-sized statue glowered over the low granite wall, ready to pounce on anyone foolish enough to threaten the two bronze cubs it guarded.

I left the lion in its permanent state of readiness, rubbing the sting from my fingers as I walked. Following the circular wall, I let my eyes wander over the more than twenty thousand names of the National Law Enforcement Officers Memorial, all cops killed in the line of duty. They went on and on. Wreaths on wire stands lined the tops and bottoms of the walls, remainders from the annual ceremony held just a few weeks before to honor all the fallen officers of the past. And add new ones to the roll. Halfway around the loop, I came across a young woman kneeling next to the wall, taking a rubbing of a name with charcoal and paper. There weren't any tears, but her face was pinched and red. I veered to one side and moved past her quietly.

I hadn't meant to stop. I'm not nostalgic. Sentiment makes me cynical and uncomfortable. But, on the way back from the Witherspoons', my hands turned the wheel and—almost without thinking about it—I steered my car straight downtown and on to the memorial.

The site was in Judiciary Square across from the venerable Building Museum, what was once the Civil War pension office, a monument for a different generation of heroes. I'd been at the dedication of the memorial in 1991, standing in a row of other MPDC cops, all of us in our dress uniforms, which we wore almost exclusively, it seemed, for the funerals of other cops. Fitting, I supposed. The feel of the uniform, like the emotion of the ceremony, had been unfamiliar. While I had agreed with the motive of the idea, I had been impatient at the time with the pomp and circumstance of the event. And not a little bit cynical. The granite slabs and bronze statues seemed a grand, hollow tribute, the kind of architectural statement that stood in for meaningful action a lot in DC.

But I had a different perspective now. Twenty more years as a cop, in a strange way, had mellowed me. I'd seen a lot of people killed, many hurt. Retirement and a battle with cancer had brought dimension to my view. I didn't have to accept the sentiment that others wanted me to see; I could decide for myself. I was looking at inanimate rock and metal, but the shapes had no particular value . . . unless I wanted them to. A monument was what you made of it. An empty gesture to some. Lasting motivation to others.

Each of Bloch's murdered cops would go through a review process to make sure their circumstances merited their names being inscribed on the wall. The cases would have to be nominated and their department, in turn, would be contacted to provide details of how and when each cop had been killed, and whether their death had been in the line of duty. It was doubtful anyone would stand in the way of the nominations, but it was still a sad and sterile bureaucratic process meant to recognize someone who'd given their life for their job. The paperwork and phone calls and interviews would stick in the craw of anyone who was in charge of their buddy's case, make them wonder why the honor wasn't automatic.

I knew all this because I'd just gone through it. For nearly six months, I'd shepherded my former partner's case through the process, making sure that he got the recognition he was due. Killed while helping to save Amanda, he hadn't even been working on an official investigation, which had made things difficult for the bureaucracy. But I'd made it my obsession for a good chunk of this year. If determination was all it took, his name would've been up a month after he'd been shot. The board had eventually seen it my way.

Cynicism had intruded at times. Not much of a trade, a life for some letters in stone. But the honor meant more to me than I'd thought. I'd been here just a few weeks ago—this time as a civilian—as the new names had been read off the list in a simple, horrible rhythm. I'd squeezed my hands bloodless as the names rolled over us, then walked away stiff-legged and barely under control when it ended. Not an empty gesture, after all.

And now I found myself standing in front of the slab where his name had been etched, looking at the single number and letter that indexed him, making him easier to find in the little white books at the entrances of the memorial. JIM KRANSKY. The last one on the block.

I rubbed my shoulder where I'd been shot by the same man who killed Jim. There shouldn't be anything to regret. But the simple fact that I was alive and he wasn't broke the logic. It seemed wrong. I stood there, looking at the wall. A soft breeze stirred the perfectly manicured trees. A siren wailed ten blocks away.

"I'm sorry, Jim," I said out loud.

It was too late for him. Too late for Garcia. And Witherspoon, and Torres, and Okonjo. Too late for twenty thousand other cops. But there were others out there. It shouldn't be too late for them. It wouldn't.

I passed my hand over the broad mane of the lion as I walked out of the memorial and, this time, it didn't hurt at all.

CHAPTER EIGHT

There were three of them, hanging on the edge of Fort Stanton Park. If my information was correct the tall black kid was Ruffy. He had on the hip-hop uniform of the day: baggy black jeans hanging below his ass, a black shirt, and a black Raiders team jacket—even though it was eighty degrees most days now. Slouching next to him was B-Dog, about a foot shorter but just as skinny. He had a Pittsburgh Pirates cap on backwards, the brim flat as an iron. Cornrows spilled down his back, tied together with a knotted Rasta bandana. The third kid could've just returned from a Redskins tryout. Six three, maybe two-eighty. This would be Tyrone. A purple Lakers tank top let him show the world what steroids and four hours doing arm curls will do for you, along with the tattoos and cuts that pronounced him a badass. Wraparound shades and a shaved head completed the look.

I parked catty-corner to them and watched for about an hour. Ruffy and B-Dog joked and hassled the girls who walked by. Tyrone kept his arms folded and scared the pigeons away. Three, maybe four times, junkies approached them. They'd talk for a minute, then Ruffy would lead them into the park a little ways. The exchange would be made, or so I assumed, and the junkie would shuffle off to Buffalo. Ruffy would come back to the corner and he and B-Dog would pick up where they left off.

I got out of the car. They spotted me before I was halfway across the street and I could see them subconsciously straighten up as they made their assessments. I was a clean-cut, middle-aged white guy in a predominantly black suburb walking toward two known street dealers and their bodyguard. From their perspective, chances were good that I was a cop.

I stood in front of them for a second. When I didn't say anything, B-Dog put a toothpick in his mouth and said, "Help you?"

"I was looking for the Three Stooges, but you guys will do in a pinch," I said, then pointed at each one. "Moe, Larry, and Curly."

"Cop," Ruffy said to no one in particular. Tyrone tried to stare me into the sidewalk.

No reason to deny it. "Guy got killed around here, not too long ago. I'm looking into it."

"People get offed all the time," B-Dog said. "Don't make it our bidness."

"Yeah, but this guy was a policeman," I said. "A cop you knew. You boys grew up around here. You knew Officer Witherspoon. You called him T."

They didn't say anything.

"He used to give you rides from the pool in the summer, take you home when he caught you out on the streets and promised not to tell your parents. His wife taught you in elementary school. Their son's just a few years younger than you."

They still didn't say anything. Ruffy fixed me with a slack stare, B-Dog focused on something over my shoulder. Tyrone continued to try to disintegrate me with his eyes.

"The way I heard it, T watched out for the neighborhood. And when he didn't like something, he took it personally. He probably wouldn't turn a blind eye to what you're doing now, but if he could cut you a break, he would."

"T was all right," Ruffy said.

"Shut up," B-Dog said to Ruffy. He looked at me. "Fuck is it to you?"

"The thing is," I said, "he was looking into something going on around here. Something that was rocking the neighborhood. Something that would've concerned you three. A lot. Like a source outside the, uh, family, shall we say?"

"Man, you don't know what the fuck you talking about," B-Dog said. "'S a quick way to get yo ass kicked."

"I don't know, B-Dog. I've been watching you and scoring deals three or four times an hour might seem good to some, but you're used to doing a lot more than that, right? You guys losing ground to someone, maybe?"

"Man, shut yo mouth. We ain't losing shit."

"Your real name is Bertrand, isn't it? I mean, no one's actually named B-Dog. Then again, no one's really named Bertrand, either, are they?"

B-Dog had decided that, cop or not, he wasn't going to be dissed. He jerked his chin toward me. "Tyrone, shut this silly muthafucka up."

Tyrone started to unwrap the two ham hocks he disguised as arms so he could open his personal can of whoop-ass on me. Which he would've, no doubt about it. Hell, I know a couple of tricks, but they won't do much for a fist backed by a twenty-two-inch bicep. But he'd only gotten his arms half undone when I slapped him with the lipstick-sized stun gun I'd been palming while I talked to them. Somewhat ineffective through clothing; just fine for exposed flesh. Like the kind sprouting out of Tyrone's Lakers jersey.

A strangled howl erupted from him as something like 200,000 volts went rocketing through his system and then he hit the ground to do the jitterbug. I stepped back and slid my hand down toward my hip. A SIG is a handy bargaining tool when trying to dissuade two gangbangers from jumping you. The next move was theirs, within reason.

Ruffy didn't take long to make up his mind. He took off across the park, fast, looking like a two-legged spider. It had probably been his MO since he was a kid. B-Dog, on the other hand, figured out after a moment that, if I was using a stun gun, I probably wasn't a cop. He pulled a clasp knife from a back pocket and moved in.

I'd made a big mistake. I should've stepped back and drawn my SIG as soon as I'd lit Tyrone up with the stun gun. Instead, my good-cop training had taken over and I had waited to see if something would develop. In the academy, they call it waiting for the "threat of imminent danger." On the street, they call it stupid.

But another thing the academy teaches is not to rely on your gun for everything. When cops across the country were found with a hand on the butt of their holstered gun, but dead from a stab wound they probably could've stopped if their hands had been free, there was a shift in training. Use your brain first, your gun second. In this case, if I'd gone for my gun, B-Dog would've opened me up like a birthday present.

So, I gave up on my gun, and just in time. B-Dog came in, swinging the knife in quick half-moons. His technique was wild, trying for a lucky cut rather than working deliberately toward getting me into a position where he could end it. He aimed high, toward my face, hoping I'd flinch. I swatted his arm away two or three times. This gave him the idea that I was afraid, so he moved a little closer. I surprised him when I did, too.

B-Dog was used to intimidating junkies and street punks. It didn't look like he'd ever heard of an arm-bar. But I introduced him to the concept by wrapping my arm through his, grabbing it on the other side, and squeezing. He hollered and tried yanking his arm away, but wouldn't let go of the knife. I squeezed more. He said, "Shit," and the knife dropped to the ground. I let up on the pressure, which he thought meant I was disengaging, so he pulled away.

But what I was really doing was giving myself room to swing a knee. Which I did at the same time that I yanked his arm and shoulder toward the ground. I wasn't twenty anymore and cancer does lousy things to your stamina, so I needed to end this quickly. My kneecap connected just above the bridge of his nose. It didn't feel like much on my end, but his body went slack, and suddenly I was holding a B-Dog–sized bag of Jell-O. The whole thing had taken maybe fifteen seconds.

I dragged him deeper into the park and propped him up against an old playground horse, the kind with the giant spring underneath. He bobbed and bounced as I held him in place. With my free hand, I took my gun out and kept it down by my side, out of sight of the street. No more tactical mistakes. Ruffy might decide to come back and Tyrone wasn't going to stay on the ground forever.

I shook B-Dog. When he started to squirm and swear, I showed him my gun. Somehow, his hat had stayed on through our little tussle, though it was skewed at an angle and now looked like a cooking pot on his head. He quieted down, but his eyes flicked left and right, looking for a way out. I shook him some more.

"Fuck you want, man?" His tone, so cocksure on the corner, was plaintive and wheedling now.

"I asked you some questions earlier, Bertrand," I said. "You can probably guess I'm still interested in hearing the answers."

"Like what?"

"A local cop gets beaten and shot to death. Street business is down. Something bad in the 'hood is about to happen. You're in the middle of it and you're going to tell me what it is."

"That all you want?"

"That's it. Some information," I said. "It shouldn't be this freaking hard."

B-Dog licked his lips and glanced down. Half of his shirt was balled in my fist. I'd shook him with every other word as I spoke. I let go and took a half step back, but kept my gun out. Give and take. If I let him pick his dignity back up off the ground, maybe he'd talk. B-Dog straightened his hat and glanced out at the street, but he didn't move off the horse.

"Three, four months ago, some spic muthafuckas start driving through the 'hood. Every day, they come through, driving slow, checkin' out the park. The street. Never cause no trouble. Just watchin'. But that mean they lookin' for an opening. They gonna close us down or take a cut."

"What do you mean 'spics'? Mexicans? Cubans? Salvadoran?"

"I don' fucking know. Spics, man."

"How would a Hispanic gang take a cut in a black neighborhood?" I asked. "Would that ever happen?"

He shrugged. "Crackheads buy from anybody that got product."

Out of the corner of my eye, I could see Tyrone getting to his feet. He stood and shook his head like a bull moose, then looked around. He spotted us in the park and started to move our way. I turned a little in place so he could see the gun about the same time B-Dog put a hand out. Tyrone stopped and watched us from a distance.

I turned back to B-Dog. "You know who they were? Which gang?"

"Fuck if I know. One of them spic gangs. Logan Circle, Woodbridge, Bowie. They everywhere, man."

"What then?"

"My boy Tone tell us, get ready for a war."

"Tone is your boss," I said.

A head tilt. Maybe yes, maybe no. B-Dog didn't want to think he had a boss, even though he was the one who stood on a street twelve hours a day dealing crack. "Tone get an idea and he tell T about the spics. Tell him if he don't want a war in his 'hood, maybe he should do something about it."

"It warms my heart to see citizens cooperating with local law enforcement," I said. "So, Tone sicced Witherspoon on these other guys, hoping he'd do his job for him."

B-Dog said nothing.

"Did it work? You guys didn't look like you were ready for a war when I showed up, you don't mind me saying."

"Things was tense for a while. Dudes stop coming 'round. Maybe a month ago, Tone say all clear and we go back to dealin'."

"Who killed T, then?"

Shrugging seemed to form a large part of B-Dog's repertoire. "Spics, man. He put the squeeze on them and they took him out."

"That matter to you?"

Shrug. "We didn't off him. And he be after us if he wasn't on them."

"Sentimental, too," I said. "So what's happening now?"

"Bidness as usual. We see any more dudes, we s'pose to tell Tone."

"And that hasn't happened?"

"Nope," B-Dog said.

"Why is business so slow?"

"Man, I look like I got an MBA? Fuck if I know. Maybe the crackheads still scared there gonna be a war." B-Dog was getting some of his swagger back now that his eyes weren't streaming anymore. He glanced out at the street again. "We done yet?"

"I don't know," I said. "But you've been very helpful."

He reached up and rubbed his forehead. It was puffy and swelling. "Man, you ain't a cop. What the fuck are you?"

I thought about it. "That is a really good question, Bertrand."

I.

It was his favorite thing to do, playing the scenes over and over in his mind, rolling them back and forth. Watching himself in his mind's eye from a distance, like a camera in a movie. He liked remembering how things went down, how he'd acted, how cool he was during it all. Each time he killed, it was a little different, but they all spooled out in his mind like an action flick and he loved sitting there and letting them play.

This one, though. It had been too easy. Disappointing.

The lock had been no problem. Torres thought he was a bad motherfucker and had only locked the knob. There were no roommates and it was still early on a Saturday morning, no random visitors to worry about. Nosing around the apartment carefully and quietly, he'd found Torres passed out on the floor with half a case of beer cans lying next to him, on the coffee table, and on top of the TV that was still playing its sports channel wrap-up show. The cop had on camo shorts and an ash-gray tank top that showed off the Superman tattoo high on his shoulder, glowing against the pale skin. Belly down, his face turned to the left. A thin line of drool hung from his lower lip and beaded on the rug, quivering in time with his snores.

Looking down at Torres, he wondered if he should wake him up, let him know what was going to happen and why. No. That wasn't why he was here. He had a purpose—a mission—and it didn't require any explanations. The piece of shit could go to his grave wondering why he'd been snuffed.

Just then, Torres groaned and rolled onto his side, revealing a short, snub-nosed .38 tucked in his waistband. Decision made. This was no time for talk.

Using a pillow to muffle the sounds, he knelt next to Torres and put two shots in the side of the cop's head. The body jerked with each one, then was still, lying just like it had ten seconds before. Tossing the pillow aside, he listened intently for five minutes. Ten. Nothing.

He reached into the backpack he'd brought and pulled out rubber gloves and a set of rain gear he'd picked up at a thrift store. He slid on a pair of safety glasses, but just then the sports show started their baseball segment. He liked baseball, so he sat on the couch and watched a few minutes of the coverage.

He swore when they announced the Rangers had beaten the Angels. He didn't care about the Angels. He just hated the Rangers. Blood from Torres's head seeped into the carpet as he watched and he moved his foot to keep it from getting on his shoe.

At a commercial break, bored, he got up and prowled around the apartment. A set of high school football trophies took up space on a dresser in the bedroom, sitting beneath framed medals and ribbons from other past glories. The biggest trophy had a marble base. He picked it up and bounced it in his hand a few times. It had a nice heft to it, so he took it and went back to the living room.

He turned the AC down to its lowest setting, then kicked the beer cans out of the way. Torres lay almost exactly as he'd found him. If you ignored the little holes. He planted his feet carefully, like a batter. Tilting his head first to the left, then to the right, he chose his spot carefully, then raised the trophy in both hands. He looked over his shoulder, winked at an imaginary camera, then brought the trophy down as hard as he could.

CHAPTER NINE

Over the next twenty-four hours, I sat in my office with my phone and let my fingers do the walking. I might not have anyone who'd be my best man if I decided to get married again, God forbid, but thirty-plus years as a homicide cop in the same town gives you contacts. And it was time to use some of them.

I'd thought about my next steps carefully and decided what I needed was an introduction. The delay made me anxious and I once again had the feeling that time was slipping past me but, while meeting with Libney Garcia and Florence Witherspoon had been easy enough to arrange, at some point I was going to have to talk to the cops that these guys worked with. And while I didn't mind cold-calling the different forces and departments and seeing how it went, I'd waste a lot less time if someone could vouch for me *before* I got there. So, I opened my little black book and started calling the captains, lieutenants, sergeants, beat cops, and DAs I knew from back in the day. I left hearty voice mail messages reminding them who I was and what great times we had and could they call me back about a very vaguely worded case I was working on, please? I wrapped up with a call to Bloch to let him know what

I was doing and that I hadn't used his name or the word "HIDTA" in any of my messages.

After the last call, I put on a pair of ripped jeans and a T-shirt and got to work repainting my kitchen. I wasn't wasting time; I was being realistic. If you asked any of the guys I'd called, I'm sure they'd remember me fondly, but my messages wouldn't be a top priority. Things like extortions and robberies and presidential motorcades were a bit more pressing than my out-of-the-blue request for help. And this wasn't something I could rush. They'd call me when they could. And if I didn't want to give myself an ulcer wondering where Bloch's killer was while I waited, I needed to keep busy.

In my kitchen, I stared awhile at the pile of brushes, rollers, drop cloths, and paint I'd picked up at the hardware store weeks ago and had successfully ignored since then. I'd never painted a wall in my life. And never would have, but while cleaning up a family-style Easter lunch, Amanda had suggested it would be good for me.

"You need a fresh perspective, Marty," she'd said. "It'll give you something constructive to do with your time. Instill a more positive outlook."

"What it will instill in me is a backache and a profound lightness in my wallet," I said.

She lifted a piece of peeling wallpaper—yellow with a pattern of quaint Amish buggies—with a fingernail. "This stuff is brown in the corners. And it's peeling at every seam. How old is it, anyway?"

I thought about it. "It's been here . . . a while."

"How long?"

"Years."

She gave me a look. "How *many* years?"

"Thirty?" I said. I diverted my gaze to the floor, ashamed. Hopefully she wouldn't ask about the linoleum. It had been there thirty-five.

"Oh my God, it has to go," she said, pinching a curling corner of the paper and pulling away a two-by-two swath without effort. I said

"Hey!" in protest, but she balled it up and threw it in the trash. "Even if it were a week old, you'd have to get rid of it. It's screaming seventies."

"That's because it *is* seventies."

She put her hands on her hips and did a half pirouette, assessing the room. "Okay, we'll need some buckets for hot water and some scrapers to get this crap off. Come on, chop-chop."

Out with the old, in with the new. We managed to get the paper off by working the remainder of Easter Sunday. Not the day of rest I'd been hoping for. Scraping the glue off the wall ruined the next Saturday. The work left me exhausted, but that had been weeks ago, and now I needed to make some progress or Amanda would stop talking to me. Patches of glue and wallpaper residue spotted the wall, giving the kitchen a glum, diseased look. Not the fresh, dynamic change Amanda had been looking for. But ripping stuff off a wall was easy. Painting was *hard*.

My cat Pierre set up camp at the doorway to the dining room and watched while I got ready. I moved the chairs and table, wrestled the drop cloths into place, taped the edges of the ceiling, and opened the legs of a stepladder. I mixed the primer and poured it into a plastic cup to start what a DIY magazine had called "cutting in." I climbed the ladder, dipped the brush in the cup, and the phone rang.

I closed my eyes briefly, came back down the ladder, and answered it. It was Bloch.

"Singer," he said. "I got your message."

"Good. I wanted to keep you up to speed. And warn you if you hear about me through the grapevine. I called in a few favors to help me run this thing down."

There was a staccato tapping on the other end of the line. It took me a second, then I realized it was a sped-up rendition of the pencil-tapping habit a lot of people have when they're on the phone. Bloch's version was sent into overdrive by his need for nicotine, apparently. "That'll make it tough to keep the investigation quiet."

"I need to get on the inside of these departments, Bloch. Which I can do if some of the people I called vouch for me. But I have to tell them something about why. And I'm going to have to tell the cops I talk to something."

He didn't say anything, so I tried to push the point home.

"How would you like it if some boob showed up at your office one day and told you he needed to talk to some of your officers because he happened to be running his own homicide case? All outside regular channels and with a very foggy mandate from a local law enforcement agency that he would rather not name."

"What are you going to tell them?"

"I don't have to lie. I'll tell my contacts that I got called in to do a favor for a task force. Which is true."

"If they press it?"

"I'll tell them to call you. Which none of them will do, because it's too much work and they trust me and they'll have heard of HIDTA. Five will get you ten that they'll just pick up the phone, call a lieutenant or sergeant they know, and ask them to play nice with me."

Tap, tap, tap. "What about the cops they get you in to see?"

"Same thing, different angle. Their lieutenant or captain will have already told them I'm one of the good guys and they should cooperate. If they push it, I'll tell them it's related to a case from your department, but that I'm not going to get in their way or step on any toes or write any reports."

The tapping slowed down. "A grain of truth goes a long way."

"Exactly."

"All right. Sorry. It seemed okay to speculate and think about how to tackle this, but then when it actually happens, and you start calling people, I realized . . ."

"That your job could be on the line?" I finished.

"Yeah."

"Try not to think of it that way," I said. "We're doing a good thing, as you pointed out to me. If we're careful not to piss anybody off along the way, and don't give them cause to think we're trying to upstage them, there's no reason they won't play ball. And let's not forget, we're working on someone else's time line. Anything we can do to head off the next killing, we've got to take."

He blew out a breath and, in that one sound, I could hear all of his pent-up anxiety and fear. "Do what you have to do, Singer. And thanks."

He hung up. I sympathized with him. It was one thing to vent to a former colleague, sharing fears and frustrations. It was an entirely different thing to authorize that colleague to start poking sticks in hornets' nests. Unfortunately, it couldn't be helped. If he wanted answers and we were going to stop whoever was killing cops, I'd have to introduce myself to the people who knew the victims best: family, friends, and other cops.

I grabbed the cup of rapidly congealing primer and headed back up the ladder. After a few minutes, I caught on to the rhythm of the strokes, taking my time, perfecting the movements. Painting was a pleasantly empty activity that lent itself to a wandering mind and I found myself thinking about the murders. Considering how I would tell the cops I would be meeting that someone was out there, methodically killing anyone with a badge. Wondering if I was right about what was going on.

Hoping that, for once, I wasn't.

CHAPTER TEN

I put the car in park and stared out my windshield across a miserable field of cars, trucks, trailers, and Dumpsters. Blue Plains wasn't the prettiest place in the world. Not far to the west, the Potomac flowed fresh and clean, but you'd never know it looking at the eight-foot cyclone fence and razor wire that guarded the city's approximately eleven zillion impounded cars. Somewhere along the fence, I'd heard, was the site of one of the original District boundary stones, placed there two hundred years ago by L'Enfant himself. The stone was moved during construction in the fifties and stolen or lost. In typical DC fashion, there'd been a replacement, but it had been buried under eight feet of fill when Blue Plains was graded to create the impound lot. The only way you could see it now was by peering down a concrete pipe.

I was pondering our region's on-again, off-again love of history when Bloch pulled up in a blue Elantra. I got out and walked over. He motioned for me to get in the passenger's seat.

"This where you bring all your dates?" I asked.

"Only the ones that want to get their car back," he said, grinning. Some of the weariness and worry seemed gone from his face. I perked up. Only a breakthrough would give Bloch a lift like that.

"What's up?"

He reached into a jacket pocket and handed me a white business-sized envelope. It was addressed to Danny Garcia, but at HIDTA, not his home. It was from the DC Department of Motor Vehicles. I peered at Bloch, who just raised his eyebrows and motioned for me to open it. I scanned the contents quickly. It was an impound notice for a 1989 Toyota Camry. The reason for its impoundment, it said in the cryptic lettering reserved for government correspondence with the public, was two unpaid parking tickets over sixty days old.

"Oh, ho," I said. "This come to your office?"

He nodded, then jerked a thumb toward the lot in front of us. "This starting to make sense?"

"You betcha," I said. "You have the original dates of the tickets?"

"Took some running down. The DC DMV doesn't exactly run like clockwork."

"Unless you like your clocks to be broken," I said. "Though even they're right twice a day. What did they tell you?"

"The tickets were from three and five days after Danny's body was found, respectively," he said.

"You know my next question."

"The registration address was the HIDTA office. Which is why the impound notice was sent there, of course."

"He have other cars?"

"Two," Bloch said. "A Corolla and a Bronco. Both registered to Danny and Libney Garcia."

I closed my eyes, thinking, remembering. "The Corolla was at the house when I talked to her. The son could've had the other one. You didn't call and ask her about the Camry?"

He shook his head. "Not until we have a chance to look at it."

"What are we waiting for?"

Bloch got a crime scene kit out of his trunk, then we went to the gate where he flashed his badge. We were ushered through to a trailer where, behind the counter, a bored-looking black lady with five-inch fingernails stopped looking at her cell phone long enough to glance at Danny's impoundment notice. Bloch told her it would be best if we went to the car rather than having it brought to us. She sighed and picked up an office phone. She said three or four syllables and hung up.

"Darnell pick you up outside," she said and grabbed her cell phone again, ignoring us as if we'd just evaporated.

We went out the door and a few minutes later a golf cart pulled up, a stoic-looking black guy in a green windbreaker and a green and yellow John Deere cap behind the wheel. He had a clipboard in his lap and nodded to us as we approached. Bloch got in the passenger's side, I climbed in the back, and Darnell took off, pushing the upper ten or twelve miles an hour that the cart could do. It made a dull whine that sounded like a large mosquito or a rip cord being unwound into infinity. Darnell drove with confidence, whizzing us past row upon row of cars.

I leaned forward. "What do you do with all of them?"

Darnell spoke over his shoulder. "Auction 'em off if they're good enough. Junk 'em if not."

"People don't come and get their own cars?"

He shrugged. "They don't care. Or they're in jail. Or they can't pay the bank and just skip town."

A minute later we pulled up to the edge of one of the shorter rows. He slowed and glanced down at the clipboard, then pulled up behind a blue Camry spotted gray with body repairs.

"Here we are, officers," Darnell said.

"We don't exactly have a key," Bloch said. "Can you help us out?"

Darnell grinned and shut the golf cart off. He clambered out, slipping something out of a back pocket as he walked up to the driver's side door of the Camry. I thought he was going to take at least a minute to fiddle with the lock, but then he stepped back and the door was open.

My eyebrows shot to my hairline. "You did that with a slim jim? Not a key?"

He grinned again. "I got it down to three seconds. You gentlemen have a good day."

He got in the cart and headed back. As I watched Darnell zip down the row away from us, I realized I was watching our ride disappear. It was a half-mile walk back to the gate. I looked over at Bloch.

He realized it at about the same time I did. "Shit," he said, watching Darnell's green jacket recede.

"Did you get the number for the office?"

"I called from my desk at work," he said. "I can buzz my guys and have them call me back."

"Three calls to save us a fifteen-minute walk?"

"Hell, yes," he said. He tossed me a pair of blue surgical gloves from the kit. "But let's see how long this takes us, first."

Bloch took the trunk so I started up front. The interior was a mess. There were stains on every inch of the gray fabric. Dents marred the dashboard and the cloth ceiling sagged where it had been ripped or cut. The backseat foot wells were full of fast-food bags and wrappers and the floor mats were covered in cinders, dirt, and the occasional leaf.

I put myself in each seat, taking on the role of someone sitting there. Where would I put my hands, how would I drop my trash, what would I be looking at? I searched the door pockets, the console, the glove compartment. I flipped the sun visors down, peeked under the seats, then took a deep breath and gingerly slid my hand between the cushions. I pulled out all the trash and carefully laid it on the ground next to the car. There were a few receipts, which I smoothed out and pocketed.

"Find anything?" Bloch called from the back.

"A buck sixty-five in change," I said. "And hepatitis A. You?"

"A flat spare, a cheap jack, and something interesting."

I climbed out of the backseat and went around to the trunk. "Oh, ho."

"You said that already," Bloch said. "But, yeah. Oh fucking ho."

Bolted to the frame was an empty three-slot shotgun rack. It was a cradle with Velcro straps that could be wrapped around the guns to hold them in place for the gunslinger on the go. Mounted on the left-hand wall of the trunk was a handgun holster that was not empty. Bloch carefully pulled the gun out and showed me. The small revolver almost disappeared in his hand.

"You know the model?" he asked, cracking the cylinder open. It was loaded.

"Smith & Wesson Model 642," I said. "A snubbie. Five rounds. As accurate as you are. Well, out to about fifteen feet."

"A good holdout gun?"

I nodded. "Very good. It's got a shrouded hammer, so nothing to snag on your clothes when you pull it out. Light. Small. Puts up with neglect."

"Like sitting in the back of a junker until you need it." Bloch put the gun back in the holster and secured it. He had already removed the tire, the jack, and some of the crap that always seems to accumulate in the wheel well. I got down on the ground and ran my hands along the underside of the frame. My hands encountered a small, rectangular anomaly.

"Oh, ho, I say. For the third time." I tugged at the rectangle and the magnet holding the box in place gave way. I stood. My turn for show-and-tell. The box had a latch but no lock. I opened it. A key chain with a plastic flag of Mexico for a fob and four keys dropped in my hand. I flipped through the keys.

"Ford," I said. "Toyota."

Bloch pointed at two others. "Those are house keys. Front and back door?"

"Or a front door and a garage," I said. I went to the front of the car and tried locking the door with the Toyota key, then plopped down in the driver's seat and tried it in the ignition. It didn't work either time. I held the key up. "Think this starts up a Corolla sitting in the driveway of a house in Chantilly?"

He nodded, then pulled out his cell phone and dialed a number. He lit a cigarette while he waited. Someone on the other end picked up and he spoke for a few minutes, walking off a little ways and staring into space like people do when they're on the phone. He waited, pulled out a small notebook and jotted something down, then turned back to me after hanging up.

"We got two keys off of Danny's body."

"An older model Toyota?" I said, gesturing at the Camry.

"And a house key," he said. "No markings on the key chain."

"Call back. Ask where the parking tickets were handed out."

He held up the notebook. "Dumont Street, Southeast."

"Not too far from where Danny's body was found."

Bloch nodded.

"You haven't thought of everything," I said. "How about our ride back to the gate?"

He pointed down the quarter-mile-long row of cars. In the distance, I could see a figure that might be wearing a green jacket get into a golf cart.

I looked at the smirk on Bloch's face and shook my head.

CHAPTER ELEVEN

"So you didn't know about the Camry?" I asked. "It's not a HIDTA car?"

We were sitting in a scuzzy booth in a doughnut shop and swatting ideas back and forth. After coming back from Blue Plains, Bloch had grabbed the keys bagged at the scene of Danny's murder and then we'd headed for the doughnut shop to grab some coffee and think. We both knew we were close to something, but wanted to get it right. My own anxiety was probably written all over my face—the clock could still be ticking down to the next murder—as it was on Bloch's, but we needed to stop and figure out what we'd just unearthed at Blue Plains.

"Nope," Bloch said, slurping through the plastic lid. He winced and pulled the lid off to let some of the heat escape. "You feel like a cop again? Sitting in a doughnut shop?"

"I never liked doughnuts," I said. "It was snapping on a pair of surgical gloves and giving the car the once-over that gave me déjà vu."

"Show me a cop that doesn't like doughnuts."

I made a frame around my face with the forefinger and thumb of each hand. "You're looking at him."

"What about coffee? You don't like coffee?"

"I love coffee, but you don't have to get it at a doughnut shop," I said. "Anyway, about the Camry."

"It's Danny's."

"But not Libney's," I said.

"Right. It's part of his undercover life."

"So, the Camry's a holdout car that says junkie or dealer all over it that his wife probably never knew about. It's got a small armory in the trunk and room for more. Which wouldn't be that unusual for an undercover cop—if his boss knew about the guns, too."

"This boss didn't know."

"You said he had a long leash. Was it this long?"

Bloch shook his head and put his coffee down. "No. I mean, a lot of cops have holdout guns. Big deal. And maybe they own a junker they drive to work. Undercover has all that and more. They have to live the life. But no cop is going to buy all that on his own dime."

I held up the two keys we'd gotten from the HIDTA evidence locker, thinking. "What's this other key to?"

"Storage facility? Apartment? Another house?"

I turned the keys over in my hand. "These keys were on his body when he was killed. They're his junkie keys, the ones he needs for the Camry. But his everyday keys were in the spare box under the Camry."

Bloch nodded, seeing it. "He was working his undercover thing, which is why we found the piece-of-shit Camry keys on his body. But he wasn't going to drive home in the Camry. He expected to swap it with something else."

"So he could go home to his normal life," I said.

"Right. Like punching out of one life and starting another."

"If he did that, he would've had to leave the Camry somewhere, right? He wasn't going to take the secret car home to his wife. But he was killed before he could do the swap."

"Which means he had another car. And it should still be wherever he left it," Bloch said and reached for his notebook. He flipped some pages back and forth, then pulled out his cell phone and dialed a number. He talked for a few minutes, hung up, said "Hold on a minute" to me, and dialed again. He waited, spoke for a minute more, and jotted something down in his notebook. He sipped coffee as he read his notes.

"It was the Bronco," he said. "It was booted, then scheduled to be towed. Probably right out to Blue Plains like the Camry. Paul Garcia paid the ticket and picked it up a few weeks ago."

"The overdue notice got sent to his home," I said, "because it's registered there."

"Right."

"Where was *it* ticketed?"

"Chalmers Street, Southeast. Near St. Elizabeths."

I frowned. "Barry Farm?"

"Yeah," Bloch said. Then, "Oh, hell. Witherspoon."

"Yeah," I said. I pulled out the fast food and gas station receipts I'd salvaged from the search of the Camry and shuffled through them like cards. "I don't know all of these addresses, but the two or three I know are all down there. Terry Street, Holtz Avenue, Fairlington."

Bloch put the lid back on the coffee and stood up. "Time to check out Chalmers Street."

I stood, too. "You think?"

We drove to the address where the Bronco had been towed. It was no surprise it had been ticketed; Chalmers was a busy street with businesses in both directions for six blocks. The sounds of honking cars, people yelling to each other, and the beeping of trucks in reverse filled the air. The neighborhood wouldn't have won any prizes for community safety, but the constant traffic and commerce at least meant it wasn't stagnant.

Bloch eased into a spot across from where the Bronco had been ticketed. The block consisted of the fifties-era, two-story, brown and gray row houses that had sprung up in the boom after World War II. They cover about two-thirds of DC and if you're an urban history buff, you can track the growth of the city by them, like counting the rings on a tree.

This clump had seen better days. There were eight separate doors in the run of connected homes. Plywood covered the windows of several and at least one had an eviction notice tacked to the door. Artless graffiti, simple vandalism, covered the porches and fronts of two. Bottles and papers had been caught and mounded in the corners where the brick steps met the sidewalk.

"Knock on some doors, see what crawls out?" I asked.

"Sounds good," he said.

We skipped the one with the eviction notice. Of the seven remaining, four were occupied. Most were black grandmothers or young mothers with two or three kids in tow. None of them recognized the picture of Danny Garcia that Bloch showed them. Or they didn't want to admit to it. In any neighborhood, under most circumstances, people denied the simplest things when asked by a cop. I'd had people deny the car on the curb outside their house was theirs, deny they lived in the house they were standing in. It was instinct. The less the fuzz knew, the better. To be honest, we half expected it. We were looking for the reaction more than anything. Did they gasp, or shake their head too much, or react strangely? Unfortunately, Bloch and I didn't get any of that.

"You want to try the more direct route?" Bloch asked me after we'd struck out on the seventh house.

"Beats knocking on all the doors again," I said.

I took the mystery key found on Danny's body and tried it on the three houses that hadn't answered our knocks. It fit into two of them but didn't work and on the third it wouldn't even go in the lock. We tried it on the house with the eviction notice, but it didn't work there, either. We stood on the sidewalk, stumped.

"This is the right place, isn't it?" Bloch asked, looking at his notebook. "Where the car got the ticket?"

"Yeah," I said and pointed to the corner opposite us. "That gas station is one of the ones we have a receipt for. And I think we passed a Burger King at the end of the block that he stopped at, too."

"What do you want to do? It wouldn't be hard to look up the landlord's name, work backwards from that."

"We're here, though," I said. I headed for the alley that split the block from the rest of the street. "Let's try one more thing."

The row backed up onto another alley where people dumped their garbage, not always with the benefit of a can or a bag. Two cars were parked there, hugging the wall so close that they almost touched. The houses had windowless, industrial-looking back doors made of steel and painted a dull black or green. I counted down the end of the row until I got to the house with the eviction notice and tried the key in the back door. No go.

I moved down the row to the houses that hadn't answered. On the second one I tried, the key went in and turned easily in the lock.

"Bingo," I said with a grin.

We drew our guns and I opened the door. Nothing came out and I fumbled around the inside wall for a light switch. A weak overhead lamp came on and we covered each other while we did a quick look around. Since the whole place consisted of the room we were in, a closet, and a bathroom, it took approximately ten seconds to ascertain that we were alone.

"I'm an idiot," Bloch said, holstering his gun. "A basement apartment. Different tenants out front. Of course the key didn't work."

"You've worked on a task force too long," I said. "It'll rot your brain, all those lackeys doing your work for you."

"Lackeys? I'm lucky they gave me a gun."

Like we'd done for the Camry earlier in the day, we split the apartment to cover more ground. I worked counterclockwise from the door,

Bloch the opposite. The place was missing the kind of cozy touches Amanda might try to put in, but for an eight-hundred-square-foot efficiency, it was packed with stuff. On the side with the longest wall, a couch and a chair sat catty-corner to each other with a coffee table between. A dilapidated end table covered with coffee rings propped up one end of the couch.

A folding cot took up another corner with a footlocker at its . . . well, feet. A card table with two cheap wire-frame chairs was pushed up against a wall near the kitchenette. The refrigerator had a plastic bucket full of single-serving nondairy creamers, a five-pound bag of coffee, and two cases of Coke. An old coffeemaker squatted on the counter with a stack of a thousand coffee filters next to it. There was no china in the cupboards, just a few dozen foam plates and cups, paper napkins, and plastic utensils. No food in any of the cabinets.

"Got something," I said when I looked in the footlocker. Inside were ammo boxes for a .38 and shells for a twelve-gauge shotgun. There were zip ties, the kind used in place of handcuffs. And there was a host of first aid supplies, ranging from the antiseptic sprays and bandages you could get in any pharmacy to some not-so-over-the-counter doses of injectable painkillers and antibiotics.

"Does it beat this?" Bloch asked from the open closet.

I walked over and peeked over his shoulder, then whistled. Inside was a small armory. Two shotguns were propped in a corner. Both appeared to have been cleaned and oiled recently. A Kevlar vest without the ceramic inserts hung from a peg. The rest of the hanger space was devoted to variations on camouflage or black clothing. Two pairs of well-worn black combat boots, identical size, were lined up neatly on the floor of the closet.

"Holy crap," Bloch said. He pushed the clothing on the hangers to one side. Several wooden pegs hammered into the wall acted as a homemade rack for a compact, crazy-looking gun straight out of the future. It was all harsh angles and made of some dull, synthetic material.

Bloch took it off the rack, holding it gingerly by the ends. He gave it a once-over, then handed it to me. It was about the length of my forearm, with a retractable stock that, if extended, would make it two and a half or three feet long.

"H&K?" I said. "An MP7, I think. Submachine gun. Not exactly standard-issue at HIDTA, I imagine."

"I think we've already established Danny didn't do anything standard. That thing is right out of *Star Wars*," Bloch said. He took the gun from me and placed it back on the rack. "You find anything?"

I showed him the contents of the locker. He shook his head. "What do we have?"

I turned to the room. "Besides the hardware? Lots of caffeine. No long-term living. No plates, cups, food. I guess that's where Burger King came in. No personal effects."

"It's a bolt-hole," he said. "Or a staging area."

"It ain't a love nest," I said. "Unless Danny was dating a gun nut with no sense of romance and a thing for carryout."

"Is that it? Did we miss anything?"

"The furniture's a little strange."

Bloch glanced in the corner. "A couch and a chair? What about them?"

"We're talking about one guy who used the place a couple hours a week, if that. Maybe crashes on the cot or grabs a cup of coffee in between meets or busts. So, why the couch *and* a chair? One chair would do it."

"Sleep. No, he's got the cot for that," Bloch said, chewing his lip. "He meet people here?"

I nodded. "Often enough that they needed a place to sit."

"Four?"

"Maybe, but probably not. Three people don't like to sit on a couch together, like ducks in a row. Especially guys. Most would sit one at each end of the couch, another in the chair."

"Three guys, meeting here, often enough that they needed a place to sit and talk," Bloch said, then glanced at the kitchen. "How much caffeine?"

"Enough to keep your squad awake for a week."

"And enough potential firepower to start a small war."

I nodded.

"Jesus," he said, running a hand through his hair. "Danny, what the hell were you doing?"

CHAPTER TWELVE

Two days after trying to cash in some favors built over a thirty-year career in law enforcement, I was starting to wonder just what kind of legacy I'd left behind. No one had phoned, dropped by, or sent a telegram acknowledging that I'd asked for some help. I would've felt better even if someone had called to say no. And, while I'd gone into the process with patience, there was a lunatic out there somewhere who had a clock ticking inside his head and when the alarm went off another cop would die. The files didn't indicate a chronological pattern to the killings, but that only meant that the next one could happen anytime.

On the other hand, the kitchen was now painted a nice, soothing shade of sage green, or at least as close as I could find to the color of the walls at Restaurant Nora. I figured I could do worse than styling my kitchen after a place that had served me my best meal of the year. If I was lucky, some of it might rub off on me next time I made something on the stove. It couldn't hurt. My cooking couldn't get much worse.

I was looking at the cabinets, wondering what Amanda thought I would need to do next, when my phone rang. I scrambled around for it in my pocket.

"Marty Singer?" A male voice I didn't recognize, high and with a slight accent I couldn't place. The syllables came rapid-fire, with the ends clipped off.

"Speaking."

"Chuck Rhee, Arlington PD. My boss said you wanted to talk to me."

I straightened up. "Yeah, I did. Thanks for getting in touch. Uh, who's your boss?"

Rhee laughed. "John Creusfeld, head of Gangs. You don't know who you're calling, huh?"

"Let's just say I made a ton of calls the last few days. It's easier to ask you than go through the list. Creusfeld tell you what this is about?"

"Something about Brady Torres and maybe a tie-in with a case in DC."

"That's it," I said. "I'm trying to connect the dots on something and Torres's name came up. It might be nothing or it might help out with both cases."

"What do you need from me?"

"What Torres was working on. Gangs he was looking into, dealers or junkies who might've wanted him gone. Especially any work that took him back and forth into DC. The victim I'm looking at was knocked off in the District and had, uh, ties to law enforcement."

"He a snitch?"

"Undercover," I said.

"Oh, man."

"Yeah," I said. "Can you meet?"

Honking covered up whatever he was going to say. He must've been driving and talking. He tried again. "I can meet, I said. What time?"

I glanced at my watch. "Give me half an hour. I can meet you anywhere in Arlington."

More honks. Rhee swore at someone or something. "Tell you what, I have to make some rounds out in Culmore and Lincolnia, check out my homies. You want to do a ride-along and we can talk? Kill two birds with one stone?"

"Sure," I said, getting a strange tingly feeling. It had been a year since I'd been in a cruiser. At least in an official capacity. Rhee asked me where I lived and told me he'd pick me up in an hour.

I changed clothes, nervous as a prom date. I didn't want to look like I was out to play cop, trying to get back in the game. I thought about what I should wear, how I should act. What about my gun? I had a license to carry and I knew I'd feel naked without it. On the other hand, there was no reason to believe I'd need it with an Arlington cop in the driver's seat.

In the end, I brought the gun, a case of caution overtaking sense. I couldn't imagine a situation where, if I had to use it, I wouldn't do so responsibly and as a last resort. On the other hand, I could visualize plenty of situations where I didn't have my gun and wished I did. I had to put on a windbreaker to cover it, which was a shame, since it was another gorgeous day and I was about to sweat my ass off.

Flipping through Torres's file again helped kill the time until Rhee pulled up in a silver Integra with custom stripes and a two-foot-high spoiler in the back. I walked out and slipped into the passenger's side. Rhee was a dark, thin Asian dude wearing a white wifebeater, baggy jeans, and black work boots. He had spiky black hair, silver wraparound shades, and a star-shaped scar on one cheek. Around his neck was a gold chain with a cross. On his left thumb was a fat silver ring. He had wide shoulders and, judging by the muscle fibers working under his skin like piano strings, maybe 1 percent body fat.

He stuck a hand out. "Chuck Rhee."

I shook. "Marty Singer."

He glanced at my clothes with a smile. "If you're trying to look like a cop, it's working."

"I was trying hard to *not* look like a cop," I said, sour.

He laughed and checked the mirror, then pulled away from the curb at about a hundred miles an hour. The Integra was a stick shift and he clutched and changed gears smoothly, like he was playing an instrument. "Some guys are just cops to the bone, I guess. No big deal. It's not like these hombres don't know what I do for a living. They'll just think you're my lieutenant or something."

"Who are you talking to today?"

"Las Chacas," he said. "Little shit Salvadoran gang in Lincolnia. If you can call it a gang. About eight girls and a handful of dudes. They hang out in malls, begging and stealing whatever they can snatch. End of the day, they pool it and rent a room at some fleabag motel. They drink cheap beer and smoke weed and fuck and trash the room until they get kicked out. Then they go to the next mall and start over."

"They sound like a waste of space," I said.

"They are," he said.

"What's your interest in them, then?"

"Grassroots," he said as he turned onto Wilson Boulevard. We got stopped every block or two by the traffic lights that seemed to have sprouted up all over Arlington. "These small fry want nothing more in life than to climb their way up the ladder, be a real gang member, man, not just some dropout in a Mickey Mouse club. So they kiss ass whenever the genuine article comes around."

"Why do they bother? The real gangbangers, I mean."

Rhee answered while he watched a girl—dressed incongruously in a knee-length skirt, silk blouse, and flip-flops—walk up Wilson Boulevard. Walk was one way to describe it. The skirt was so tight that she had to take steps that seemed half the length of her normal stride. Rhee grinned, loving every mincing step. "Eh, they gotta recruit, too. They take like one out of ten of the little fish. And the ones they don't take . . . well, who wouldn't mind having a bunch of groupies tripping over you, giving you pot and booze and pussy without you asking? Even if they are, for the most part, completely worthless."

"So you build up relationships with the little gangs," I said.

"And cash in once in a while on the big ones," he said. "None of these kids have what it takes to make it into the real gangs, but they don't know that. They give it the old college try anyway, try to impress the hard-core homies. Go stab somebody or torch an apartment building or be a drug mule to San Antonio. When that happens, shit can go wrong. Then they freak and come running to us."

"And you flip them."

"Sometimes. Not always. The smart ones realize there's no going back if they talk to us. They clam up after we save their asses. Then we have to let them go. Lost opportunity. But even those usually give us something we can use. Where we picked them up, what were they doing when we did, that kind of thing. They know they'll get the yellow light when they go back to their homies, but that's the price you pay for talking to the cops."

"Yellow light?"

He glanced over at me. "Medium-level punishment. Gang makes a big circle. You get in the middle, then they beat the shit out of you for a ten count. Well, not every time. Sometimes, if they're feeling generous, they just stab you once and then drive you to a hospital. Kick you to the curb outside the ER and take off."

"Nice," I said. "Was Torres doing this grassroots stuff when he got killed?"

Rhee shrugged. Traffic broke for a two-block stretch and he shifted to fourth. "Kind of. Brady was impatient, always wanted to go to the top and make the big bust, haul in the head of the gang. He didn't want to do the legwork to get there. He could get under your skin. But he was a smooth talker, man. Six months on the street and he was chatting up hard-core homies like they were related. Milk-white kid with red hair, shit."

"Did he get too close? Somebody get nervous and take him out?"

He made a face. "I don't see it. The big gangs have to be plenty pissed to take out a cop. They'll do it, if they have to. But they have to get the nod from a bunch of honchos way up the food chain. Do it without approval and you're fucked, end up in a garbage can in little pieces."

"That's the, uh, green light?"

"Beyond green light, man," he said. "Green light means they just kill you. This is green light plus."

"They do it because of the heat?"

"Yeah, but not just the way you mean. You kill a cop, everything stops everywhere," Rhee said. "No drugs, no parties, no money changing hands. Three, four months, everyone in the gang has to lie low. And these boys don't exactly keep a savings account, right? Even a couple weeks out of action hurts. If you're talking months, then these guys are stone-cold broke. With every cop on the squad breathing down their neck."

"So Torres wasn't bothering them enough to bring that on?"

Rhee shook his head. "Not unless he was hiding it real good. Gang unit is tight. We all know pretty much what everyone's doing. No one else is looking out for us, so we have to."

"Is it that bad?"

"I don't know. It's better than it was. I've been with Gangs for eight years and it ain't the best thing for your self-esteem, man, I can tell you that. First, everyone thinks the unit is a cutout, brought in by the mayor or the chief to headline a press conference." His voice dropped an octave. "*City Official Declares War on Gangs with Elite New Unit* and that kind of shit. So, the rest of the force thinks we're a bunch of props. Or, no, wait, we must've got kicked out of our old units because we're fuckups and troublemakers, right? And if *that* isn't it and we actually do our job, well, it must be because we're all on the take."

"Because you're consorting with the enemy," I said.

"Every day, man. And you don't do it in a uniform or a shirt and tie, you know what I mean? You want to tell a bunch of schoolkids to just say no, wear a badge and a hat. You want to know who's driving up 95 with six hundred pounds of dope in the back of a U-Haul, then you gotta play the part."

"Isn't Creusfeld on the warpath? I hadn't read or heard a thing about Torres's killing until a few days ago," I said. "I mean, if no one is looking out for you . . ."

"Then we look out for ourselves," Rhee said. "Sure. Three Musketeers and all that shit. But you heard what I said, right? Half the department's looking for an excuse to close the doors on us. If we go bananas and start putting people in the ground, Gangs is over."

"So?"

"So we wait. And when we know for sure who put our boy Brady down," Rhee said, turning to me and smiling, all teeth, "then life gets hard for that individual. Very hard."

We were both quiet for a few minutes.

"What's the theory on Torres, then?" I asked. "If he wasn't bothering anyone enough to get knocked off and he was in tight with the right people, where's that leave you?"

Rhee was quiet, then shrugged. "I wish I knew."

CHAPTER THIRTEEN

We arrived at the stretch of suburban consumer hell known as Seven Corners. Every road in Northern Virginia seemed to come together at this one spot with all the charm of a train wreck. Parking lots and strip malls and traffic lights radiated in every direction. The road was twelve lanes wide in some places, if you counted both directions and all the turning lanes. At ten o'clock in the morning, we were one of hundreds of cars choking the road.

Rhee took a left off of Wilson Boulevard and we headed down Route 50 at a stop-and-go pace for a mile before turning into the parking lot of an older, beaten-down-looking strip mall. A beauty parlor and a mattress store held down the middle of the row, flanked by a "party warehouse" on one side and a 7-Eleven on the other. The party store was dark and the posters in the windows were yellowed. It was pretty down in the mouth for a place purporting to sell fun. How many foil hats and noisemakers do you have to sell to make a living, anyway? The mattress place and the beauty parlor were almost as dead as the party store. The only life was a group of kids hanging out in front of the 7-Eleven.

Rhee pulled into a free space in front of the mattress store, put the car in park, then turned to me. "Okay, two of the girls over there are in Las Chacas, but I don't see Rico, the leader. He's probably still working off a hangover in a Motel 6, but if these cuties talk to me, it'll save some time. Hang tight."

He got out of the car and sauntered over to the little group. There were four kids altogether, all of them girls. They wore nearly identical combinations of skin-tight jeans and pullover tops. Two sat on the curb, one checked out something through the window of the store, and the last leaned against one of the pillars holding the veranda roof up. The first two noticed Rhee as he got close, but there was none of the scrambling around or straightening up that I was used to seeing when cops made contact with gangs. Or kids, for that matter. They seemed relaxed, chatty even. The girl who'd been looking in the window turned around and walked over to join them, popping gum.

Rhee's body language was confident, cool. He slouched, his hands in his back pockets, while he talked. He must've led with a joke, because the girls all started to laugh. He made some kind of gesture to go with the joke and the girls all laughed again. He talked some more, then listened, asked a question and got some nods, then fingers pointing out toward Seven Corners. Another question, then shy nods. He turned toward me and made a "hold on" kind of motion, then went inside the store. The girls looked over at the car with idle curiosity, then went back to staring at nothing.

Five minutes later, Rhee came out with a plastic bag ready to burst, which he handed to one of the girls. He waved and said something, but they'd already torn into the bag, spilling sodas and chips onto the ground.

Rhee got into the car. "Okay, *las chicas* didn't know for sure, but they think Rico actually is at a Motel 6, the one off Columbia Pike. So, that's where we're heading."

"What was the joke?"

"Huh? Oh, you know, the usual. Talking smack about how bad their guys are in bed. They love it. I was lucky it was all the girls, though. If there's even one macho asshole there, they don't say a word. You never deal with the ladies if there's a dude around. And you can't joke with most of the homies. They think they're in a war or something. Gotta stay *strong*. Can't laugh at a joke or you look weak."

"And the little bag of goodies?"

Rhee waved dismissively. "Thirty bucks. Junk food. Keeps them happy, saves them three or four hours of panhandling at the malls. These kids are so poor, most of them don't eat but once a day anyway. And they'll remember me for it. Next time I come around, they'll give me Rico's shoe size if I ask. As long as I don't tell *him* where I got it."

"Don't a bunch of Latinas think it's weird to trade jokes with a Korean cop who's trying to pump them for intel about their *jefe*?"

He grinned. "We're all outsiders, man. As long as I don't look like a gringo or flash a badge, I'm in tight."

We joined the line of traffic heading down to Columbia Pike, passing the area known as Culmore. This was ground zero of the Salvadoran population in Virginia and pretty much the whole DC area. Business signs were in Spanish first, with English, if it was listed at all, below.

"We didn't see any of this coming," I said, looking out at the rundown neighborhood. "We all thought the black gangs had dibs on the worst of the drugs and the violence."

"The pulse of history, man," Rhee said. "Someone else gets on top once in a while. You know how it started? Why the Salvadoran gangs are so prevalent?"

I shrugged. "A little bit. You probably know it forwards and backwards."

"Want to learn?"

"We got time. Lay it on me."

Rhee grinned. "In 1980, while you were busting crooks in DC and my older sister was falling in love with Duran Duran, El Salvador has itself a twelve-year civil war. Bunch of people get killed, even more get the hell out. They trickle north, but Mexico isn't much better than home. And LA is just over the border, looking pretty good to a bunch of people who live on five bucks a month. But LA ain't ready to welcome a bunch of piss-poor Central American refugees with open arms. The blacks and the Mexican gangs start pushing the Salvadorans around."

"And they push back," I said.

"Right. Now, normally, these refugees would get their asses handed to them by any number of gangs in LA that would line up for the pleasure. But these fuckers weren't bean farmers, man. They're rebels, army deserters. They got five, ten years of combat experience in the *jungle*. They're not going to take shit from anyone. People learn real quick not to mess with the Salvadoran *maras*, the gangs, and pretty soon we've got a real success story, the American Dream come true. The gang carves out some breathing room, starts to spread, and puts down roots."

"What about recruitment? Some of those ex-rebels have to be out of the picture by now, right?"

"Sure. That was in the early nineties. But there ain't never been a shortage of poor, displaced Central Americans, homie, especially around here. And even the ones who are trying to be decent can be part of the problem."

"Like?"

"One scenario, happens all the time. Mom and Dad emigrate from El Salvador to make money in the US, leave their kid back home with Grandma. The parents work their asses off. Ten years later, they finally get enough cash to bring him along, but now their cute five-year-old is a surly teenager who doesn't know a lick of English. He's supposed to fit in overnight. And maybe he has a new little brother or sister half his age who speaks the language and acts American and is the apple of Mama and Papa's eye. Now the first kid's pissed off. He's a second-class citizen in his own family. He's got no identity. He finds the gang, or the gang finds him, and they've got a new recruit who doesn't have the first idea about the Salvadoran civil war and wouldn't care if he did. He's just mad and wants to make somebody pay."

We spied the motel a minute later and Rhee pulled into the parking lot. We sat and took stock of the place, a two-story, run-of-the-mill flophouse.

"Which one?" I asked.

Rhee puffed his cheeks, then blew out a breath. "I could ask the front desk, but the clerks get a little skittish if they think the gang might take it out on them for ratting to the cops. Let's try something else."

He got out of the car and I followed, adjusting my jacket. Rhee noticed and said, "You packing?"

"Yeah."

He looked troubled, but just said, "This isn't a bust. Just an info session, okay?"

"I'm not here to put holes in anyone."

He nodded, then motioned for me to follow him. We walked along the cracked and weedy pavement slabs that fronted the first-floor rooms, heading for an external second-story set of steps. Rhee took them two at a time and we followed the platform balcony around until it turned a corner, putting us in the rear of the building. The back of the motel overlooked a lonely patch of asphalt populated by two Dumpsters and bordered by a chain-link fence. On the other side was a used car dealership partially hidden by its own chain-link fence and that strange plastic curtain stuff that they weave in between the links.

At the end of the balcony, in front of the door to what must've been the last room in the place, was a pile of cans and pizza boxes. A mountain bike hung half over the concrete knee wall, its front tire missing. As we got closer, I could see a grubby denim jacket on the ground with a battered Washington Nationals cap nearby.

"What do you think?" Rhee asked, nodding at the mound of garbage. "Think we found our party?"

He walked up to the door and tried it. Finding it locked, he cupped a hand and squinted through the window, then went back to the door and banged with his fist a half-dozen times.

"Rico! *Vámonos, hombre*," he yelled, kicking the door. Another three or four minutes of this and eventually the door cracked open. A creaky voice asked in Spanish what the hell we wanted. Rhee ignored it and pushed his way in. I followed a few steps behind, wanting my eyes to adjust.

It was my nose that needed the adjusting. The smell of days-old pizza, beer, puke, and sweat hit me like a hammer. I took shallow breaths and waited while my eyes got used to the dim light.

What I saw wasn't anything to write home about. A typical crummy motel room. Two twin beds, a cheap table with two chairs, and a TV bolted to a faux-wood credenza that was, in turn, bolted to the wall. There were beer cans and cardboard Budweiser boxes everywhere. Two open pizza boxes decorated the table where a family of flies landed on and contaminated what remained. The TV screen was smashed and there were small shards of the glass on the floor. The AC fan was on, but it was broken, so the only noise was a low buzzing sound not unlike the flies on the pizza.

A guy and a girl were still fast asleep in the bed nearest the door. A guy was passed out on the floor. A girl in biker shorts and a halter top had answered the door and backed away, standing bleary-eyed by the foot of the second bed. Rhee opened his mouth to ask her something when at that moment the toilet flushed and a guy in jeans and no shirt walked out of the bathroom.

He was a scrawny, pockmarked sort of kid, with skinny arms and a potbelly. About five eight and a hundred and nothing pounds, with black hair and black eyes. A tremendous scar ran along the right side of his scalp, white against his skin and dark hair. But the most arresting detail was on his face. Across his forehead, in large block letters, were the letters "MLA." Several black teardrops were inked below his left eye. Tattooed Gothic script flowed around his nose and cheeks, with stylized skulls, women, and numbers dripping down his neck where they joined a score of others on his chest and stomach. I'd seen gang members proclaim their loyalty before, but never like this. He could've been wearing a mask.

Both Rhee and the tattooed dude froze. The scene seemed to crystallize and slow to a crawl. The smell and the heat faded away, but the buzz from the broken fan seemed to get louder. My arms and legs felt leaden, even though my pulse jumped up a notch. I was very careful to keep my hands motionless and visible.

"This isn't Rico, I guess," I said after a second.

"Nope," Rhee said, not taking his eyes from the other guy. He said something in Spanish, very fast, too fast for me to follow. The tattooed guy watched us, his liquid black eyes moving slowly back and forth. There was casual menace in the set of his face, but he was as still as a stone. After a second, he replied, in a soft voice completely at odds with the body it came from. Rhee said something else and got a shrug in return. There were a few more exchanges where Rhee did most of the talking and the other guy said very little, if anything. Then Rhee nodded and stepped back, away from the door. I followed his lead. The tattooed guy very deliberately reached down and picked up a grimy T-shirt from the floor, slipped it over his head, and walked out the door without looking back. The deadbeats in the bed and the guy passed out on the floor slept through the whole thing. The girl who'd answered the door watched us.

Rhee seemed pretty cool, but I let out a shaky breath. "Who was that?"

He shook his head. "Never seen him before. I asked him his name. He said Cuchillito. Chillo for short."

"'Little Knife'?"

"Yep. Well, kind of. Chillo actually means snapper, like the fish. But in this case, it means knife."

"Chillo a first or a last name?"

"More like a brand name, I think," Rhee said.

"I'm guessing from his ink that he's not one of the benchwarmers you're looking for?"

"Fuck, no. That's the real deal, a dude from the *mara*. Wasn't expecting that. Maybe this was just a party, but I doubt it. My boy Rico here has some explaining to do."

Rhee went over to the bed and slapped and poked the guy in it until he groaned and sat up. It was another skinny Hispanic kid, but without Chillo's tattoos and menace. Rhee handed the kid an opened beer and started to pepper him with questions, but the kid was hungover and sullen and eventually stopped talking altogether. The girl began to snore. The guy on the ground moaned and rolled over onto his back. Rhee tried a few more times to get Rico to talk, his voice going from wheedling to flat and threatening. I heard him say the name "Chillo" several times. But the kid just sat propped against the headboard like a lump.

Rhee swore and straightened up. "This piece of shit isn't going to give us anything. Rico, I'm telling you, you start playing with those guys and you're going to end up deader than dirt. Or in jail for life. You understand, *chico*? You know something, you better tell me. I'll be around, okay?"

The kid watched us, resentful, as we walked out of the room and into the cleaner air of the parking lot. Rhee closed the door behind us and, this time, did blow out a breath.

I looked at him. "'Deader than dirt'?"

He shrugged. "All I could think of."

We headed back to his car and got in, but Rhee sat without starting it. "This is weird," he said.

"Which part? I thought you said the gangbangers came around once in a while."

"Yeah, but after they leave, punks like Rico can't shut up about how they're going to be in the real *mara* now and how things are going to change. They puff up like a blow-up doll until a couple weeks go by and they realize the only reason their homie came around was to score some dope for the night."

"Rico didn't look forthcoming."

"No, he didn't," Rhee said.

"And the Illustrated Man wasn't exactly, uh, voluble."

"No, he wasn't. He was as surprised as we were. But he could tell it wasn't a bust. Either that, or he's stone cold inside."

"Both," I said. "That piece of work could pull your heart out without blinking."

"Rico knows that better than we do."

"So Rico is scared," I said.

"Or we're hassling him just as he's making the grade. Maybe he got the call-up to the big leagues. And we made him look bad by showing up," he said, thinking out loud. "Can't help his case if they know we can find Rico anytime we want."

"That would explain the pouty face."

He sighed and started the car. "Any of this help you out?"

"No, not really," I said. "But it's been fun."

CHAPTER FOURTEEN

As a kid, I read comics about Superman and his home, the Fortress of Solitude. I can't recall how the artists portrayed Superman's Arctic home, but I'd always envisioned him sitting on a chaise longue made of ice or steel—Superman doesn't experience discomfort—doing the *New York Times* crossword puzzle or whatever it was superheroes did to unwind after defeating the Lex Luthors of the world.

The point being that even Superman needs a break.

I'd been working on Bloch's cop killer for a week solid and felt run down. There was a time when I could've done that week on no more than a few hours of sleep. Cancer and age made that kind of stamina a memory of the distant past, but the tradeoff had been wisdom. The kind of wisdom that tells you that sometimes you're more effective when you take a rest, that running yourself into the ground doesn't always solve the case. In fact, might even make a solution more elusive.

So, I tucked all my feelings of guilt and fear into a back corner of my head—not easy to do, when I expected to get a call from Bloch any minute—and called my old partner Dods to invite him to a cookout.

"A cookout?" he said. "What the hell, Marty?"

"What's wrong? You have a problem coming over?"

"No," he said. "It's just . . . you've never had a cookout before. Do you know how?"

"Of course I know how," I said.

"Really? You have a grill?"

"No."

"How are you going to have a cookout, then?"

"I'll do what everyone else does. I'll buy a case of beer, order takeout from Rocklands, and heat everything in the microwave."

"I think you're missing the point," he said. "But we'll be there. Margie's gonna be ecstatic. Who else is coming?"

"I'll ask Amanda, see if she wants to bring any friends," I said. "It'll be small."

Everyone congregated in my backyard, sitting at an old picnic table, moving carefully to keep from getting splinters. Amanda had brought Zenny and Jay, her grad friends from GW, who listened in rapture as Dods regaled them with stories about life as a career homicide cop. The guy could find humor in just about any situation, which was a useful trait for staying alive and sane in our line of work. Even better, he loved to play the ham. My sense of humor tended toward the internal and sarcastic, which Dods was good at as well, but he was even better when he had an audience to play to. His broad, Slavic face was lit up like a lightbulb and his hands were held wide in an "it was this big" gesture.

I watched from the kitchen window as I cleaned up, one of those people who can't sit for very long. Or maybe it was just experience. Dods would inevitably get around to roasting me and it was always smart to excuse yourself before the guns swung in your direction. Or, maybe it was because I'd hoped the cookout would act as a pick-me-up, but what had really happened was my feelings of loneliness had been brought into stark relief. I wondered what it would look like with Julie sitting there, pushing a strand of hair out of her face as she listened. Or Kransky and Dods together, two ex-partners, swapping stories about me. It hurt to think about. When I let myself open that door, sitting at a picnic table chuckling at one of Dods's jokes didn't seem to fit. I'd originally hoped the get-together would pull me out of the dumps, but it seemed to be having the opposite effect.

I was scraping the last of the baked beans back into its take-out container, Pierre skulking around my legs looking for scraps, when I saw Amanda glance around, looking for me. She stood while the others were still laughing at something Dods had said and came toward the house. She poked her head into the kitchen, holding a hand out to keep the screen door from banging.

"What are you doing in here, Marty?"

"Just trying to get a jump on cleaning up," I said. "I'll be out in a sec."

"You should be enjoying yourself."

"I am. I enjoy cleaning."

She made a face. "Seriously, come out and join us. Relax. Laugh a little. That was the whole point, right?"

I shrugged. "True. And who knows when we'll get the chance again."

She came all the way inside, a concerned look on her face. "What's that mean?"

I tried to wave it off, but I'd let my mouth run ahead of my brain again. "Nothing."

Amanda folded her arms and leaned against the doorframe. "Hey, give me some credit. Did the doctor call? Has something happened?"

"No, it's not that. I . . ." I gritted my teeth.

"What, then?"

I put the container in the fridge and rinsed my hands, dried them on a dish towel. It gave me a good excuse to not look at her. "Look, I'm happy that you're graduating, that you're moving on. Very, very happy. If anyone deserves some good news in life, it's you."

"But?"

Okay, now I had to look. "I'm trying to get used to the idea that in a few weeks you could be leaving. Maybe for good. Maybe more importantly, I'm trying to adjust to the idea that you leaving should bother me so much. I've gotten through fifty-odd years with about four important relationships in my life. At some stage, all of them involved the person leaving, changing, progressing, doing something different than I was."

She was quiet, her face expectant.

"I'm saying that you leaving bothers me. A lot. We've helped each other in the last six months, but I feel like I've gotten the better end of the deal."

"That's up for debate."

I brushed that aside. "Long story short, I don't want you to leave, even though you've got every right to. I'm trying to work around that right now, but what can I say? It's depressing."

She walked over and put her arms around me. Her grip was strong. She stepped back and looked me in the eye. "First, I may not leave. They haven't exactly been beating down my door with job offers. Second, even if I end up leaving, we'll cope. You'll miss me, but you'll find a way to deal with it, the same way I'll have to, wherever I end up. Third, you're part of my life and nothing will change that, especially not something as meaningless as distance and time. Like it or not, you're my family, Marty. Which means, wherever I go—if I go—we're connected."

She hugged me again and I hugged back, hard. After a moment, though, my stomach broke into a long and protracted gurgle that felt like a lawn mower had started somewhere south of the border. Amanda, her head tucked into my chest, started to laugh, her body shaking in my arms. I laughed, too, and it felt good.

"So much for our Hallmark moment," I said, letting her go.

"We're too cynical for it anyway," she said, smiling. She squeezed my arm. "Come on, Marty. Leave this stuff for later. Come out and sit with your friends."

"Go on out. I'll be there in a sec," I said. "I'm going to grab some more beer for Dods before he guts me."

"Don't be long," she said and went outside. "I don't want to have to send him in after you."

I reached into the fridge for another six-pack, but paused at the sink again, watching as Amanda rejoined the group. The tableau was perfectly framed by the window. Dods had her laughing before she was done taking her seat and I smiled. It was a snapshot of joy and friendship and I wanted to tuck it away.

She was right. And she was wrong. We all cope. We're all connected. And we hope the love we share with others will get us through bad times. But it doesn't always erase the pain, the loneliness. It isn't always enough.

I put a smile on my face and went outside with the beer.

CHAPTER FIFTEEN

It seemed like a good time to get ahold of Bob Caldwell, the DEA agent who had collaborated with Danny Garcia in the past. The number Bloch had given me rang fifteen unanswered times. I hung up and thought about it. I could try calling later or I could get my ass in gear and actually chase down a lead. So I got in the car, pointed it toward Seventh Street, and in fifteen minutes I was cruising DC's somewhat underwhelming waterfront—about a block wide and ten blocks long—looking for a parking space. I squeezed my car next to a parking meter by the Harbor Patrol building, then headed up the boardwalk that fronted the marina.

Bloch had told me "the waterfront" and not much else, so I had to settle for walking up to folks who seemed like they might own a boat and asking if they knew a Bob Caldwell. I got a lot of blank stares until I remembered the name of the boat—*The Loophole*—and then I had his slip number in a matter of seconds. Trust people in DC to not know a person but instantly recognize the name of a dog, house, or boat.

I took my time walking down the cement-slab boardwalk, admiring what I saw, from dart-shaped pleasure craft to worn-out houseboats.

Bumpers and lines squeaked and creaked with the Potomac's gentle tide, and the smells of the crab shacks and fish stalls on Water Street a few blocks away set my stomach rumbling in a good way. If I closed my eyes and ignored the joggers, security helicopters, and the jets taking off from National Airport, I could be in a small fishing village on the Chesapeake.

The person who'd recognized Caldwell's boat told me he was moored at the Gangplank marina, about a third of the way down the waterfront. The pier was fenced off with a security gate, but someone had propped open the chain-link door with a cooler to make it easier to bring stuff down from their car. A static security camera was trained on the entrance. I pulled out my cell phone and tried Caldwell's number again. Ten, eleven, twelve more rings and no answer.

No sense wasting the trip. I clomped down the ramp and through the gate, trying to look like I belonged. There were scads of boats, though, and I wasn't sure how to find Caldwell's. To keep up the illusion for anyone watching, I didn't want to stoop and stare at the slip numbers. Then I remembered Bloch had said *The Loophole* was a sailboat. Most of the craft in the slips were pleasure craft or barges, so I headed for the only group of masts I could see.

The first four or five weren't what I was looking for, though I did appreciate the names: *Sea Pub*, *Roman Holiday*, *Play Date*. *The Loophole* was the last one I checked, a long, slim sailing yacht, maybe thirty-five or forty feet long. A little ragged around the edges, but at least it appeared used, unlike some of the yachts that still had their white winter shrink-wrap clinging to their hulls like bandages.

There was no one on deck, so I shouted Caldwell's name at the boat a few times. When there wasn't any answer, I walked down the graying wooden pier and leaned across the short stretch of water so I could put my hands on the side of the boat. I hunched a bit and peeked inside a porthole, but between the glare on the glass and the fact that the window was tinted, I didn't see a damn thing.

When I straightened up, there was plenty to see, since there was a gun in my face.

Holding it was a plump white guy with graying hair who had damn near magically appeared on deck. He was in a kneeling position, leaning over so he could cover me. A neat, salt-and-pepper beard ran along the edge of his jaw, or where his jaw would be if he'd been thinner. The perfect line of the beard and his clean-shaven cheeks emphasized the chipmunk-roundness of his face. He wore a Hawaiian shirt with a pineapple and orange-slice pattern on it, khaki shorts, and deck shoes. He could've been an insurance salesman on his day off. But I paid less attention to what he looked like and more to the chunky black handgun pointed at my face. The analytical, professional side of my brain tried to ID it—maybe a .45 ACP or an old Browning Hi-Power. It didn't really matter. The more emotional side of my brain recognized that, at this range, a cap gun could take my head off.

"Who the hell are you?" the guy asked. His voice was hoarse, all gravel and sand, like he'd spent his life as a rock 'n' roll roadie instead of a DEA agent.

Keeping very still, with my hands held against the gunwale of the boat, I said, "Marty Singer. I guess Sam Bloch didn't tell you I might drop by?"

"Who the fuck is Sam Bloch?"

I said, slowly, pacing my words, "MPDC lieutenant with HIDTA. One of the cops on his team, Danny Garcia, was killed a few months ago. He asked me to look into it and said a guy named Bob Caldwell knew Danny from working with him back in the day. He thought Caldwell might be able to give me a handle on what Garcia was looking into before he was taken out."

The guy seemed to think it over, or that's what I'm assuming he was doing, since he didn't blink or even look away for what seemed like a whole minute. My arms started to cramp from holding my weight against the boat. It was like holding halfway through a push-up. I needed to stand or let myself slide into the water between the pier and the hull.

"Is that good enough or do you need something else?" I asked. "A note from my teacher, maybe?"

"You with MPDC?"

"Was."

"Department?"

"Homicide. Retired."

"Got any ID?"

I shrugged, no mean feat in my position. "I do, but it won't mean anything to you. I'm not official anymore. No badge."

He seemed to think that over with the same fish-eye stare as before.

"Can I at least stand up?" I asked. "My arms are about to fall off."

"Let's see that ID," he said. "Right hand only, slow."

I reached back, pulled my wallet out, and opened it so he could see my Virginia driver's license through the little plastic window. I squeezed the wallet, hoping the whole thing didn't drop into the Potomac with a slip of the fingers. He glanced at it, nodded with a quick jab of his head, then he stood and the gun disappeared under the Hawaiian shirt, though not before his eyes did a quick scan of the dock. All while keeping me in line of sight.

"You *are* Bob Caldwell, right?" I asked, straightening up.

"That's me," he said. He stooped to retrieve an aluminum cane that I hadn't seen while I was busy looking at his gun. He took three gimpy steps toward me, then leaned over and gave me a hand up to the deck. A blurry blue tattoo decorated the inside of his forearm. "Sorry for the rough welcome."

I heaved myself onboard. His grip was meaty and surprisingly strong. "Do you really not know who Sam Bloch is?"

"I know who he is. I wanted to see if you did."

"Jesus," I said. "I'm glad I stuck with MPDC if this is how paranoid life in the DEA is."

"Hold on a sec," he said, then limped over to the stairs belowdecks. A second later he came back carrying two lawn chairs. He handed one to me, then unfolded and sat in the other with a groan. He'd oriented his chair so he could keep an eye on the docks. His gun had to be digging into his gut, but if he was feeling any pain, he didn't show it.

"What's the limp from?" I asked.

He took a second to fish out a pack of cigarettes, tapped the pack until one fell out, lit it. It was a clove and a puff of its sweet, acrid smoke wafted toward me. "Accident. Working on this damn boat. The jib got wrapped around the mast, so I thought I'd scramble up there like a goddamn monkey and fix it."

"Less like a monkey and more like a gorilla?"

"Shit, more like a hippo. Fell off and landed kidney-first on a cleat. Real smart. Some nerve damage. Don't know if it's permanent yet. But I walk with a cane now."

"Where's the paranoia from?"

"Twenty years in the DEA," he said, taking a drag. "Live and learn. Don't and die. So now I don't climb masts and I point my peashooter at people who try to look in my windows."

"I called," I said. "Twice."

He shrugged, unapologetic. "Caller ID. Didn't know your number."

A small crowd of people walked by on the boardwalk, chatting and laughing, probably late lunchers trying to get crab cakes before the fish markets closed. They were thirty yards away, but Caldwell's eyes followed them until they were almost out of sight.

"You're on disability?" I asked.

"For now. The pay is good and the workload is great. But I'm really just killing time until retirement. The day that happens, I'll throw off the lines, put Jimmy Buffett on shuffle, and sail *The Loophole* down to Saint Thomas. It's going to take two months and I'm going to love every fucking clichéd minute of it."

"When's the happy day?"

"Soon. Second week of July. I'll finish up disability, take a week's vacation, then walk in with my papers." He finished the cigarette in record time, then flicked the butt into the water. Smoke from his last drag wreathed his beard and curled around his head. "You're retired. What the hell are you still doing around here? Got kids, family? It can't be the PI work."

I shook my head. "I'm not a PI. This is a favor."

"You must owe somebody big," he said. He folded his hands over his belly, which swelled underneath the Hawaiian shirt. "Anyway, you wanted to ask me something. About Danny."

"Bloch said you might've done some work with him, maybe some liaising between DEA and HIDTA."

Caldwell's face flickered, like a light had passed over it. "Fucking Danny. Getting killed."

"You knew him pretty well?"

He shrugged. "I worked with him on a few cases, though not as many as you might think. It's all drugs, but our circles didn't really cross much, you know? He was an intense little dude. Could work a street. I mean *work* it. He could be a buyer or a junkie or anything in between, just perfect. Me," he gestured toward his body, "I'm a fat white guy. Maybe I could bankroll a deal or act like a retired hippie who needed to score some weed, but that's about it. No way I could keep up with him on the street."

"What did you end up doing, then?"

"Surveillance, trained other guys at HIDTA, helped with some busts when I could squeeze into a vest. Smoothed things over when things got chippy between the DEA and the other agencies or departments."

"You know what Garcia was working on when he got killed?"

"Bloch doesn't know?"

I shook my head. "He said Garcia was on a long chain, barely kept him up to speed."

Caldwell laughed, shook his head. "Big surprise. I haven't worked with HIDTA in a while, but Bloch is a by-the-book kind of guy. Garcia was the exact opposite. Creative, an artist. Improvised all the time. Street-smart, talked a mile a minute. He probably had no time for Bloch. Fact, I'd be shocked if they touched base more than once or twice a month."

"Did he ever tell you about the cases he was on?"

Caldwell pushed himself out of his chair and limped over to a cooler, holding on to a bulkhead for support. He pulled out a can of Miller Lite, held it up for me. When I shook my head, he closed the cooler and limped back over to the chair, where he fell into it so hard I thought the whole thing was going to snap in half, but by some miracle the nylon and aluminum held. He cracked open the beer and slugged back a third of it.

He shook his head. "Like I told you, I haven't worked with HIDTA for a while. And, while I got along with Garcia better than Bloch probably did, it's not like he told me his innermost thoughts."

"Why would Bloch tell me to talk to you, then?"

"Well, I worked with him more than anyone else at the DEA. Maybe he thought I'd have some insight," he said. He lifted the can, hesitated, then put it back down. "You know, not sure it's worth mentioning, but I do know he hated the Latino gangs that had made inroads around here in the last few years. Took it personally, I think."

"You collaborate with him on that?"

He made a face, jerked a thumb toward his chest. "Forget something? Gringo *gordo*, remember? We teamed up on the black gangs, crack dealers, the white kids running meth labs out in the boonies. I only know about the Hispanic thing because he talked about it all the time."

"He hate anyone in particular?"

"Salvadorans. The ones moving into all the Latino neighborhoods, taking over, you know? Those guys don't just deal drugs and make money; they want to rule the place, own every part of it."

"You think he might've been looking into one of them?"

Caldwell held his hand up. "No idea. I just know he felt that special something for them."

I nodded, thinking it over. A boat passed by, ignoring the "no wake" rule, and the waves it kicked up rocked *The Loophole* gently from side to side. "You know a guy named Terrence Witherspoon?"

He stared at me, which I realized now was his way of thinking hard about something. Then he closed his eyes and put his head back. His lips moved silently. He opened his eyes and shook his head. "Witherspoon's common enough, but I don't know the name, sorry. Should I?"

"Not really," I said. "It was a long shot."

"You gotta cover all the bases," he said.

"True," I said, then gestured at his arm. "So, how long were you on the force?"

His hand, which he'd raised to take another swig from his beer, froze in midair. "What?"

"Your tattoo," I said. "It's the old MPDC logo. I'm going to guess you didn't get that when you went into the DEA."

He looked down at the inside of his forearm like the tattoo had suddenly blossomed under his skin. "Yeah, it's been a while. I was a beat cop for three years before I chucked it all to go down to Quantico and try out for the Feds. I thought it would be more exciting than scratching my ass in a cruiser. Big fun."

"Was it?"

He snorted. "About as much as falling off my mast twenty feet up."

"Be careful what you wish for," I said.

CHAPTER SIXTEEN

A week after talking to Danny Garcia's widow, I was back out in Chantilly to talk to his son. Ten minutes into the drive, I found myself whistling "Chantilly Lace" and I realized I'd whistled it the first time out, too. It's an easy song to hate and impossible to get out of your mind once it's sunk its claws there.

I managed to clear my head by reviewing the case out loud, sometimes shouting the questions I wanted answers to anytime I had the urge to purse my lips. Why was I driving out here again, exactly? What did I think Paul Garcia would be able to tell me about his father that I hadn't already learned? Danny had taken obvious pains to shield his family from his work. No, "shield" wasn't a strong enough word. Danny had lived a double life. The chances that his son knew something about what he did in the force hovered somewhere between zero and none.

Maybe.

And that maybe was why I was taking the time to drive out to Chantilly. An intense, dedicated family man might feel the need to protect a wife or young children from the brutal realities of being an undercover cop. But what if his son had become a man, served in Iraq and Afghanistan, seen calamities and horrors on par with the ones his father had seen? Maybe Danny, accustomed to adopting an entirely new persona at home for years, had decided to open up and share a little of his undercover life with a son who shared similar, if not exact, experiences.

Maybe.

I parked in exactly the same spot I had the previous week and looked the house over. This time, the Bronco was in the driveway behind the Corolla, gleaming in the sun. It had been washed and the asphalt of the drive was stained a dark black where water had sluiced off to the curb. A garden hose was coiled on the grass. It could've been a scene of summertime bliss—but the shades were drawn and the home radiated stillness.

I went up to the door and knocked. I heard some bumping around inside. The curtain might've been drawn back from one of the windows. I resisted the urge to slide my hand down to my gun where it rested in its holster—the instinct and training built up from so many years of knocking on doors where the reply could be automatic gunfire. But I relaxed. I'd been here once already. This wasn't a shoot-out in a crack house. I was here to talk.

The door opened. Standing in the doorway, based on the picture I'd seen last time, was Paul Garcia, Danny's son. He was about five nine and broad across the shoulders. He seemed chubby, but it was what guys call "hard fat." To call him clean-shaven was an understatement. He had pale skin that was so devoid of facial hair that it almost glowed, and a Marine-issue haircut that showed scalp. Brown, almost black, eyes stared back at me. He had on a camo T-shirt, Umbro shorts, and flip-flops.

I introduced myself and explained why I was knocking on his door. "You're Paul Garcia?"

"Yes, sir. My mother said you'd been here before."

"That's right," I said. "I'm looking into several cases for a friend, murder cases, including your father's. I wonder if you have a minute to talk?"

He didn't reply, but stepped back and motioned me into the house, then gestured to the same spot I'd sat in when I'd talked to his mother. Paul sat on the couch across from me. The flip-flops and casual wear seemed out of place when compared to how carefully put-together his mother had been.

He cracked his knuckles, then rested his hands on his knees. "How can I help you, sir?"

"You were in Iraq, is that right?"

"Yes, sir. And Afghanistan. The Twenty-Fourth MEU."

"MEU?"

"Marine Expeditionary Unit, sir," he said. He almost saluted.

"Your mother said you mustered out recently?"

"Last year, sir."

"That long? You still seem to be very, uh, Marine-like, if you don't mind my saying."

"I applied to the police academy right after I shipped back, sir. It's a lot like the Corps."

"Only softer?"

A trace of a smile. "It's not Camp Lejeune, sir."

"And you haven't graduated yet, I take it?"

The trace disappeared. "After my father was killed, I requested a leave of absence so I could help my mother."

I nodded. "Paul, did your father ever talk about what he was working on? What he did day to day?"

"No, sir. My father was undercover, I know that. But he went out of his way to keep his work at the office, so to speak."

"Why would he do that?"

He made a small motion with his shoulders. Not quite a shrug. "He didn't want to upset my mother. Wanted to keep his work life separate from his home life."

"But he didn't open up to you?"

"No, sir."

"Even though you'd probably seen stuff overseas that was at least as bad as anything in DC? Probably worse?"

He took a moment to answer. "I think he might've told me about it once I'd become a police officer myself. But until then, I believe he wanted to keep things the way they'd always been."

"With you in the dark," I said.

"Yes, sir."

"Did that bother you?"

"When I was younger. But in the Corps you get used to the idea of need-to-know. He did it for a reason and that reason was good enough for me."

"Did your father have any friends on the force? Guys who came over, shared a beer with him, that kind of thing?"

"Not really," Paul said. "When I was younger, before my father went into undercover work, there were a few friends who came around."

"Bob Caldwell?"

He nodded slowly. "He knew my father from way back. I believe he works for the DEA."

"Nobody else?"

"No, sir. He tried to keep his lives separate, like I said."

I nodded. I was getting nowhere. These were all things I'd already known or surmised. I tried a different tactic.

"What was your time in Afghanistan like?"

"Sir?"

"I only know what CNN said. What was your time like there?"

"Tough. Hot. Scary."

"The firefights were scary?"

He shook his head. "We had training to help with that. It was the IEDs and the snipers and the guerrilla attacks they'd pull that gave guys nervous breakdowns. Never knowing if the man you were helping clear some rubble with was the one shooting at you that night."

"Did you lose a lot of guys?"

He nodded, said nothing.

"Are you still tight with the men who came back?"

Paul's lips pinched together and the skin around his eyes constricted. "Yes, sir. It's a bond you can't buy, you can't fake."

"So there's something special you share with the men who saw combat together?"

"Very," he said. "You watch out for each other, you have each other's back. It's no shame if your buddy gets shot in the field. But it's on you if you let him down."

"Sounds like you've had experience with that," I said.

There was silence. I'd seen small rocks rolled over and over in a river's flow, black pebbles ground and polished until they gleamed like marbles. Paul Garcia's eyes were just like those river stones. Flat, glittering. He stared straight through me, and his voice was flat.

"I was ten weeks in-country. Little town called Kandahar. It was supposed to be an easy walk-through, but none of it's easy. We knew that, prepared for it. Problem is, training doesn't cover everything. We knew that, too. Six Hummers trying to get from one side of town to the other. Shouldn't be that hard. Enemy activity was supposed to be low. This was part recon, part showing face. Remind the locals that we hadn't pulled out. Five minutes into town, an IED takes out our number three vehicle. Standard tactical approach. Split the line and take out each half."

I said nothing.

"I was on point in the first ATAV. We came under fire and the second IED went up. The driver and my lieutenant were hit right out of the gate. I was on the mount gun. Armor took most of the bullets meant for me, gave me enough time to bring the M60 around."

Paul hadn't moved while he spoke. His hands were still clasping his knees, his back still perfectly straight, not even touching the cushions of the couch. If he'd blinked I hadn't seen it.

"The firefight lasted three hours. We were pinned down for every minute of it. Number two had been hit just as hard as we were. Number three was gone, flipped over. Couldn't even see four, five, and six through the smoke. We found out later that they'd decided to make a tactical retreat, figuring they could wait for backup, then rush the bad guys. Problem was, this was supposed to be a low-threat recon mission, so there *was* no backup. Three hours went by and the shooting stopped. Just like that. One minute, a thousand rounds a second, like it was the end of the world. Next minute, nothing. Silence. We thought we'd held them off, but the reality was they'd done the damage they wanted. They'd simply decided it was time to cut and run."

Paul's eyes regained focus, seeing me for the first time since he'd started talking. "My lieutenant bled out while we waited for that backup. The driver is at Walter Reed, learning to walk again. Number two lost another one. The guys who hit the IED were gone, but four through six walked away without a scratch."

The air in the room was stifling. The decorations and tidy appointments in the room and the near-summer May morning outside all seemed obscene in light of what Paul Garcia was describing. I wonder if he and the other survivors of all the wars that ever were walked around thinking the same thing, that the world that they'd fought so hard for was so trivial, so without meaning or cause, that it was like some terrible joke. Someone had conned them, a great swindle that they'd fallen for the moment they'd signed their name on the dotted line.

Paul suddenly got to his feet and, with a tight "Excuse me," hurried from the room and down a hall. I heard a door open and close, then a bathroom fan masked all other noises. I stood and paced the living room, finally stopping by the TV with all of the family pictures on top of the cabinet. I looked them over again. The family portrait of Danny, Libney, and Paul seemed almost mocking now; I was sure it had been taken before Paul had shipped out to Iraq. I thought somehow that, if it had been taken after, I would see it in the face staring back at me.

Near the back was a blurry, low-quality snapshot at odds with the other more staged studio pictures. It was in a simple black frame with one of those cardboard tripods in the back. I picked it up. A candid shot of a younger Danny Garcia wearing a Dallas Cowboys jersey and sporting a puffed-out grin, like he was valiantly holding in a mouthful of beer after being told a really good joke. The lighting was poor, but I could see it had been taken in someone's backyard. A thinner Bob Caldwell in a Hawaiian shirt and khaki shorts was caught in mid-guffaw. Apparently, he'd heard the same joke. He was about to slap Danny on the back, maybe in jest or maybe to keep him from choking. A grill was going in the background and the chef, a big guy wearing a number 69 Redskins jersey, had his back to the photographer. There were a few out-of-focus people in the background, including a gaggle of skinny white, brown, and black kids wearing mismatched fluorescent shorts and tops, swinging on a jungle gym. I wondered if Paul was one of the kids.

I put the picture back as I heard the toilet flush and the bathroom door open. Paul reappeared a second later, looking pale and smelling strongly of mouthwash.

"Is there anything else I can do for you, Mr. Singer?" he asked.

I smiled politely and gestured to the picture. "Looks like a good time."

His eyes flicked to the picture. "It was."

"Any special occasion?"

He thought about it before answering. "It was the summer before my father started working undercover. A celebration. Undercover was an assignment he'd always wanted."

"There weren't any more picnics? No more happy times?"

His gaze seemed to sink into the picture. He gave his head a little shake. "Those days are gone for good."

CHAPTER SEVENTEEN

My oncologist's office was in Old Town Alexandria, in an unassuming brownstone building not far from where George Washington ate the occasional meal and danced the cotillion with powdered and bewigged colonial ladies. I normally enjoyed going to Old Town—the place was cute as a bug and appealed to my love of history—but today was my cancer checkup, and I was so distracted that I barely saw where I was going on the drive down, let alone the architecture or the cobblestone streets. I could've been driving into an airplane hangar or a meatpacking plant for all the impact it had on me.

In the waiting room, I fiddled constantly with my watch, picked up and put down all the magazines, crossed and recrossed my legs three dozen times. I'd forgotten to bring a book, something I'd done on most of my trips to chemo, though I wondered if anything I read would've actually registered. My nervousness was obviously irritating the one other person in the room, a well-dressed older woman with a perfectly stationary mane of white hair that swept back from her forehead in a rounded wave. She was trying to read a copy of *Chicken Soup for the Soul*, but my jitters seemed to have gotten under her skin. From her sidelong glances and sighs, she had obviously reached the stage where she found it impossible to ignore me and now even my breathing was starting to peeve her. She was anointed in a lavender perfume that, even across the room, made my eyes water and my nose itch, adding to the list of small, annoying body movements I was making.

Just as I thought she was going to jump up and stab me in the eye with the sign-in pen, my favorite nurse, Leah, came out of the magic door and called my name. The old biddy, who'd been there longer than I had, huffed and said "Really!" under her breath, just loud enough for me to hear. As I walked by, I stuck my tongue out, but she'd already buried her nose in *Chicken Soup*.

It wasn't nice, but hey, I wasn't a cop anymore.

The office was familiar territory by now, full of desks, countertops, scales, charts of the human body, and filing cabinets. I knew their three examining rooms intimately, had studied their framed copies of great American landscape art minutely. They administered chemo in a large room in the back of the office that I called the lounge. A half-dozen comfy chairs with access to various medical apparatuses were arrayed in a semicircle. I was also familiar with each lounge chair, since they were where I'd spent three to four hours once a week for three months—give or take a few—and had a succession of antinausea, cancer-killing, and chemo-flushing chemicals pumped through my body. It was like having my oil, transmission fluid, and brake lines flushed.

This time, however, Leah led me back to one of the examination rooms. She was a cute Asian girl with about as positive an outlook as you could have and still be an oncology nurse. Her well-timed wise-cracks and zero tolerance for self-pity had kept my head above water through some rough patches.

We went through some medical rigmarole. My life as a patient had been made easier by the insertion of a Mediport, a little gadget surgically implanted near my collarbone that let the nurses draw blood and access my bloodstream without jabbing me every time. Leah used it to draw some blood, which she took away with a smile and a sidelong remark about how fat I was getting. I'd lost thirty pounds since the day I retired.

I was feeling positive, both physically and mentally. I'd tried to take charge of my futuré and done some reading on my disease. No, make that a *lot* of reading. My prospects seemed good. I'd handled the symptoms of the cancer and the side effects of the chemo well. The pain had receded, or the medicine had made it seem so, and I hadn't exhibited any setbacks. All signs were up. Colorectal cancer was one of the most survivable cancers—we'd caught it fairly early—and once my doctor had scaled back the chemo so that I didn't pass out afterward, I'd taken to it just fine. Many victims of CR cancer had to have partial or full colostomies and that had never been mentioned for me. Any day I didn't have to poop in a bag was a good day.

Dr. Demitri came in about ten minutes after Leah had departed. He was a stocky guy with the black hair and sun-soaked tan of his Mediterranean ancestors. He could be locked in a box for a year and he'd come out looking like he'd spent a week at the beach. The white lab coat and tie looked perpetually out of place to me. Maybe it was insensitive, but I always pictured him in a blue and white striped shirt, holding a jug of wine in one hand and a fish in the other.

He smiled, we shook, and he sat down.

I coughed and sat back, trying to smile.

He shuffled through papers in a dossier with my name on a red tab in the corner and I felt the first stirring of dread. He was taking too long to talk. The air-conditioning kicked on and the rush of air seemed very loud.

"It didn't work, did it?" I asked, trying to take the sting away by preempting him.

He canted his head. "I wouldn't say that. The chemo treatment didn't work to the extent I'd hoped. That doesn't mean it didn't do something."

"Come on," I said. A rush of peevishness and fear bubbled up, fast, from somewhere deep down. I'd sat on my emotions pretty well for three months and was only just realizing how close to the surface they really were. "Don't bullshit me."

He held out a hand to placate me. "I'm not, Marty. If I've learned one thing in twenty years of oncology work, it's that you can never lie. You can't even sugarcoat. It doesn't get you anywhere. Not only is it unethical, it's unfair, and can make things a lot worse in the long run. So, if I say the chemo did something, believe me, it wasn't ineffective."

"How effective? What did it do? What didn't it do?"

"The simple story is that I'd hoped that the cancer would be highly receptive to the chemo. That the chemo would, in effect, take it out. What happened instead is that it was moderately effective and reduced the disease by a considerable amount, but not one hundred percent."

"Was it because I couldn't take the full dosage you'd started with?"

He shook his head. "No. What I'm seeing is that the cancer was partially resistant to the chemotherapy we launched at it. This happens sometimes. Doubling your dosage wouldn't have done much to the cancer, but it would've done all kinds of things to you."

I closed my eyes. Emotionally, I saw myself crawling across a sliver-thin bridge. On one side, despair. On the other, pity. I took a deep breath and opened my eyes. "So where do we go from here?"

"It's your red blood cell count that tells us the chemo wasn't one hundred percent effective, but we need to take a look inside to see what's left. It would be something like the first time you had a sigmoid-oscopy. The difference is that we would be prepared to do surgery if what we found would respond to what we call a local excision, or partial removal of the colon."

"Poop in a bag," I said in despair.

Demitri smiled despite himself. "Not necessarily. Think in terms of baseball. A home run would've meant the cancer is gone. A triple or a double might mean there's so little cancer that a simple excision is called for and you'll just need recovery time. A, um, single would be partial or total removal of the colon or maybe another round of even more aggressive chemo, the kind that keeps you in bed twenty-four/seven. I don't think that's where we are."

"What about a bunt?"

"That's where the baseball analogy starts to break down. If you had, uh, struck out, we wouldn't be having this conversation, we'd be rushing to surgery. Or talking about palliative care."

"What did I hit, then?"

"Let's call it a double with a chance to steal third," he said, smiling. "We'll get you into surgery, take a look around, and, if things look good, we remove what we need to, to make you better. If not, we regroup and talk about options."

I took a deep breath. "When do we have to do this?"

"Sooner the better, Marty. Cancer is a replicative disease. It's not going to stop for very long."

"I'm . . . involved in something that needs my attention. And I don't know for how long. Can I afford to put this off, say, a month?"

He sucked in his lower lip, thinking, then shook his head. "I can't recommend it. Anything more than a week would make me nervous."

I thought of the bronze lion, the one-inch-high names carved into a wall nearly a city block long. "There are lives on the line, Doc."

He nodded a little, then looked at me square. "More than yours?"

My phone rang that evening, just as I was about to sit down to a hearty meal of watered-down vegetable soup and white bread—a meal that three months of dealing with chemo side effects had made normal. And, while my nausea had been under control for a few weeks, the news I'd gotten from the doctor threatened to undo all that. I thought I'd better stick with the regimen.

"Singer," I answered.

"It's me," Bloch said. "Got a sec?"

I glanced at the bread lying on my plate like a piece of bathroom tile. "Sure."

"You know that snubbie in Danny's car and the guns we found at his love nest? I took them to the lab and had them test fire some rounds, then ran them through IBIS."

"Do I want to know what the results were?"

"They came up in seven unsolved shootings from the last ten years. Southeast. Prince George's County, Maryland. Northern Virginia. Most were fatalities."

I whistled low. "Unsolved?" I said. "Assumed to be drug violence, gang-on-gang kind of stuff?"

"Yeah—hey, you okay? You sound funny."

"I'm fine," I said, and tried to inject some enthusiasm into my voice. "What about those shootings?"

"Three of them were drive-bys, but no ID of the car. One report of a group of three or four guys involved, but—okay, this is gonna shock you—no witnesses and no one willing to talk to the cops about it."

"Any connections between the shootings?" I asked.

"You mean, besides drugs? Like, were they all the same gang?"

"Yeah."

"Negative," Bloch said. "These were equal-opportunity assaults. Victims were black, Hispanic, the odd freelancer."

I was quiet. "You thinking what I'm thinking?"

"I think so. I wish I weren't."

"Danny was moonlighting," I said. "Taking out drug dealers and gangbangers on his own time."

"Looks that way," Bloch said. "If he wasn't already dead, I'd kick his ass."

"The guns, the cot, the medical supplies . . . that place we found was his staging area, his command post."

We both thought about it for a second. I don't know if it's every cop's desire to go rogue, but I know it sure as hell goes through your mind once in a while. Particularly after a bust gone bad. Or, worse, a bust gone perfect . . . and then the guy walks thanks to light sentencing or a technicality.

"He did it," I said. "Lived the dream."

"Probably got sick of seeing guys he'd busted back on the street in a week."

"Or, being undercover, saw a ton of action he knew he'd never be able to pin on anyone," I said. "And he had everything he needed to work it."

"Sure. He had a decade of street experience. Any hard-to-get intel he couldn't squeeze from his contacts, I delivered from HIDTA sources. Then he probably picked up a couple of off-record guns on busts or through his contacts, stockpiled some medical supplies, and kept his nose clean the rest of the time. I gave him all kinds of slack on the job, so he had plenty of time to plan his takedowns."

I sat down at the dining room table and put my feet up on the chair across from me. "You know, if reports say a drive-by, my experience as a detective tells me that's at least two. Witnesses say maybe three or four. And everything about the bolt-hole says at least three to me."

"You're thinking his partners were the other guys who got killed? Someone's murdering the whole crew?"

I sighed. "I don't know. It fits nice and neat on the surface, but what were the connections? These were cops from all over the Metro area. Different ages, different departments, different squads."

"I can dig a little on my end, see if there's a connection."

"Okay," I said. "Just to cover all our bases. If not them, who else could've been working with him?"

"Hell if I know. I'll look at the other guys on my squad, but all these undercover boys are lone wolves. I can't see them wanting to share."

"Not with something this crazy," I said.

"Hell, no. Jesus, can you imagine? Sitting around the doughnut shop, 'Hey, remember that time we sprayed down the Eleventh Street gang?'"

"This changes our position," I said.

"What do you mean?"

"Well, with all due respect, this doesn't sound like the serial killer with a thing for cops that we thought we were after. Danny's murder sounds like some guy moonlighting who got whacked by bad guys when he wasn't paying attention."

"Either way, it got him killed. And, either way, we're still looking for the guy who did it."

"Sure, but we're not searching for the Son of Sam. We could just be looking at a drug bust gone bad. With a couple of unrelated murders that happened to occur around the same time."

"I'm not going to believe that," Bloch said, sounding ready for a fight.

"Ease up. I'm just putting it out there," I said. "I'll keep digging. All I'm saying is, the goal is to stop whoever's killing cops, not to give ourselves a pat on the back proving a conspiracy theory."

He was quiet. Wounded, maybe. I felt for him. We were making headway, but what we were finding took some of the air out of his balloon. He'd been sure we were looking for the next big serial killer, something that would justify the flack he'd been given by the other departments, something he could hold up to them and say, *See? You should've listened to me.* What we were uncovering—as much as it pained me to say it when talking about other cops—were routine murders, easily explained by that all-encompassing motive, greed.

His voice was tight, but he said, "You're right. This isn't about me. We still got to stop whoever it is. Keep pushing on those other killings. I'll let you know if I find anything else. Sorry if I ruined your dinner."

I stared at the soup, now cold. "No worries. It was already a goner."

II.

White was a lousy color for couches. And carpet. And pillows. When it got dirty, it was a motherfucker to clean and never did look quite right again. Spill some red wine or some Chinese takeout on it, you might as well throw the whole thing out and get a new one, because stains were something that the honeys picked up on right away. And then it was all over.

He could show them the whole apartment—the glass and steel and leather, the thousand-dollar stereo, the half case of Cristal in the fridge—and if they saw one damn stain on the couch, they'd be up and out of there. Lucky for him, low lighting worked wonders on just how bad some of those stains looked. And with the music going good and enough booze in the glass, it didn't hurt his chances of slipping his johnson where he wanted, either.

But another thing bitches couldn't abide was a messy pad. So he took an hour every day to make up the living room and the bedroom, even if that meant he had to shove most of his shit in a closet. You never knew when you were going to talk some sweet young college thing—tired of doing it in frat houses—into coming back to your place. Didn't need her walking out on you because you lived just like the dudes she was trying to get away from. And when you were twenty years older than them, you needed every play in the book.

It was that time again. He'd just put the stereo on, to give himself something to listen to while he cleaned the place, when he heard a knock on the door. Curious, he went over and opened it, smiling wide when he saw who it was.

"Hey, man," he said, stepping back to make room. "Thanks for coming by. That was pretty lucky. I almost didn't hear you knocking with my music going on."

CHAPTER EIGHTEEN

My phone rang again early the next morning. I reached over and answered it without opening my eyes. I didn't want to pick it up. Somehow, I knew who it was and what he was going to say.

"Singer."

"We have another one."

A cold ache swelled behind my breastbone. I opened my eyes. "Where?"

"Rockville. Cop named Clay Johnson. Killed in his apartment a few days ago. I haven't been paying enough attention or I would've heard about it as soon as it happened."

"MO fits?"

"All the way," Bloch said. "Beaten to a pulp."

"Think Rockville PD will talk to me?" I asked.

"I've already called in some favors," he said. "Though I didn't really have to. Rockville hasn't lost one of their own in thirty years. They want to nail whoever this is and they don't care who they have to hold hands with to do it."

"So they'll take the help, but they'll want their share," I said.

"Yes. Which is fine. That's what I was after in the first place. But don't give them anything unsubstantiated. Go up to Rockville and see what you can find out. If Johnson's case is related to the rest of these, maybe it'll shed light on Okonjo's killing. If not, we can decide where it fits with the others."

"I'm on my way," I said, and hung up.

◆ ◆ ◆

A tired-looking homicide detective met me by the front desk at the Rockville PD headquarters. He was a heavyset black guy, maybe five nine, with a salt-and-pepper mustache. He wore a plaid blazer and green Dockers. Police work is the only profession I know of where the black guys dressed as bad as the white guys.

"Singer?" he asked, holding a hand out.

He had a thick hand that I had trouble getting my own around when we shook. "That's me. Call me Marty."

"Charlie Goodwin. A Lieutenant Sam Bloch said you were willing to come up and help us with Clay Johnson's murder. Said it might have something connected to a couple other cases in the District?"

"Arlington, too. Maybe," I said. "Nothing's for sure yet, but Johnson's death comes at a really weird time to be coincidence. Sam asked me to look into it and a few others."

Goodwin motioned for me to follow him through the security door and down a hall. I got a good look at Rockville PD HQ. It was like every other station I'd been in, with the same smell of burnt coffee, disinfectant, and cologne lying heavy on the air, along with a subtle office odor of paper and copier ink. Energy-efficient compact fluorescent bulbs gave off a ghastly sterile glow that might save the city money but bounced off every surface and made the room look sick.

"How's it going so far?" I asked as we walked.

"We've been giving it everything we've got."

"I hear a '*but*' in there."

"But we're chasing our damn tails because we got the message from higher up to do what we had to do, but not too publicly, if you can believe it." Goodwin had a voice with the richness and timbre of an opera baritone. "It's not even an election year and the mayor's got a wild hair about not looking too partial in the prosecution of crimes. We're under a microscope, everyone making sure we don't spend an unfair amount of time on a cop's murder when there are so many others deserving of our time."

"Like meth labs taking out their owners in a blaze of glory," I said. "Or six-time DUIers running over pedestrians out by the mall."

"I see you're familiar with our work," Goodwin said, amused. "Bloch says you were a homicide dick for twenty years."

"Thirty."

"Seem like fifty?"

"Some days," I said. "Others, it seemed to flash past, when we were hot on something and cases were falling our way."

"Ain't that the truth," Goodwin said.

"You're okay with me poking my nose in this thing?" I asked.

Goodwin shrugged. "You check out. And it'd be nice if you share."

"I can do that," I said. "How about your higher-ups?"

"Can't say the captain would be too happy if he knew a freelancer was running around with this thing."

"But what he doesn't know won't hurt you?"

"I wouldn't mind an extra set of legs on the case," Goodwin said with an easy smile.

"I won't tell if you won't."

We arrived at what once would've been the bullpen but now would be called a cube farm. Goodwin took the lead, weaving between desks until he got to one with his nameplate on it. A half-wall separated it from the next cube. I picked a chair in the empty cube and watched as Goodwin sat down heavily at his desk and tip-tapped on his computer keyboard. After a minute, he stood and went to a block of printers at the center of the room. He drummed his fingers impatiently on the plastic tray, then grabbed a handful of pages spat out by the nearest printer, which he stapled with a *kerchunk* and brought back to me.

"Evidence list and autopsy," he said. He talked to me over his shoulder as he went around a cube wall. "Look through that while I get you the case file."

I flipped through the stack of sheets, trying to get a high-level view before diving in. The autopsy and crime scene report portrayed the same god-awful tableau as the other murders. Johnson had been killed in his own apartment, a fate he shared with Torres, though the location was an anomaly compared to the others. Minor, maybe. The problem was that, since the crime occurred in a home, nearly every item the man owned was included on the evidence list, which ran to ten pages. Not everything had been tagged, bagged, and brought in, of course, but anything of note had made it onto the list. Johnson had been found on his living room floor, so the TV, the magazines, the end table, the lamps, the ashtrays, the knickknacks, damn near everything was there.

Goodwin came back with a cardboard box, the kind with handles and a lid. Johnson's name and initials, along with the date, had been scribbled on it in Magic Marker. "This is the summary stuff. If this isn't enough, let me know if I can get you the other ten boxes."

"Thanks. Can we talk about it for a minute before I jump in?"

He eased into his chair and put his hands behind his head. "Shoot."

"You were investigating officer on the scene?"

"Yes."

"Give me the rundown."

Goodwin closed his eyes. "Forced entry into the apartment. Lights were on when we got there. Clay was on his back in the living room, all beat to hell. He'd tricked the place out like a real bachelor pad, trying to impress. All glass and steel. White leather couch, fake white bearskin rug, blond hardwood floor. So the blood just stood out everywhere. Just pulsing, man, you know? Even though he'd been dead for a while."

I glanced down at the autopsy report. "ME put it at thirty to thirty-six hours?"

Goodwin nodded. "Clay had a couple days off coming to him, so no one down here noticed when he didn't show up."

"Murder weapon?"

"A .38, through the mouth and out the back of the head. Slug lodged in the wall. The postmortem stuff was done with the steel leg from an end table. No prints."

"Anything bug you about the scene?"

Goodwin scratched his nose and put his hand back behind his head, all without opening his eyes. "Besides the almighty postmortem beating he took?"

"Something stand out about it?"

"The killer either worked himself into a rage or started the day absolutely out of his mind to go off on the body like that. Almost certainly male, considering the strength it took to break Clay's bones."

"What else?"

"Not a robbery. Wallet, laptop, watch, electronics, and stereo all untouched. Service weapon holstered and on top of a dresser in the bedroom. No witnesses, no security tape. Alarm system wasn't activated, but that doesn't necessarily mean anything. His ex-wife said he forgot to turn theirs on the whole time they lived together."

Goodwin went quiet. I gave him a minute. "Is that it?"

"Well," he said, hesitating. "It was forced entry, like I said." He stopped.

I looked at him, then nodded. "Gun's in the bedroom."

"Yeah," he said. "Doesn't make any sense."

"What kind of door?"

"Standard steel frame, foam core. Nothing special."

"How many locks?"

"Three. Chain, dead bolt, knob. All busted up good."

"Take even a big guy a couple of tries to kick that in," I said.

"And Clay's going to sit on his leather couch, sipping a beer, waiting for them to get done?" Goodwin shook his head. "The door's a put-up, done after the fact. He knew the killer."

"Neighbors report anything? The noise must've been terrific."

"No. Adjacent unit was empty and the place is full of single renters who either aren't there half the time or don't care. None of the neighbors we interviewed even knew his name. We had to tell them the apartment number before any lightbulbs went on."

I gestured toward the sheets. "Says he was divorced. You looking at the wife?"

"Mostly. Tamika. That woman can hold a lot of hate. Clay left her in a lurch with three little girls about six months ago. Went off to chase after something younger and sweeter."

"She didn't kick that door down," I said.

"I guess you haven't met Tamika Johnson," he said, almost smiling. "Woman's six foot, two-forty. She'd make some NFL team a fine middle linebacker. But, no. We're thinking maybe murder for hire."

"And that takes a ton of legwork," I said. "Warrants, phone records, canvassing, interviews."

"Manpower we don't have," Goodwin said, spreading his hands. "Hence my eagerness to learn what you find out."

"Hence. I like that."

"I read it in a book somewhere. I try not to say it 'round the office. They hear me using works like that, they might bump me up to captain."

I grinned. I liked Goodwin. He seemed like a guy I could've worked with ten, twenty years. "You don't mind me saying, you don't seem, uh, broken up about this. Johnson have some kind of reputation around here?"

He let out a gusty sigh. "Clay had too much attitude. He was a showboat, liked to talk about all the college girls he was banging.

Badmouthed his family, how he was glad to leave the wife and kids behind. Some guys liked the act, but for a lot of cops, family's all they got, you know? They understand a divorce, separation—hell, cheating on your wife, maybe. But no one wants to hear about it all the time."

"Anything to build on there?"

He shook his head. "No one hated him. They mostly wanted him to shut the hell up and do his job."

I jerked a thumb at the box. "All right. Let me get lost in this stuff, see if I find anything."

"Knock yourself out, my man," he said, spinning in his chair so he could face his computer. "You know where to find me."

CHAPTER NINETEEN

I hunkered down across from Goodwin and started sifting through the box. A familiar feeling of calm washed over me. Early on in my homicide career, I used to hate this part of the process, the drudgery and tedium of going through rafts of paper, notes, and pictures. But at some point, I turned a corner. I looked forward to the task. Not just the paper-chase aspect of it, but the methodical examination of things, whether it was people or tire tracks or reams of computer printouts. A sense of calm eventually replaced the irritation and toward the end of my career I felt the most at home in the details. Maybe it was because I learned that a lot of cases got solved right here, in the box.

I began by skimming the items, getting a sense of what was actually in the treasure chest. As I removed each report or list or printout, I organized it, putting like with like until I had a dozen stacks filling the desk surface. I could feel Goodwin's gaze flick over to me from time to time, gauging my work and getting the unspoken sense that he approved of what I was doing. I almost blushed. It had been more than a year since I'd worked a case. Granted, I'd been a homicide cop when

Goodwin was still in high school and I shouldn't have given a rat's ass what he thought, but it was nice to think I'd still get a 10 for technique.

Once I had everything situated just so, I ignored all the piles and went back to the evidence list. It would've been better to give Johnson's apartment a look-see, but I didn't have that kind of time or authority. Maybe if I found a golden nugget for Goodwin, he'd let me tag along to visit the scene, but until then, this would have to do.

I grabbed a pen and forced myself to concentrate on each line of the evidence list, reading the description of the item, deciding whether it warranted more thought, then ticking it off if it didn't. In this manner I got to know everything there was to know about Clay Johnson's apartment. The DVDs he owned, the beer he drank, the mail he received, the North Face jacket and Timberland boots and the black Kangol cap he seemed to prefer based on the wear and tear. Riveting stuff. At the end of every page, I gave myself permission to look up and blink. On the fifth of these mini-breaks, Goodwin glanced over.

"Coffee?"

"Christ, yes," I said. "I'm about to start in on how many pairs of underwear the guy had."

He got up, then came back a few minutes later with two navy-blue Rockville PD mugs. The coffee was steaming hot and good. My surprise must've showed on my face.

Goodwin grinned. "Not bad, huh?"

"What happened to the sawdust and pencil shavings?"

"I get this at a coffee roaster in Bethesda and bring it in."

"You import your own?" I asked, incredulous.

"Life's too short to drink bad coffee, man."

I slurped some more and got back to reading. I really was looking at the number of pairs of skivvies Johnson owned—and T-shirts, and trousers, and belts—swimming in the relentless details, and nearly missed it. It was a fairly innocuous line: *(1) Sports jersey, maroon and gold [Redskins].* It had come right after *(4) Dress shirts, long sleeved, blue.* But something snagged at the edge of my attention when I saw it. The list indicated that it hadn't been brought in. No real reason to haul it from his closet to the station.

"Goodwin," I said. "I need to see something from Johnson's place. Any chance I could get access?"

"Have to be a real good reason. You got something solid?"

"I don't know," I said. I marked the line where the jersey was listed. "I need to see this."

He glanced at the sheet. "You can't afford your own?"

"It wouldn't fit anyway. It's just a hunch."

He handed me the sheet back. "Sorry, my friend. Everything not bagged was released to Tamika Johnson."

I pulled out my phone and punched in Tamika Johnson's number from the phone number list on the stats sheet. She answered after three or four rings. Her voice was slow, Southern. Carolina or Georgia, maybe. I introduced myself.

"Just one question, Ms. Johnson, and then I should be out of your hair. Among Clay's effects was a Redskins jersey. The officers here didn't think it pertinent to the case and gave it back to you. Do you still have it?"

"Lord, that thing? Clay wore it every Sunday during the season. I hated it."

"Can you describe it for me?"

"Well . . . it's a Redskins jersey. Maroon and gold."

"Yes, I know," I said. "Does it have a number or a player's name on it?"

She sighed. "He was so immature. Thought it was a big joke."

"It had a number, then?"

"Yes. He had it custom-made. It had 69 on the back."

I felt a tingle run up my spine. "Any lettering?"

"No," she said. "He used to tell people the number said it all. What a jackass."

"Thanks for your time, Ms. Johnson," I said, and hung up.

Goodwin poked his head over the cube wall. "Got anything?"

I thought back to a picture I had seen, one with Bob Caldwell, Danny Garcia, and a host of blurry figures in the background. A man had been working the grill, a big man, blurry and indistinct, but wearing a Redskins jersey with the number 69 on the back.

Goodwin cleared his throat, raised his eyebrows. *Well?*

"I don't know what I've got," I said. And meant it.

CHAPTER TWENTY

I left Rockville after another couple hours. Goodwin hadn't pressed me for info, even though he knew I'd seen something. I promised him I'd share whatever I could, when I could. He accepted that and I'd headed out. But since I was on the north side of DC and there were still a few hours of daylight, it made sense to take a swing at Okonjo's case. The file said he'd been shot in the parking lot of a bar called Rudy's on Rockville Pike.

The Pike was a never-ending strip mall that ran in a gentle curve north-northwest from DC until it hit the city of Rockville like the last link on the end of a chain. The mattress discounters, restaurants, fabric stores, and nail shops went back two or three blocks on either side of the road, some buried so deep in the sea of retail it was a miracle any of them stayed in business.

Rudy's pool hall propped up the end of a row of these shops on Broadwood Drive, a lower-rent location than front and center on the Pike. At three in the afternoon, the neon beer signs were just dull green and orange tubes hanging in the window, and five empty parking spots out of seven told me how busy it would be. Four more storefronts—a

Chinese restaurant, an Asian grocer, a taco carryout joint, and a convenience store—made up the rest of the strip, which stared directly across Broadwood at a nearly identical lineup of stores. Which, in turn, were cookie-cutter examples of any commercial strip in a two-mile radius. It made me wonder if buildings ever got depressed or suffered from identity crises.

I parked and walked into Rudy's. It was open but just barely. A TV game show flashing dollar signs and beach vacations kept the only waitress mesmerized at the far end of the bar, while a bartender—biting his lip while he concentrated—changed the handles on the beer taps. A half-dozen pool tables took up one side of the large room, their felt tops scarred and ripped. Sconces and billiard lamps gave off a muddy light, relieved by the occasional blinding offer from the TV. The place stank of bleach and beer, the signature off-hours odor of bars the world over.

I went up and introduced myself to the bartender. He was a chubby, balding guy in his early thirties. Green polo shirt over a T-shirt, jeans, and a name tag that said "Teddy." His hands looked clumsy and swollen as he spun the tap handles. I told him I was there to talk.

"You mind if I keep working?" he asked.

"Not at all," I said.

"What are you looking for, exactly?"

"A cop was killed here a while back. Isaac Okonjo, a Montgomery County deputy sheriff."

"Oh, yeah," he said. "God, that was shitty. We had to close down for a week, then the place was deserted for another couple days after that. I almost didn't make rent."

"For what it's worth, he was in worse shape."

He bit his lower lip as he concentrated on getting the last tap off. "Sorry. That was a lousy thing to say. You just think about how things affect you, y'know?"

"It's natural," I said, trying to stay agreeable. "What can you tell me about him?"

"The cop?" He shrugged. "Not much. I never saw him before." He called over to the waitress. "Nance, do you remember that guy, the black cop that got killed here a few weeks ago?"

The waitress tore herself away from the latest talk show. Her gaze was unfocused, like she had to concentrate after watching the tube. "Huh? The cop? Yeah, that was sad."

She came down from the end of the bar. She was in her twenties, with frizzy blonde hair pulled back in a ponytail, and she had on a green polo like Teddy's, but with a black half apron across her hips. As she came up to me, she pushed out a pink bubble of gum, then cracked it. "You a cop, too?"

"Was," I said, turning my attention to her. "I'm looking into the shooting for a friend."

"They catch the guy who did it?"

"Not yet."

"We talked to the police that night, but I don't think I helped much. I was inside the whole time and didn't see a thing."

"Well, maybe you noticed something that you didn't realize was important at the time," I said. "You never know what could help. You might have something buried deep that could crack the case open."

"You think?" she said, getting excited. "That would be cool."

"So, you working the night he was killed?"

"Yeah."

"Was he a regular?"

"No, never saw him before," she said. "I only remember him because he made this big entrance, walking through the door with his arms spread and said 'My people!' in this big, booming voice like some African king. He seemed like a funny guy. Wanted to get to know everyone at once."

"Did he come in with anyone? Have any friends here?"

Nance thought about it. "I don't remember any. He hung around the pool tables. He was a terrible shot and didn't mind losing, so people wanted to play him. He got chummy, buying drinks and stuff, but that's about it."

"He leave with anybody?"

She glanced at Teddy, who shrugged. "Honestly, I didn't see. But there was hardly anyone left to leave with."

"He stayed for last call?"

She nodded. "And a little bit past."

"Where'd they find the body?"

Teddy chimed in. "Back lot. Busboy found him when he took the garbage out. The light's bad back there and he thought the guy was passed out at first."

"Any reason for him to go out there?"

"That's where most of the parking is," he said.

"Did he fight with anyone? Is it a rough crowd here?"

Both of them shook their heads. "No," Nance said. "The regulars are pretty laid-back. Anyway, he was so freaking big, no one wanted to find out how tough he was. And with Moonpie around, too, there wasn't going to be any trouble."

"Moonpie?" I asked.

"Yeah, this other guy, a regular. Huge, too, like your guy. Hands like this." She held her own hands about a foot apart. "His face is round as a plate. Everybody calls him Moonpie."

"Black? White?"

"Black, too, but not . . . African, like the other guy, you know? Just black black. Is that okay to say?"

A tingle started near the back of my skull. "I'm not really qualified to judge."

Nance giggled.

"Do you know Moonpie's real name?"

"Y'know, I don't," she said, sounding surprised. "I probably checked his ID, but I was looking for numbers and a face, I guess."

"Hold on a sec, will you?" I said, and ran out to my car to get my files. I came back in, leafing through the photos Bloch had given me. I found a staff picture of Clay Johnson and held it up for both of them to see. The one where he'd been beaten to a pulp probably wouldn't have done much for the ID. Or their emotional well-being. "Is this, uh, Moonpie?"

Nance squinted at it, then nodded. "That's him. Oh. Do you . . . ?"

"Think he did it?" I said. "No."

"Then, if you have his picture . . . is he . . . ?"

I nodded. "I'm afraid so."

She put both hands to her face. "Oh my God."

"Clay, that was his real name, right?" Teddy asked. "I remember him now."

I'd almost forgotten Teddy was there. "Yeah."

"Took me a second. He hung out at the bar a lot. He liked making time with the girls who came in. He left with someone that night, in fact."

"A woman?" I asked and he nodded. "What time?"

Teddy pursed his lips. "Early, I know that. One drink in. I could tell he was pretty pleased with himself for scoring so quickly."

"Would you ever mistake Moonpie for the other guy, Isaac?"

"Maybe," Nance said, doubtful. "I mean, they weren't twins. But they were both kind of chubby. And huge. And, uh, black."

"So I gathered," I said.

"Maybe at a glance or if it was dark or something," she said. "Then, yeah, maybe."

"Did they see each other? Know each other?"

They glanced at each other, shook their heads. Both were more subdued than when I'd come in. Teddy said, "Moonpie . . . Clay, whatever . . . he stayed at the bar, just hitting on chicks. The other guy played pool all night, like Nance said."

"What happened to him?" Nance asked in a small voice. She didn't sound excited to be part of a murder investigation anymore. "How did he die?"

I thought about reaching into the file folder and showing her what some people are capable of, but it would've been gratuitous and smug.

"He just did," I said, tired. "That's really all that matters."

I walked out the back door and looked around. In front of me was an asphalt lot like a million-billion others, with sloppy white lines showing you where to park and a couple of light poles jutting out of the ground. A Dumpster and the compressor for the AC were next to the building, hidden by a cheap vinyl fence about seven feet high. I slid the crime scene photos out of the envelope, then glanced at the autopsy report. Traffic on the turnpike buzzed a few blocks away, a honk or two telling of distant anger. A starling flew down from a wire and pecked at a piece of crust, then flew off. The tingling feeling I'd had inside the bar was still with me.

Okonjo's body had been discovered on the left side of the lot, between the Dumpster and the first row of parking. I paced it off from the back door, trying to get the location right. He'd been found lying with his arms wide, face up to a starless sky, shot twice in the back of the head near the base of his skull. Exit wounds had obliterated much of his forehead. Judging from that information, I was going to go out on a limb and say the shooter was shorter than the six six Okonjo and that he shot him from behind. My deductions, however, would probably not get me the Detective of the Year Award.

I walked around the Dumpster, on the far side of the fence, which put me behind the Asian grocer's. I glanced at the steel door. The grocer would've been closed at three in the morning. As would the restaurant next to it. Quiet. Secluded. I stood at the corner of the fence in such a way that I was hidden from view from anyone coming out of Rudy's but could still see most of the parking lot. Swaying a little bit, I found a sweet spot between slats of the fence where I could see the door without losing my position. The smell wasn't great, but that wouldn't have been much of a worry. Just at that second the compressor turned on with a sound like a jet engine and I jumped about two feet off the ground.

Once my heart started again, I turned back to the parking lot. I made a gun out of my thumb and forefinger and said, "Bang." Or, I think I did. I couldn't hear myself over the industrial roar of the AC unit behind me. I let my arm fall and stared at the asphalt, thinking.

Three in the morning. Terrible lighting. Stark, blurring details. You're tired. You've been hanging out for two or three hours, waiting for him to show. You catch a glimpse of movement through the fence as he finally comes out the door. A big black man. This is it. He can't hear you, the AC's on full blast after a night of smoking and booze and bodies and the compressor is going like gangbusters. He walks at an angle in front of you, oblivious, intent on getting to his car. You step forward and pull the trigger from ten feet away. No one hears the shots or, if they do, they don't know what they've heard. He twists at the last second or maybe you roll him over to make sure. And you find out . . .

"You got the wrong guy," I said.

CHAPTER
TWENTY-ONE

"What are we doing here, again?" I asked.

"It's a surprise," Amanda said for the fifth time, an impish grin on her face.

We were back on the George Washington University campus, in an auditorium called Phillips Hall, mid-afternoon on a Friday. At about the same time most people in DC were loosening ties and thinking of sixteen-ounce drafts, I'd been commanded to dress as though going out for an embassy soiree. I had on black slacks, a gun-blue dress shirt, and a black blazer. I was allowed to skip a tie. The ensemble gave me a cool, hip look while avoiding the migraine ties always seemed to give me. Losing the tie also let me sidestep the awkward look from my recent weight loss; my neck now swam in the size 17 collars that used to be snug when I buttoned them. Amanda wore a sleeveless, shimmery lavender dress and black heels, which put her at nearly eye level with me. We were the tallest, best-dressed, ersatz father-daughter couple on campus.

Amanda took my arm and hurried me through the auditorium lobby, keeping me from getting a look at the billboard, then snatched a program before I could grab one from the nice girl handing them out. Big double doors led into a darkened corridor that deposited us into the cavernous auditorium's main seating area. Whatever it was we were going to see, it wasn't very popular. The place could probably fit a thousand, but only the first three rows were filled and, assuming the mystery event was going to start on the hour, it was getting close to showtime. Amanda dragged me down to the tenth row, end, then made me take the seat on the inside.

"This is just an experiment," she said, turning to me with her big eyes. "Here's what I want you to do. You're going to sit here and listen for one hour. At the end of that hour, you'll tell me what you think. If you don't like it, I'll never ask you to sit through anything like it again."

"What exactly is being performed?" I said. "You're making it sound like we're here for an autopsy."

"That might be your reaction after it starts. I'm just asking you to listen with an open mind. Don't bring any preconceptions to the music."

"So, it's music, at least?"

"Yes, Marty. It's going to be music."

"Why are we sitting ten rows back, then? Don't we want to hear it?"

"I don't want you to be influenced by anyone around us. A lot of the audience is going to be made up of music students who have some strong opinions about what they hear."

"And tenth row means I can get up and leave without anyone seeing," I said.

She glared at me. "Don't even think about it. Promise me you'll hang on for the hour."

"Without even knowing what it is first?"

"Marty," she said. Warning me.

I held up my hands. "Okay, one hour. I promise."

There was that low murmur that you hear in theaters and auditoriums as people tried not to make noise finding their seats, but saw
friends or whispered to companions or swore as they stubbed their toes.
A low-wattage excitement ran through the tiny audience. I felt a little
thrill of anticipation myself. It had been more than a year since I'd even
gone out for a movie and . . . well, I don't know how long it had been
since I'd seen live music. And, hell, I'd just gone out to dinner a few
nights ago! I frowned. What did I do with my time? Sure, cancer fills
up your day-planner, but still. I needed to get a life.

The overhead lights went down and the whispers stopped, then the
curtains swung away from center, revealing six musicians illuminated by
the soft glow of footlights. One guy was on drums, another at a baby
grand piano off to the right. A third kid was on an upright bass and a
girl was on guitar. Two more players, an older black man and an Asian
girl, made up a tiny horn section front, stage left. The crowd broke into
applause and there were a few whoops. The musicians on stage tried
to ignore it, but the kid on the bass grinned ear to ear as his friends
shouted his name.

The drummer clicked his sticks lightly, setting the tempo. I expected
the whole ensemble to jump in, but the piano player started a soft,
almost introspective stop-and-go solo. It lasted just a minute when the
piano paused and the bass player, all business now, slipped in with a
short, barely audible riff that repeated and swelled. The drummer came
in with a cool hi-hat and snare rhythm that had me thinking of Scotch
and velvet and smoke. The instruments eased into the pattern seam-
lessly. After another minute, the black guy stood up, trumpet in hand,
and started to blow.

I stifled a groan. It was jazz. I hated jazz. You wouldn't know it to
look at me now, but I'd dedicated every waking moment of my early
years to punk music. In the early 1970s I was young, angry, and looking for something to give me a voice. Punk was it. Everything else was
a sticky sweet anthem for singles' bars, a look back to the Summer of

Love, or the black hole of Your Parents' Music. Even as I got older and my tastes changed, I couldn't wrap my head around jazz. All the random, off-key honking made me antsy and gave me the urge to run away.

Amanda punched me in the arm and I looked over. She was glaring again and mouthed the words, *You promised.* I let my head loll to one side with my tongue falling out of my mouth, but turned my attention back to the stage when Amanda wouldn't look at me.

The trumpet player had sat back down to applause and the Asian girl stood, a sax half her height dangling from a strap around her neck. Still staying inside the structure of the rhythm and the original riff, she took off where the trumpet had ended, her fingers flying up and down the keys. She, in turn, gave the stage to the piano. The piece uncurled in front of me, flying around the room and finally coming in for a landing with the same drawn-out, two-note riff that the piano had started with, dying out entirely with the second of those two notes. I let out a breath as the audience went nuts.

Amanda was grinning at me. "Well?"

"What was that one called?"

"So what."

"Huh?"

"'So What.' That's the name. It's a classic. Miles Davis, John Coltrane, Bill Evans. Catchy, isn't it?"

"It was okay, I guess."

"So you were tapping your feet because you were nervous, huh?"

"Quiet, please," I said. "The musicians are playing again."

I stopped kidding around and paid attention to the rest of the set, trying to relax and soak it in. Thirty years in law enforcement makes you a judgmental kind of guy and I found it hard to forget what I thought, forget the things I'd told myself, and just listen in the moment. It helped to watch each instrument in turn, rather than let my mind wander on its own. The jazz combo was in full swing, each player doing their own thing, but obviously very aware of what the others were doing. After peering at them for five or ten minutes, even I—with the musical sensitivity of a concrete block—could see that, while they all were careful to stay within the framework of the piece, they were given permission to go off on tangents, as long as they came back to the original at some point. They weren't just improvising, they were inventing.

It wasn't all my cup of tea. Some pieces were more avant-garde than others, going too far out on a limb for my tastes. I drew the line when I couldn't tell if the musician had made a mistake or was ad-libbing. But it was, by far, the best jazz experience of my life. I might not run out and buy the complete Blue Note boxed set, but I was impressed. The combo finished up with a furious sax solo that made it pretty clear the little Asian girl with the big horn was the first among equals and the audience, filled out to the sixth or seventh row now, erupted into applause. I found myself clapping hard enough to knock my hands off. The whole ensemble was grinning like the bass player had been at the start. They gave nervous, perfunctory bows, as though unused to playing in front of an audience. Eventually, the applause died off, the lights came up, and the musicians descended to seat level to chat with friends and colleagues.

Amanda turned to me, one eyebrow raised. "Try and tell me you didn't like that."

I cleared my throat. "Well, given the choice between a murder scene and another jazz concert, I'll take the concert. But only if the victim isn't somebody important."

She stared daggers at me and I laughed as we moved from the row of seats and back out of the auditorium. "Okay, it was good. No, it was great. I could do without the dead-cat noise in the middle, but I really liked it. What was that slow piece towards the end?"

Amanda ran her finger down the program list. "'Wise One.' It's a John Coltrane piece."

"Funny," I said. "It seemed to be everything I dislike about jazz. Too schmaltzy, too contrived. Rainy streets and cigarettes and French cafés. Then I realized it's what came after that was the schmaltz. This was the real deal."

She covered her mouth in mock surprise. "Why, Marty Singer, I think we might make a jazz aficionado out of you, yet."

I held up a hand. "Easy. Old dog, new tricks, remember? Give me some time to adjust."

She took my arm again to lead me out of the darkness. "Oh, Marty. Don't you get it? Life's nothing but new tricks."

CHAPTER
TWENTY-TWO

At almost any time of the day or night, the steps of the Portrait Gallery on Seventh Street were a good place to meet someone. The broad granite stairs gave you an elevated view of the ruckus at street level while keeping you insulated at the same time. This was important because the whole other side of the street was just one face of the massive Verizon Center sports arena, the premier venue for the city's hockey and basketball teams and every other attraction that didn't require a football stadium. The sidewalk teemed with jerseys and warm-up jackets plastered with school insignia or professional logos most nights of the week. Fans pushed through each other to the doors or past them to the pubs to grab a seat to watch their game. Scalpers and the homeless tried to take advantage of the crowd, getting in people's way, both of them trying to make a living off the frenzy for sports and entertainment.

For someone like me, the steps were also nice in that the doors behind me were permanently closed, so I felt secure sitting on the top step in a little bit of shade, waiting for my date, Jake Valenti. Jake was a criminology and sociology professor at Georgetown who had taken a deep interest in the culture of gangs in general, and the rise of Hispanic gangs in particular. One of my calls for help to other cops still on the force had put me in touch with him and he'd agreed to meet me as long as it was on the Portrait Gallery steps around six o'clock.

I got there early, sat on a stone step, and watched the scene for half an hour while my butt went numb. As five thirty became six o'clock, a trickle, then a wave, of red-sweatered fans came down the street and up out of the Metro toward the Verizon Center doors. DC's hockey team, the Capitals, apparently had a game. I didn't follow the sport myself, but I could read and you'd have to be deaf, dumb, and blind not to see the team's logo emblazoned on nearly every flat surface around the arena. A small drum corps kept up a steady cadence to get people's blood going. Drunk fans spilled out of bars chanting, or trying to chant, the team's cry of "Let's Go Caps!" but it came out sounding more like "I Grow Cats!" or "Let's Make Hats!"

One of the blobs of red detached itself from the mob and crossed the street toward me. If it was Jake, he was about five five, thin and hawk-nosed, with receding brown hair. He wore dress slacks and leather bucks that just didn't seem to mesh with the hockey jersey on top. But that could describe most of the fans I was watching. He smiled at me from the bottom of the steps, then watched his footing as he came up.

"Mr. Singer?"

"Just Marty," I said, rising to a half squat and extending a hand. We shook and he sat next to me. "Jake? Or is it Dr. Valenti?"

"Jake is fine," he said, then smiled. "Unless you're a regular on the Caps Internet forums. Then you'd know me by Howlin' Wolf."

"Let's stick with Jake."

He put his hands on his knees and rocked back. "Phil Ricci over at the Alexandria police department called and told me you could use a primer on local gang culture. Specifically, the Salvadoran *maras*?"

"Maybe," I said. "I tend to get in trouble when I make too many assumptions. But, yeah, in essence, I'm working on a case where they keep cropping up. They might be the motivating force behind a lot of trouble that's been happening lately. Or they might just be an easy target to finger since they're around."

"What's going on, specifically?"

I gave him what I knew, trying to keep out my own deductions and guesses. He listened intently without nodding or interrupting, just rocking a little in place. Besides Sam Bloch, I gave him the most complete picture of anyone that I'd talked to. When I was done, he nodded to himself while he digested what I'd said.

"Were the scenes marked up or decorated in any way?"

"Not the scenes, per se," I said. "In four out of five cases, though, the bodies were severely beaten."

"Pre- or postmortem?"

"A little pre-, mostly post-," I said.

"Mutilated?"

"No trophies, if that's what you mean. Not, uh, dismembered. Beaten all to hell, though."

He rubbed his hands on his knees. "Do you have the crime scene photos with you?"

"I do," I said and handed him a folder with copies of the photos. He put on a pair of gold-rimmed glasses. My estimation of Howlin' Wolf went up a notch as I watched him sift through the glossies. The circle of professions that could look at these pictures without flinching was pretty much limited to soldiers, cops, nurses, and doctors. But Valenti's face remained expressionless and once or twice he peered closely at a photo, lifting his glasses to try and make out particular details. He put two of the batch aside and flipped through the rest, back and forth.

"Find something?" I asked.

"Yes," he said, drawing the word out. He picked up the two he'd put aside. They were from Okonjo's and Clay Johnson's scenes. "These are very different from the others."

"The victim that wasn't beaten. I told you about him," I said. "But that last one looks just like the others."

"The lack of beating is the obvious standout in the one case. But number five is different for a more subtle reason." He picked up the set of the first three photos. "These are the same because of one physical detail."

"You can tell that without seeing the autopsies?"

"Oh, no. I'm no crime scene pathologist. I can't tell you anything medically. I'm talking culturally, from a gang point of view. Specifically, from the viewpoint of a member of one of the *maras*."

The streets were alive now with sports fans and even across the street we had to huddle a little to hear each other. "You can tell something just from the pictures?"

He nodded and flipped through the pictures, pulling out Danny Garcia's. "See the hands? The way the fingers are lashed together?"

I studied the picture. "Yes."

He shuffled the pictures again. "And this one, Terrence . . . Witherspoon. The fingers aren't taped but appear to be snapped, bent back."

I frowned. "Not in the same way as Garcia's, though."

"Not when the picture was taken, but how about before rigor mortis?" he asked. I didn't say anything. "And this one, the last one."

"Brady Torres."

"Yes. Same extensive trauma, though even more vicious than the other two. His arms appear to have been broken—which is why he doesn't look like the other two—before the fingers were stacked."

"Stacked?" I asked. Then the light went on. "Oh. Oh, hell."

"Stacking," he said. "Slang for making gang sign. Each of these three bodies exhibit postmortem beating, in part, because the killer was trying to get the fingers to stack a particular way. He didn't always have the time or opportunity to tie the fingers together for the stack and so was forced to break some fingers until they conformed. The other two victims, even though one was beaten, do not show stacking."

"How the hell did I not see this?" I said.

"It's a relatively new tendency among Salvadoran and Mexican gangs. It's totemic, a way of laying claim to a killing without actually taking a . . . trophy, as you put it, or making an announcement. They think they're being cryptic, though of course everyone in the know gets what's going on. Which is the point."

"What do you mean?"

Valenti took his glasses off. "These are almost always retributive killings, not regular 'hits.' For cowardice or going to the police or threatening the existence of the gang. It's a way of degrading the victim, owning them. It's saying that the victim no longer is his own being; he belongs to the *mara* after death."

I chewed this over for a second. "What does the stacking mean specifically?"

Valenti pulled out Danny Garcia's picture again. "This one is the best example. Roughly speaking, his right hand is stacking the letter P. The fingers of his left hand are making an E."

"Which is?"

"The code takes a little deciphering. PE is short for *Para Él*."

"'For him'?"

Valenti nodded. "Short, again, for *Esto es para Él*. It's a corruption of an old catchphrase meaning 'This is for Him,' meaning God. It's been used many ways in the past. As a battle cry, a plea for salvation, a way of absolving oneself—or dodging responsibility—before committing an atrocity."

"What's its application here?" I asked. "It fits everything you mentioned."

Valenti handed me the photos. "Like a lot of groups, gangs take things that are culturally familiar and turn them to suit their own needs. They no longer believe in God, they believe in the gang. So the *Él* in the phrase isn't the Divine, it's the figure that embodies the group for them."

"The gang," I said. "Or the gang leader."

He nodded. "It's not worship, of course. The act of swapping God for a gang leader as the object of devotion is tongue in cheek, a cultural wink and nod everyone understands. But as a way of making a statement—for these punitive killings, for instance—it's perfect."

"I kill this person, or these people, for him. And, by extension, for the good of the gang."

"Exactly."

I stared at the stack of photos for a moment. "So, the two killings are different because they're missing this stacking. If there's no message, there's no connection."

"Probably. Well, I'd say definitely in the case of the one victim, who was not beaten. Then again, his killing could be connected in a less retributive way. Who knows what the circumstances are—that's more your realm."

We'd been talking for a while now and the streets were thinning out. The drum corps had packed it in and the area had returned to its normal decibel level. It was a strange thought that the building across the street now held almost twenty thousand people who I couldn't see or hear. Valenti checked his watch.

"Game time?" I asked.

He smiled. "They'll be dropping the puck in a few minutes."

"Big game?"

"We're meeting the Penguins in the playoffs. It's going to be a bloodbath," he said, then grimaced. "Sorry. Poor choice of words."

"No problem," I said. "One last question, then. Who, in this area, does this?"

He pursed his lips. "Only one I know of, though these things spread as the idea gets more popular. Fads, so to speak. Look for a Hispanic gang. In this area, that means MLA. Mara Loco Asesinos."

"One of the Salvadoran *maras*."

"No, Marty. *The* Salvadoran *mara*." He stood up and brushed himself off. "Feel free to call me if you need any more background. I hope this has helped."

I shook his hand. "Unfortunately," I said. "It has."

CHAPTER
TWENTY-THREE

My phone rang. On the screen was a number I vaguely recognized, but no name. I answered.

"Singer?" The voice was lightly accented.

"Rhee?"

"Yeah. I need to talk to you."

"Okay," I said.

"There's a pull-off on 66 west, just after Ballston. Mile marker 25. I'll have a flat tire there that I'm going to need help with. You *capisce?*"

"I *capisce*. When?"

"Soon as you can get there."

"On my way," I said and hung up.

I hurried to my car and headed out. Rhee didn't seem to be the cloak-and-dagger type, but neither was he a prima donna. If he wanted to play it safe, then there was a reason. The thought made me jumpy. I checked my mirror for a tail and made a handful of unnecessary switchbacks and detours before grabbing the ramp to 66. After that point, my caution became moot, since two dozen cars could've qualified as a tail, including the guy camped out on my bumper for ten minutes while he talked on his cell phone.

Alertness was a good thing, though. At mile marker 20 I caught sight of Rhee's silver Acura. He was pulled off to the side of the road with his hazards on and the jack out by the passenger's side of the car. I was in the center lane when I saw him and had to do a near-suicidal swerve to the right. There was a shower of gravel as I whipped off onto the shoulder and several drivers laid on their horns to let me know what they thought of my driving. I, in turn, let them know they were Number One in my book and put the car in reverse. I'd overshot Rhee's car by about a quarter mile and it took several minutes of cautious backing up before I was close.

I got out. Rhee was squatting by the back wheel and appeared to be fiddling with the lug nuts but it was obvious the tire was fine.

"I thought you said marker 25," I said as I walked up to him.

"Can't be too careful," he said, having to yell over the traffic. He gestured for me to join him down by the tire. I took a knee. It was a slower process than I would've liked.

"Please tell me this is worth it," I said. "It's going to take me an hour to get back up."

Rhee turned his head to me, his eyes obscured by his wraparound shades. "You wearing a wire, Singer?"

"Am I what?" I looked at him like he was crazy. "No, I'm not wearing a wire."

He went back to the lug nuts. "Care to prove it?"

I shook my head in disbelief and unbuttoned my shirt. He gave a quick glance and then raised his head, searching my face. After a second, he nodded. "Okay."

"What the hell is going on?"

"Some weird shit is going down and I'm not going to be played, that's what."

"I'm not here to play you, Rhee," I said. "You want to tell me what's got your panties in a twist?"

He picked up a rag and wiped the hubcap down. "Two days ago, I did a ride around over in Culmore. Like you and I did the other day so I could talk to Las Chacas. And I get the same treatment from the little shit up in Culmore that runs things that I did from Rico."

"Won't talk to you," I said.

"Right. I joke, I threaten, I lecture. Nothing. They won't talk. But they seem scared, not pissed. So, I drop the name Chillo. Just to see what happens."

"Throw something at a wall, see what sticks."

He nodded. "Well, this wannabe gangbanger, Hervé, it's like I snapped him in two. He starts crying and talking fast. My *español* is good, but even I couldn't keep up. He was, like, hyperventilating. I tell him to shut up and slow down."

I winced as a semi went blaring past, the chatter of its air brakes shaking the ground around us. Rhee took a second to gather his thoughts.

"Hervé talks. Gives me more than I bargained for. Long story short, Chillo is a hired gun, on loan from another *mara* in Texas. Some *chavala* up here asked for him."

"I'm going to go out on a limb here and guess that doesn't happen all the time."

"No. They send members back and forth a lot. Ship them out if they're in trouble with the local cops, that kind of thing. But this is different. Chillo is here on request."

"Did Hervé tell you for what?"

"With a little encouragement," Rhee said.

"And?"

"He said he was up here to kill people. To kill cops."

I let the roar of traffic blot out my thoughts for a half minute. It probably shouldn't have come as a surprise, but it did. Cops get killed in the line of duty. It happens and it always will. But the killings are unintentional. Sure, there's intent to pull the trigger, but it's after we bust down a door or get caught in the crossfire. Cops are *not* supposed to be targets, singled out and hunted down.

I pushed my anger away. "I appreciate you letting me know, Rhee, but why are you telling *me*? Why aren't you comparing notes with Arlington Homicide? Why are we talking about this on the side of the road?"

Rhee was quiet for a second. "It gets better."

"Yeah?"

"Gangs is short-staffed because of what happened to Brady. So, we have to divvy up his territory until they bring someone else on. The ride-along you did with me was in his territory. I knew some of Las Chacas from before so naturally it became mine."

"Okay."

"Day before I find out about Chillo, I head out to check in with a little gang cell in Arlandria, smaller and dumber even than the ding-dongs in Las Chacas. They were all Brady's people. I don't know them from a hole in the ground. So I play it cool, try not to spook them."

"Right."

"So, I go up to their leader, fat guy named Rudolfo, outside a restaurant. I don't get two words out before he hands me an envelope, then scoots inside like I'm going to shoot him."

My stomach felt cold and hollow. "How much?"

"Two thousand."

Cars passed. A plane flew overhead. "How often would Brady have checked in with these guys?"

"Every two, three weeks."

"Anyone else try to push an envelope on you?"

"Two more."

"Shit," I said. "*Shit*."

Rhee nodded. "I figure Brady was only squeezing the littlest guys."

"Too scared to say no to a cop and too scared to tell their boss."

"Yep."

"Then he gets greedy or someone blabs and the head honcho realizes he's being bled by a cop," I said. "He needs to set an example so his people don't think he's soft. Or start cooperating on a bust."

"But you don't do that lightly," Rhee said. "Don't want to use your own people."

"So he goes up the food chain, gets the green light to ace Torres, and asks for someone who can do the job."

"They send Chillo, who takes Brady out. And does such a good job that *el jefe* says, 'Hey, you wanna do a couple more for me, amigo?' And there goes your undercover dude."

I stared at the ground. It all made unfortunate sense about Torres. But Danny Garcia, on the take? Possible, but I wanted to think it was unlikely. Terrence Witherspoon? Not in a million years. Still, it was a lead. "That's why you didn't go to Homicide?"

Rhee gave me a look. "I told you what everyone thinks of Gangs. Half the departments want to bring *us* up on charges. I'm supposed to tell Homicide I've got the cop killer sitting in Motel 6 but, by the way, the reason he's here is because our boy Brady was taking in sixty grand a year in squeeze money from local dealers? You mind keeping that part our little secret?"

"Rhee, you'll have to tell someone sometime."

He grinned, but there wasn't any humor in it. "I am, Singer."

I lifted my head. "Ah. You want *me* to pee in the punch bowl."

"You're investigating it anyway. If you figure out Chillo is behind the other thing, then you take him down for it. Justice is served."

"Means and ends?"

"In this case, yeah," he said, then lifted his hands. "Look, it may not even matter. Arlington Homicide is on Brady's killing like white on rice, so the whole thing may come out tomorrow."

"In which case, Gangs gets implicated anyway."

He shrugged. "Yeah, but I won't have been the one to say it."

"You could preempt them. Be the hero. The one who's big enough to admit that, yeah, we've got dirty cops, too."

"I think when you say 'hero' what you really mean to say is 'fall guy,'" Rhee said. "Singer, no one's going to give me a medal for lifting the lid on Brady. Gangs would disown me, the other departments wouldn't want me, and the DA would use me to prove a point, then spit me out."

I said nothing. He was probably right.

"What really needs to happen is that whoever thinks they can kill cops, dirty or not, needs to go down. And you're in a position to make that happen."

I was quiet, thinking. Something occurred to me. "That stuff about the wire," I said. "You were afraid I was with IAD."

Rhee shrugged. "If you knew about Torres being dirty before he was killed, I would've been the perfect patsy to try to break the case open. I told you, I'm not going to be played. If you were wearing a wire, then I'd say thanks for the help with the flat and drive off."

I nodded, watched as the cars zoomed past. "Can I tap you for some help on this if I need it? I'm off the books as it is and this thing just got bigger."

"As long as we're not talking grand jury kind of help. I'm looking to stay behind the curtain, like I said."

I nodded. "Thanks for the intel, Rhee," I said. "I know it wasn't easy."

He tilted his head, a *whatever* gesture. "Someone's got to know."

I nodded again. "We all done?"

"I hope so," he said. "My knees are fucking killing me."

CHAPTER TWENTY-FOUR

At my request, Bloch came out to my house in Arlington to talk about where we were with the case. I was tired of driving to every godforsaken corner of Washington, DC. It was about ten o'clock, early enough to be called morning, late enough to miss the worst of the traffic. Though it wasn't even June, the DC region was true to its meteorological form, with both the temperature and the humidity in the mid-eighties and the promise of a brutal summer to come. When there was a breeze—almost never—the air moved reluctantly, with an attitude.

I didn't do heat well. I was five degrees away from turning the AC on, although it seemed like a violation of some unspoken rule to even think about doing it before July. It was still spring, technically. You were supposed to enjoy the seasons in all their aspects. Take the good with the bad, the hot with the . . . hotter. The AC wasn't supposed to go on until all the grass turned to straw and the sidewalks were hot enough to melt sand into glass. Anything else was Wimp City.

So I was on my porch toughing it out, with dark crescents of sweat under my arms and a coffee cup in hand when Bloch arrived. He got out and walked toward me, smoking. I hadn't noticed before that he had bad posture, a slouching, crumpled kind of walk. Maybe the heat got to him, too. He flicked the butt into the street and blew a lungful of smoke into the atmosphere as he walked up to my porch.

He stopped at the foot of the steps. "Singer."

"Bloch," I said. "Get you some coffee?"

"Absolutely," he said. I led the way through the living and dining rooms and into the kitchen. I saw him jump as he passed through the kitchen archway.

"Jesus Christ," he said. "What was that?"

I turned around from the coffeemaker, pot in hand. "What was what?"

"The thing that ran past me."

"Oh," I said. I poured him a full mug, handed it over. "My cat, Pierre."

"What do you feed him? Gunpowder?"

I topped off my cup and put the pot back with a clatter. "That cat has genes that start in Africa. He's my backup when I run out of bullets."

Bloch took a sip, then gestured at my kitchen table. "You mind if we stay inside? It's already in the eighties out there."

"Wimp City," I said.

"What?"

"Nothing," I said with a little smile. Bloch took a seat while I put milk and sugar on the table. My case notes were already spread out on the surface and I had to shuffle some things around to make room. I grabbed my cup and sat down across from him, then flipped to the first page of my notebook. "Ready? You're going to have to hold on with both hands."

I gave him everything, starting with my interviews with the Garcias, my run-ins with Chuck Rhee—who I didn't name—and the latest news that I stumbled on mostly by accident, that Isaac Okonjo had almost certainly been killed by mistake, and that the real target had been Clay Johnson. I relayed how Witherspoon had probably stuck his nose out too far. I told him about Jake Valenti, my gangs expert, and his theory about the "stacking." Bloch listened intently, taking sips of his coffee a few times, but otherwise letting me finish the whole thing without interruption. When I got to the end, he closed his eyes, soaking it in.

"Torres was dirty," he said.

"Yes."

He opened his eyes. "How do you know?"

"A source," I said.

"You won't name him?"

"No," I said.

"Really?"

"He isn't exactly taken with the idea of being a whistle-blower. Wouldn't do much for his advancement opportunities if word got out he was the one to finger Torres for us."

Bloch fiddled with his coffee cup. "If Torres was on the take . . ."

I shook my head. "This guy is clean. He's got no reason to help me or you except to give us a hand catching whoever's knocking off cops. If it becomes really important, like if whoever it is doing this might walk, then he'll step up."

"I could find out," he said.

"Then you lose me," I said. "I told this guy I wasn't going to hang him out to dry."

Bloch nodded, accepting it. "Who was paying Torres?"

"A Salvadoran gang called Mara Loco Asesinos."

"MLA," he said, sounding surprised.

"Brady was squeezing the little guys at the end of the food chain. Someone in the MLA found out and called in an out-of-town hitter.

I'm guessing that there're only a few *chavalas* around here with the clout to do that—"

"Just one."

"—and that you probably know the identity of that individual."

"If it's really the MLA, then it's Felix Rodriguez."

"Okay," I said.

"Where do the other killings fit in?"

I shrugged. "Witherspoon nosed around, making life uncomfortable for an enterprising young Hispanic drug dealer looking to open up a new distribution point in Barry Farm. Danny Garcia gets whacked while working undercover or moonlighting. Rodriguez probably had more than a little to do with both those things. I think you'll have grounds for suspicion."

"What real cops call 'clues,'" Bloch said.

"Exactly."

"We know Danny was moonlighting," he said.

"Yes."

"We don't know that he was looking at the MLA when he was killed."

"We don't know that he wasn't," I said. "And, judging by what Bob Caldwell told me, Danny had a special hatred for Hispanic gangs. Gave them special attention."

"A Salvadoran *mara* would fit the bill," Bloch said.

"It would."

"And Danny had his finger on the pulse. He knew who was making a move and when. So he might've known about the *mara* trying to expand and was looking to get more intel or screw up the process or something."

"It fits Danny's MO," I said. "Maybe he thought he could take them out himself at some point. If not—if it looks too big for him and his vigilantes—he hands it over to you and says, 'Hey, boss. Look what I found.'"

Bloch scrubbed his face with his hands. "Moving on. Okonjo was a mistake, almost pure coincidence."

"Yep. Well, not a total coincidence. Someone was out to kill a big, black cop that night. It was Okonjo's rotten luck to like the same bar Johnson did."

"If you're right, then his murder and Clay Johnson's are essentially the same."

"Right."

"And Johnson was the real target. Why?"

I shrugged. "Not sure about that yet. I've still got some legwork to do, things I want to check out."

"Think he was in it with Torres?"

"Like I said, I don't know. I haven't seen a connection on Torres's end, but we're operating in the dark. Anything I say would be a guess."

We were quiet for a long time. The coffeemaker made small hissing noises as condensation hit the hot plate. Bloch stared into the middle distance, drinking his coffee and thinking. After another minute, he put his cup down and leaned back in his chair, lacing his fingers together behind his head.

"There's no serial killer," he said.

"Well, there's a serial killer," I said. "Just not the Hollywood-style maniac with a hockey mask and a thing for cops."

"It's all just gang shit," he said, a note of amazement creeping into his voice. "Some punk wants territory or money or dope and he's mad that we're in his way, so he just starts shooting cops to get what he wants."

"That's how they do it," I said.

"Not here it's not. It's time to run this motherfucker into the ground."

"What's your next move?"

"Well, the irony is we were already watching Rodriguez and his little band of merry men. There was enough to move on him before, but I wanted something bigger and badder."

"Guess you found it," I said.

"No kidding." He sighed. "It'll take a little bit of time to get the warrants, contact all the agencies and departments that want their finger in the pie, put a team together to take this guy out. I'll have to go official now, no more under-the-covers investigating. But we can't take too long or they'll ship this guy Chillo out in the middle of the night, try to put him out of reach."

"Might've already happened," I said, getting up and filling both our cups.

"Maybe," he said. "It would be the smart thing to do, get out from under us. But these guys aren't the KGB or anything. They like to party, score some dope, make some money before they head back. They've probably treated Chillo like a potentate, at least for a couple of weeks. He might hang around and milk it for all it's worth."

"Potentate?" I said.

He smiled. "I'm a words guy."

"Nice," I said. "You think Chillo would stick around long enough to get picked up?"

"I hope so." He swirled the coffee around in his cup. "What're you going to do in the meantime?"

"Run with it. See if I can find something else on Johnson that will help your case with Rodriguez or tie the screwup with Okonjo to him. Better to have five homicides to pin on his shirt than three."

He nodded, then said, "You know what bothers me?"

I sat back in my chair. "Is it over?"

"Exactly. If it really is Rodriguez, he obviously doesn't think twice about killing cops or anyone else who proves to be a minor inconvenience to his plans. Is he stopping at five? Or is there someone else that he's got a problem with and we're just in the middle of the run?"

"Another reason to move fast," I said. "But careful. We don't want to rush it and have him walk."

"I don't want another cop to get shot, either," Bloch said.

Pierre slunk back into the kitchen, if that word could be used to describe any movement of a twenty-two-pound cat. "Careful, Bloch. There's a smilodon behind you."

"Huh?" Bloch turned around. Pierre tried to meow, but no sound came out, so it just looked like he was opening his mouth wide in an attempt to intimidate Bloch. Bloch stared at him for a minute, impressed, then turned to me. "Smilodon?"

"The proper name for a saber-toothed tiger," I said. "You're a words guy. I'm a history buff."

"You're a strange dude, Singer," Bloch said. He leaned over and wiggled his fingers. Pierre walked over and rubbed his face against Bloch's hand. "But you do good work."

CHAPTER
TWENTY-FIVE

Amanda called me not long after Bloch left. I was cleaning up, getting ready to leave and almost missed the innocuous little buzz.

"Hey, kiddo," I said. "What's up?"

"Marty!" she said, her breath fast, excited. "I've got news."

"Good or bad?"

"Both. Neither. I don't know," she said. "I just got calls from a counseling center in Austin, a women's shelter in Chicago, a clinic in DC wants to interview me, and the director of a youth group in Baltimore asked me to have coffee with him next week."

"That's . . . that's . . ." I said, trying to catch up. "That's a lot."

"A lot? It's great! I haven't had a job offer since I worked at a shoe store in the mall."

"Hey, don't get ahead of yourself," I said, cautious. "An interview is one thing, a job offer is another."

"Oh, Marty. Don't pee in my Wheaties."

I smiled, even though I felt a little tug on my heart. Austin and Chicago were pretty far away. Whatever. The least I could do was be happy for the poor girl. "Amanda, that's fantastic. It was just a matter of time before someone saw your potential. Is the pay good? Are these the kind of jobs you wanted?"

"The pay sucks. If I wanted to make money, I'd run a hedge fund."

"Good point," I said.

"It's the work that's important to me and all of these places do great things. I know you wouldn't be too happy with me moving to Austin or Chicago, but the other two might come through, too."

"Anything can happen."

"Don't sound down, Marty," she said. "Be happy for me. I told you, we're connected. Being a plane flight away isn't going to change that."

"I know, kid," I said, forcing a hearty tone into my voice. Maybe now wasn't the time to tell her that I had to schedule cancer surgery. "I'm happy for you. Tell you what. Keep me in the loop. We'll go back to Nora's the minute you get your offer. On me."

"That's sweet, Marty."

"One condition."

"What's that?"

"You can bring Zenny and Jay, but no existential arguments. Acceptable topics are your job, football, or guns."

"They won't have much to talk about, then."

"That was kind of the idea," I said.

She laughed. "I'll call you tomorrow, Marty."

I was about to hang up when I heard her call my name again, tinny over the short distance. I put the phone to my ear again. "Yes, ma'am?"

"You never told me how the doctor's appointment went," she said. "How did it go?"

"Ah," I said. My mind raced through all the options, the thought that her future was spooling out in front of her, while mine was . . . unknown. Did she really need to know the details? She'd drop everything to stay and help me through whatever my disease had in store for me, no matter how much I might protest. And it would cost her all the opportunities she'd earned. Make all the obstacles she'd overcome meaningless.

"Marty?"

"It's fine," I said, a little too quickly, then cleared my throat. "I'm fine. The doc said he's got some more tests he wants to run, but he always wants to do that, you know? Anything to make another buck off the insurance companies."

"That's great news," she said. "I was so afraid . . . well, I'm just really glad. Look, I've got to get going on some paperwork the clinic wants before my interview, but I want you to tell me about it later, okay?"

"Sure," I said, then we said good-bye.

I hung up and put the phone in my pocket, then leaned against the counter and stared out the window. Around me, the noises of an empty house filled the silence. A gurgle as sink water settled in the pipes, a ticking sound as a beam or a joist somewhere settled a fraction of an inch. The refrigerator hummed, then went quiet. I hadn't noticed the sounds as much before. When people enter your life, they expand your world. But when they leave, the void is that much greater. The question is, can you fill it up again? Or does it just stay there? A hole in your heart, empty and waiting.

For the third time in ten days, I pulled up to the curb outside the Garcia home. The Corolla and Bronco were both in the driveway, exactly what I was looking for. I wanted both Paul and Libney to be there when I questioned them. Why I wanted to question them was another thing entirely. Bloch seemed content with my report on the situation and was gearing up for a big bust on Felix Rodriguez and the MLA, but something wasn't sitting well with me. While Bloch scratched around for warrants and signed requisitions for body armor, I figured I might as well keep poking around until I stopped feeling weird about the situation. Back in the day, that usually meant starting over and talking to everyone I'd talked to once—or twice—again.

Paul Garcia didn't seem surprised when he answered the door and saw me standing on his porch.

"Paul, I'm sorry to bug you again," I said, "but I was hoping I could talk to you and your mother once more."

His eyebrows rose slightly. "I thought we answered all your questions, Mr. Singer."

"You did. Thank you," I said. "But unfortunately I've got more. Under every stone are two more stones. This shouldn't take long."

He thought about it for a moment, then opened the screen door and ushered me in. I followed him from the foyer into the living room, which still retained its hushed, closeted feel. He motioned me to take a seat as he walked down the hallway toward the bedrooms. I took a look around as I waited, did a double take when I saw something missing. I got up to take a look at the TV set, but at that moment, I heard some murmuring and then Libney Garcia, wearing a long, cotton sleeping gown, appeared out of the darkness looking woozy and half asleep. Paul shuffled behind, a hand out to steady her as she went.

I stood. "I'm sorry to bother you, Mrs. Garcia. I just have a few questions and then I'll be out of your hair."

She nodded, though I'm not sure it was in response to anything I'd said. Her head might've been bobbing. Paul guided her to the couch. She eased down most of the way, then fell onto the cushion. Paul sat next to her, holding her hand. I frowned when I saw her eyes, then glanced over at Paul.

"She's on Xanax," he said. "She's having panic attacks at night."

I nodded. "I'm sorry. It's understandable."

"What was it you wanted to talk to us about, Mr. Singer? I'd like my mother to rest as much as possible."

"Of course," I said, then paused to gather my thoughts. "What did the two of you know about Danny's work?"

"You ask this a'ready," Libney said.

"I know, Mrs. Garcia. Can you tell me again?"

She closed her eyes and swayed in place, then opened them. "He work for the police."

I nodded.

"He work undercover. He arrest many bad men."

Libney's voice trailed off. I glanced at Paul. He shrugged. "That was about it. My father worked undercover, mostly with gangs and drug dealers. He never brought his work home, so we were in the dark most of the time."

Libney nodded.

"Did he ever mention working with other men, other police officers?"

Paul looked at me blankly. "He didn't talk about it. If he had, I'm sure he would've mentioned working with other police officers, yes."

"What about off the record?"

They seemed confused. "What do you mean?" Paul asked.

"I know Danny hated drug dealers and gangs of all types, and especially Hispanic gangs. We all know that sometimes the legal system can be slow and a little uneven when it comes to prosecution and punishment. It must've made Danny angry to see some of the crooks he crossed paths with never face jail time."

"Probably," Paul said, frowning. "Wouldn't anyone?"

"Yes," I said. "But not everyone had the kind of access and specialized knowledge that Danny did. Or the particular desire to get certain gangs off the street."

Paul's face, normally round, hardened, seemed to become defined along planes and angles as I watched. "What are you saying?"

I took a deep breath. "Paul, it's pretty clear your father was moonlighting in his spare time."

"Moonlighting?" Libney asked.

"Chasing and sometimes killing drug dealers," I said. "We found a small apartment in Southeast where he stashed weapons and planned his hits."

"What?" Paul said, looking shocked. "Jesus."

"I take it you didn't know about it?"

"No," he said. "How do you know this? It doesn't seem like my dad to go off on his own."

I gave them the abridged version of Danny's hideout and the ballistics matching that Bloch had been able to do through IBIS. Libney glanced back and forth between us, not comprehending. Paul said some things in Spanish and I watched her face crease as she began to understand what we were talking about. She replied, then turned to me.

"You say he kill some of these bad men?"

"Maybe," I said, hedging. "We don't know for sure."

She shrugged. "What's the difference?"

"Mama," Paul said, then said some more things in Spanish. Explaining the legality of the situation, maybe, and what was wrong with it. Maybe he could explain it to me when he was done.

"Is he in trouble?" she asked me.

"Danny?" I said. "No. It's not something anyone's really interested in pursuing legally. But if we knew more about what he was doing, obviously we'd have more information that might help us find and build a case against whoever murdered him. And the other officers who've been killed."

Paul cleared his throat. "Do you think there's a connection?"

"No, we *know* there's a connection," I said. "We know who is responsible for most of the deaths, but not all."

"Who is it?"

"The head of a local Salvadoran *mara*."

"What's his name?"

I shook my head. "I'm sorry, I can't tell you that. But he was probably involved in at least three of the killings, including Danny's. There are two others I want to clear up, however. They don't have the clear connection that the others do."

"Could they be accidents?" Paul asked. "I mean, random killings, instead of connected to this *mara*."

"Sure, they could. But I'm not real fond of complete coincidence. Especially when the unconnected murders bear all the physical hallmarks of the other killings."

"Then you just haven't found the thing that connects them," he said. "Find that and you can pin the other killings on the *mara*."

"Maybe I have," I said. "See, when we found your father's apartment, we found signs that indicated that it was more than just Danny doing the freelancing. There might have been up to three or four of them all working together to take out drug dealers and crooks in their spare time."

"So you think one of the murdered police officers was working with my dad on this?"

"Yes," I said.

"Which one?"

"We don't have much pointing to either Terrence Witherspoon or Brady Torres, two of the other officers killed. They stirred up trouble on their own. But it's the odd man out in this situation, Clay Johnson, who might be the one we're looking for."

Libney raised her head when she heard Johnson's name. "Who?"

"Clay Johnson," I said. "He was a police officer with the Rockville force. Do you happen to remember him?"

She asked Paul something in Spanish. He shrugged and replied. She turned to me.

"He's a big man? Black?"

"Yes."

"He and Danny used to be frien'. Years ago. They met at the academy."

"Did they stay in touch afterwards?"

"A few year," she said. I was looking at her, but out of the corner of my eye, I could see Paul staring straight down at the floor. "Danny went undercover and then we never have friends over or see anyone."

I stood and walked over to the TV stand. "Paul, the last time I spoke with you, there was a picture here, taken years ago. It seemed like your father, Bob Caldwell, and someone like Clay Johnson having a good time at a picnic. But you told me that you didn't know any of the other victims when I asked."

His eyes flicked up to meet mine. He didn't say anything.

"The picture isn't here now," I said, and paused. "Is there anything you want to tell me?"

"No, sir," he said, staring back at me. A change had come over him as my line of questioning had become obvious. He had straightened up where he sat and his face became impassive. Excessive formality—the unbreakable, millennia-old protection of the foot soldier—now enveloped him like a shield.

"No one's going to dishonor your father's memory, or hurt you or your mother, Paul," I said. "But I can't say the same about anyone else. For all I know, the killer is planning on murdering another cop, maybe another officer that worked with Danny in this off-hours stunt. If you know anything, son, you have to tell me."

"Sir, I don't know. I was very young when my father knew these people—"

"You were almost a teenager," I said.

"—and I don't remember the picture you're talking about."

"You don't remember it?" I said. "Or saying how that had been the last of the good times?"

He looked at me, his eyes flat. "No, sir."

I returned his stare, giving him the chance, willing him to say something. When he didn't, I nodded. "Well. Maybe we'll be in luck and no one else will get hurt. My colleague is planning a raid on the gang's headquarters. I just hope it's soon enough to save anyone else who they may have targeted."

Libney seemed about to say something, but Paul made a small motion with his hand and she went silent. When he spoke, his expression was tense. "When is this raid supposed to happen, Mr. Singer?"

"I don't know, exactly," I said. "Soon. If everything goes well, I'm sure Detective Bloch will be in touch to get your help with the prosecution. And to ask you some other questions."

"Will you make sure to tell us anything you know? We'd like to know when my father's killer will be apprehended. And punished."

"I'll do my best, Paul," I said. His gaze held mine for a moment, then he nodded. There wasn't anything else to say. I thanked them and left, taking my time walking out to my car, giving them every opportunity to stop me and tell me what they were hiding.

CHAPTER
TWENTY-SIX

I called Bob Caldwell from my office. I hadn't heard from Bloch, but I knew there wasn't much time before his raid and, having been blown off by the Garcias, I was hoping maybe Caldwell would be willing to tell me something—anything—about Danny's after-work hobby of taking out drug dealers on the QT.

The phone rang about ten times before his voice mail came on and I hung up. I waited five minutes and tried again. I let it go eight times and hung up. I had done some doodling on a scratch pad while waiting for him to pick up. I had written "Danny—moonlighting" and then "partners?" next to it. Below those I'd jotted down "Felix Rodriguez" and drawn two arrows to each of the other words. In my boredom, I'd traced the words a half-dozen times and put small stars and squiggles radiating outward. So many, in fact, that there was no way I could use the paper to take notes, so I ripped that off and wrote everything down again. I tapped my fingers on my desk. I'd decided to call one last time when it rang in my hand. It was Caldwell.

"You wanted to get ahold of me?" he asked, his gravel-rock voice coming over the line along with the background noise of the waterfront.

"I've got a few more questions for you; thought it would be easier to catch you on the line than having you stick a gun in my face again."

"What do you need?"

"We found some interesting things lately, chasing down some leads on Danny Garcia's case. I thought you might be able to clear some things up for me."

Caldwell's breath came heavy and labored over the phone. "Yeah? Like what?"

"The primary thing is that it's clear Danny liked to go hunting for scalps in his spare time."

"What do you mean?"

"Busting dealers off the clock," I said. "We found a cache of his down in Southeast. Not exactly a little getaway in the Hamptons. A cot, a kitchen, some guns. A med kit good enough for light combat. It looks like he used the pad to stage his side jobs."

Caldwell whistled low. "You're shitting me."

"The thing is, Bob, it was too well-outfitted for a single guy. I mean, you can't measure these things, but it didn't look like he was doing this solo."

"You're looking for someone who might've been running with him?" he asked.

"Yes. Not to bust them, necessarily, though it would be nice if they left things like this to, you know, our legal system. But maybe the guys who knocked Danny off know who these other moonlighters are, you know? If they got it out of Danny before they killed him—and we know they broke half the bones in his body before he died—then there's a good chance he might've given up a couple names. Names of guys they're going to want to add to the list."

"Assuming there were others," he said, his voice even.

"Sure. But it's safer to go with that than it is to throw our hands up and decide there wasn't anyone else involved. Because if we're wrong, then another cop might die."

"You know who did Danny?"

"An out-of-towner from one of the Salvadoran *maras* is looking good for it. Chillo is his name."

"Never heard of him. Who ordered it?"

"Felix Rodriguez. Heads up the MLA in these parts."

He swore. "That piece of shit?"

"Looks like he did two of the others, too," I said.

"Who else?"

"A beat cop named Witherspoon and an Arlington detective named Torres. In the Gangs unit."

"They knew Danny?"

"No. Looks like they just got on Rodriguez's hit list for sticking their noses in it too far. But I'm almost sure that Clay Johnson was mixed up in it."

"Clay Johnson? Who's that?"

"Rockville PD. Killed with the same MO as the others. I'm surprised you don't remember him, Bob. I saw a picture from a barbeque years ago. It was of you, Danny, and Clay in the background."

"You know from when?" he asked. "I don't keep track of all the parties I go to."

"This was at Danny's," I said. "Maybe ten years ago."

"I don't know, Singer. Before he went undercover, Danny and me got together a lot. There were always other cops showing up. Friends of friends. After he got the nod to go undercover, he stopped calling unless it was about business. Guess he got into the role."

"So you don't know Clay Johnson?"

"Nope. Sorry."

"You wouldn't happen to be the third guy on Danny's team, would you?"

He laughed, a coarse sound. "You gotta be kidding. You saw me, right? I'm an old white guy with a bum leg and a sixty-pound spare tire. I got thirty-five years in, Singer, and I'm a couple months from retiring. Why the hell would I be running around blowing dealers away after hours when I could be on my boat drinking beer?"

"You don't have to be an Olympic athlete to pull a trigger or drive a car, Bob," I said. "You just have to be willing."

His good humor drained away. "You can get fucked, Singer. Danny Garcia was a good cop, but if he wanted to waste his time capping punks who were going to get aced by their twenty-first birthday anyway by some *other* punk, then that was his business. I got the rest of my life to live and I can tell you the plan doesn't include dragging ass around Southeast looking to get shot. I'm sorry about those other cops getting killed, but it sounds like you'd be better off running them into the ground instead of giving me a hard time. Now, you got anything else on your mind?"

"That's about it," I said, but I only got half my sentence out before he hung up. I put the phone down carefully. It had been a while since someone had told me to get fucked. It was a refreshing twist to the normal, implicit "fuck you" I'd been getting from everyone else.

CHAPTER
TWENTY-SEVEN

I was looking at ties at the downtown Macy's.

It had already been a long day, but I wanted to talk to Bloch. I'd called and he'd asked me to meet him at a noodle house downtown in the Penn Quarter. I told him I wouldn't be able to stomach the smell, so we settled for meeting at Macy's instead, where the odor of thirty kinds of perfume lingered in the air, even in the men's section. It wasn't much of an improvement over the noodles.

"Singer."

"Bloch," I said, turning from a table of ties.

He stood beside me and picked up a tie, rubbing the material between his thumb and finger. "Four-dollar coffees, seventy-dollar ties. I gotta get out of DC. I can't afford this place."

"It's the same everywhere," I said. "They keep cops' salaries a hair under the living wage. Keeps us hungry."

He snorted for my benefit and we started walking. Just two regular guys, meeting mid-afternoon in a department store to talk about multiple homicides, gangs, and drug raids.

"You said you had something for me?"

I hung back to make room for a trio of twenty-something girls to pass, their eyes glittering with the prospect of shopping. It was never a good idea to get between a predator and her prey. "Yeah." I explained the Redskins jersey and the picture I'd seen at the Garcias' house. "I'm no sports historian, but I don't think there was a number 69 about the time that picture was taken. And, with Johnson's reputation as a womanizer, it would fit his . . . uh, juvenile sense of humor. So, it's not much, but it got me wondering if that was Johnson in the photo. When I asked Paul Garcia and Bob Caldwell point-blank if they knew the other victims, though, they both said no."

"Maybe it was a chance thing. One cop passes another in the hall, says, 'Hey, I'm having a cookout at my place this weekend. Want to come over?'"

"And he runs the grill? And happens to be one of the victims in a serial slaying of cops?"

He made a face, impatient. "It's strange. So what? It's not against the law to lie. Doesn't mean there's a conspiracy."

I looked at him. "You seem pretty eager to make excuses for a guy who begged me to look into this thing. What happened to doing the right thing?"

"We *are* doing the right thing. Felix Rodriguez did this and we're going to nail his ass to the wall. I appreciate what you've done for us, Singer, I really do. I couldn't have gotten anywhere without your help on this. But Rodriguez is our man."

We'd walked all the way to housewares. The row after row of convenient household goods, gleaming under soft fluorescent lighting, depressed me for some reason and I made a motion to turn us around. "You're talking like this is a done deal."

"Not exactly. But I got some good news today. We got the warrants to hit Rodriguez at home. Full-on raid with complete multijurisdictional support. We're going to clean up that shitbird's nest and put him and Chillo and the rest of his homies away for twenty to life, times three."

"You can pin everything on him?"

"Garcia, Torres, and Witherspoon for sure. If a murder weapon turns up that helps us out, then they might go down for Okonjo and Johnson, too. We're taking this to federal court. They'll stomp on them with both feet."

"Sounds nifty," I said. "What are you thinking Johnson's connection was?"

Bloch seemed uncomfortable for the first time. "I don't know. I was hoping your trip to Rockville would let us tack that on top. Maybe he was dirty, like Torres. There's a connection somewhere."

"But you're going to go ahead with a raid."

He checked his watch. "Twenty-four hours from now."

"Jesus," I said. "You can't wait? If you're right about Johnson, a little more work and we might dig up the evidence you need to tie that to Rodriguez. Make things airtight."

"Or Rodriguez might ditch the gun that shot them all," Bloch said. "Or Chillo might be in a car heading back to Texas. No, I want to move now. We've got enough on him to hold him by the short and curlies as long as we need to. We'll backfill the shaky stuff later or hit the jackpot when we tear his place apart."

"You mind if I keep digging in my spare time? I still think there's a connection we're missing."

We'd come full circle and found ourselves back in menswear again. He straightened a crooked "Sale" sign. "Be my guest. But you might want to reserve a spot on your calendar for tomorrow night."

My eyebrows shot up. "You want me to ride along on the raid?"

"Really and truly," Bloch said. "As an observer only, of course. But I thought you might want to see the object of your search up close and personal. I'll even let you kick him in the nuts if you want. After I do, of course. What do you say?"

My mouth went a little dry. Another chance to play cop a year after it had stopped being a job. "Sure."

"Great. I'll let you know where the meet-up is. We'll fit you with a vest. You can back me up on the briefing. Hell, I should let you run it."

"A raid," I said, musing. "Maybe we'll get some answers."

"We've already got them, Singer."

I kept my mouth shut and went back to looking at ties.

CHAPTER
TWENTY-EIGHT

For fifteen different reasons, my stomach was twisted into a tight knot that felt like everything from my throat to my navel was made up of a hard, oaken core. It was 4:03 a.m. and I'd been awake since three. I'd already had two cups of coffee and held a third in my hand. Cancer was possibly gnawing away at my lower intestine and, if it wasn't doing the job, then the residual chemo drugs were. Which reminded me that I was putting off a surgery that might save my life in order to lock up someone to whom life was as cheap as it gets.

But the main thing that had my guts in an uproar was that I was sitting in my car under a flickering sodium light in an empty Safeway parking lot in Culmore, half an hour away from taking part in a raid on one of the most violent gangs on the East Coast.

I was early. Zero hour was 5:00 a.m. Everyone taking part in the bust would be arriving at the "neutral zone," the parking lot, in the next few minutes for a final briefing before we kicked the doors down and made the collars. I passed the time emptying my mind. Taking increasingly smaller sips of coffee was my only ambition.

Bloch pulled his blue Elantra into the lot at a quarter after four, parking next to me instead of stopping window to window. I got out, opened his passenger's side door, and slid in. Bloch punched on a small dashboard light. He looked at me, grinning through the baggy lids and sallow complexion of someone pulling too much overtime.

"This is it, Singer," he said, holding up a folder. "One no-knock search warrant for 1803 Landsdowne Heights Apartments. By the power vested in me by Judge Carrie Peterson of the United States of America, I hereby proclaim we shall kick some ass."

"You went federal? Didn't shop it to the state?"

Bloch's smile turned upside down. "The local DA is a prick. He wanted six more months of surveillance, then a complete case review. We can't wait that long. I've got a good thing going with the US attorney's office, so . . ."

I nodded. I'd been in Bloch's position before. As the guy in charge of the investigation, you can shop the bigger cases around to different district attorneys and federal assistant US attorneys—AUSAs—to try to get the best result. It was a balancing act between success and payoff. Sentencing often got more severe as you went from local to state, state to federal, but sentencing didn't matter much if you couldn't get the DA or an AUSA to take the case in the first place. So you knocked on doors until you found a prosecutor that was willing to play ball. An AUSA is giving you a hard time on getting a wiretap? No problem, go to a local DA and ask him to adopt the case at the local level. Looking for the harshest possible sentencing for a gangbanger who's killing cops? Go to the US attorney's office and get the killer tried in federal court. Bloch was in a good position: he'd been blown off by the state DA—which might have a better chance of conviction—but he was tight with someone at the federal level. It would be a harder conviction to get, but if he got it, the bad guys wouldn't see daylight ever again.

"Think you can wrap everything up in one go?" I asked.

"You know Mike Gilmore, the AUSA over at the US attorney's office? Says it's a no-brainer pulling Hobbs Act on these shits."

"Ah," I said. "I'm getting a warm, fuzzy feeling."

The Hobbs Act was the iron fist in the velvet glove of criminal prosecution. Actually, there was no velvet glove. Although originally enacted to take on labor racketeering cases, increasingly it had been used to crush "violent criminal enterprises" like gangs into smithereens. Prove that your perps had a habit of shooting people and disrupting businesses and you were on your way to a Hobbs Act violation. Sentencing was draconian. Less than a twenty-year stint was almost unheard of. And since it was a federal charge, there was no parole. You get fifty years? You serve fifty years. Cops were known to burst into song and crooks who knew the system rolled over like puppies when an AUSA confirmed the Hobbs Act could be used on a case.

Bloch grinned. "I know, makes you want to cry, doesn't it? We've got so much to pin on Felix Rodriguez and his little MLA, he could get minimum sentencing and still be in lockup until the Second Coming."

I sipped my coffee, put it in a cup holder. "Who's on the crew this morning?"

"I made a couple of calls," Bloch said. "We got eight, including you and me. I'll introduce everybody when they show up. Arlington County PD has four, so they'll be tactical lead. Guy named Chuck Rhee is one of them. Made a special appeal to be included."

"Gangs," I said. "He's a good guy to have."

"You know him?"

"A little," I hedged. "I know he wants to show Gangs isn't made up of losers and crooks."

"He a cowboy?" Bloch asked, frowning.

"No," I said. "I don't think so. Just has a chip on his shoulder. Small, but noticeable. Probably unhappy that Torres confirmed the Gangs stereotype."

"So, he's your source?" Bloch said, smirking.

I grimaced. "You were going to find out sooner or later."

Bloch waved a hand as if to say *don't sweat it*. "I saw his file. All that *mara* experience he's got, I'm glad to have him. As long as he doesn't go apeshit when we get inside."

On cue, Rhee pulled into the lot in his souped-up Integra, with an Arlington PD cruiser and a white pickup in tow. Everyone parked together, bunching up near the lamppost. Bloch and I got out and walked to the front of his car. Rhee and a beefy, middle-aged guy got out of the Integra, while two white guys in their twenties emerged from the cruiser. A short, athletic-looking blonde woman hopped out of the pickup and headed over to us. She had a ponytail coming out the back of a black, logo-less baseball cap. Everyone except Rhee, Bloch, and me were wearing paramilitary blue-and-black tactical BDUs and boots. Rhee, in designer jeans and a ripped T-shirt, could've just stepped out of a club, while Bloch and I had on khakis and sweatshirts and could've come from Walmart.

Expressions and body language matched the way I felt. A little nauseated from the early morning and too much caffeine. Keyed up, but under control. Excited, but keeping a lid on it. I nodded at Rhee. He grinned and nodded back. Bloch introduced himself and then asked Rhee to do the intros for the Arlington group. The beefy guy was McDonald, the two twenty-somethings were Huston and Carlson. The blonde told everybody her name was Ramsey and that she was a US marshal.

"I thought there were two of you coming," Bloch said to her, looking down at a list. "Louis Chaco?"

"Louis got appendicitis yesterday, late," she said, pronouncing it "Lou-ee" in a thick Southern accent. "He's in the hospital getting his belly stitched up. Sorry, Lieutenant. I'm the only warm body."

I could tell it bothered Bloch, but didn't say anything. He fished out a cigarette, lit it, and introduced me. When he got to the part about me being retired, Huston and Carlson exchanged a quick glance, but otherwise no one blinked. I sat on the hood of Bloch's car as he opened his folder. He took out a set of photos. A trail of smoke from his cigarette followed his hand as he passed them around.

"Okay, folks. Here's our target. Landsdowne Heights, unit 206. Your average shithole garden apartment, it's just missing the garden. Here's a picture of the door to the building and the unit entry. There's one stairwell, locked from the bottom up, halfway across the building. As long as we clear it on entry and keep our backs to it, we should be fine."

"I know those apartments," Rhee said. "They all got balconies."

"They do. We need coverage. Anyone?"

I was suddenly interested in my shoes. No one wants to be out of the action, watching a back door in case the bad guys make a run for it. But you also don't split up cohesive teams. Chuck Rhee and the Arlington cops were the largest tactical group, so they would be the ones to go through the door. Bloch was the case agent in charge and I wasn't even a licensed cop, so the obvious choice was Ramsey. Inevitably, the decision would seem sexist, with no consolation that the choice would've been the same if she'd been male.

She knew it, but raised her hand anyway. "I'm it, I guess. Takes a woman to do it right."

Bloch nodded his thanks, smiling a little. He collected the first set of photos and handed out another. "Here are the personnel targets. Felix Rodriguez is our primary. Thirty-three years old, five nine, one-thirty-five or forty. No visible tattoos. He actually has a mess of them, but they're on his scalp, chest, and back. With his hair grown out and a long-sleeved shirt, he looks completely normal.

"This guy, on the other hand," Bloch continued, pulling out a second photo and passing it to his left, "would stand out on Mars. Martin Julio Benavides, a.k.a. Cuchillito, a.k.a. Chillo. He's the real deal, lady and gentlemen. Twenty-eight years old, five six, one-fifty. Time in for manslaughter, battery, rape, weapons possession, you name it. We think he was a heavy borrowed from a San Antonio *mara* to put the hit on a half-dozen cops around the Metro area to, uh, facilitate Rodriguez's dreams of expansion. I want him. Very badly. Very *very* badly. If it were a trade between pulling in Rodriguez or Chillo, I'd settle for Chillo. But we're going to nab both."

"How are we going to pick him out?" McDonald asked. The pictures hadn't reached him yet. Bloch gestured for Rhee to hold the photos up. Chillo's sleepy-eyed, nightmare face, covered in tattoos, stared back at us.

"Jesus fuck," McDonald said. "Okay, I'll remember him."

"Weapons?" Huston asked.

Bloch glanced at Rhee. "Detective, you might have better intel."

Rhee's expression didn't change, but I could tell he was pleased Bloch had deferred to him. "Rodriguez is probably packing or has access, but I don't see him throwing down. He's lasted this long because he uses his head more than his stones. He knows, or thinks he knows, he can get a lawyer to bail him out in a day. Why get shot by a cop when he could be out tomorrow?"

"What about Scarface?" McDonald asked.

"Chillo? Different story," Rhee said. He glanced at Bloch. "Would this be his third fall?"

"Yes."

Rhee shook his head. "Prison don't hold the same fear for these dudes that it does for regular crooks. Back in San Salvador, it's like Holiday Inn to them. Still, Chillo's probably had a taste of the good life. No reason to go to jail now, right? So, he ain't going to roll over for us. He's a dangerous motherfucker. Expect the worst."

"How do we know they're in the same pad?" Ramsey asked Bloch.

"Detective Rhee here has been keeping an eye on things for me. It's pretty clear that they want to ship Chillo out ASAP, back to San Antonio where he came from. He's been in DC for a couple weeks enjoying himself. Smoking dope, screwing, doing his thing. But he's their smoking gun. We've got intel that Rodriguez is getting nervous having him around. So he's keeping him close, real close, until they can get him in a car bound for Texas."

"Civilians present?" This was from Carlson.

"There are three girls who hang around. Maria Paseo is Rodriguez's girlfriend, the other two are passed among the gang members. All three are probably there. And there's at least one child under two, a little boy. He's Rodriguez's kid by the girlfriend."

Carlson grimaced. "Complicated."

Bloch nodded. "Not easy. That's why I asked specifically for you all. Every one of you has a reputation for being solid. I need us to be on the same page: we cuff Rodriguez, keep the noncoms quiet and safe, and dogpile on Chillo when we see him."

Everyone was quiet then, for a second, thinking. Then I felt their attention swing to me. Bloch did, too, and met it head-on. "Marty here has thirty years of experience with the MPDC, which is more than any two or three of us put together. I realize it's highly unorthodox to have him in the crew, but we wouldn't be conducting the raid without Marty's legwork in the investigation that's led to here. He'll be sixth man in the stack. With orders," Bloch raised his eyebrows meaningfully at me, "to play it cool and let us do the heavy lifting. We don't want to screw up his retirement."

"I'll try not to shoot myself," I said.

"Any questions?" Bloch asked, spreading both hands and looking at each member in turn. "Okay, let's—"

Rhee's cell phone rang, a jangly hip-hop beat. He snatched at it and checked the screen, then emphatically raised a hand for quiet as he answered. We watched him, puzzled. Rhee spoke rapid-fire Spanish, his answers clipped and staccato. At one point he turned around and scanned the street bordering the Safeway, his eyes roving back and forth. I could see Ramsey listening intently as Rhee spoke. About halfway through his call, she swore softly, an expression of worry and surprise on her face. Rhee spoke a little more, forced a laugh, then hung up.

"Someone made us?" Ramsey asked him when he put the phone away.

Rhee nodded, concerned. "That was one of the *chicos* I got contact with. Not one of Rodriguez's crew, but deals with him. He called me and told me to stay away from the MLA tonight, 'cause he was cruising with some homies and told me there's a bunch of narcs in a Safeway parking lot ready to bust the place. Didn't want me to get shot if I was out chatting up the Latinas."

"He's talking about us," Ramsey said.

"He just drove by and saw us?" Bloch said, stunned. Our heads swiveled around, scanning the parking lot, as if the guy were hiding behind a shopping cart.

"Two minutes ago, man," Rhee said.

"You think he'll warn Rodriguez?" I asked.

"Don't know, Singer. He might. To earn some points, maybe? Or he might just stay away, hoping not to get caught in the crossfire." Rhee consulted Bloch. "What do you want to do? Cancel and rewind?"

Bloch bit his lower lip and thought for a second. He looked at me.

I shrugged. "Might be our only chance at Chillo."

Bloch turned to the group. "Fuck it. Get your vests and guns. It's on."

CHAPTER
TWENTY-NINE

Moving at double-time, we hurried to trunks and backseats to grab flak jackets and guns. What should've been a semi-leisurely activity—almost a ritual to help calm the nerves—was a rushed affair. I fumbled with the straps of my vest and had to take a breath and concentrate on each buckle.

"Who's got the long gun?" Bloch yelled. He had donned a blue windbreaker with large yellow letters spelling out "HIDTA" on the back.

"Here," Carlson called back.

"What do you have?"

"M4."

"That'll do," Bloch said. He tossed me a HIDTA jacket identical to his. "Let's move it, people!"

I slipped the windbreaker on and jumped in the passenger side of Bloch's Elantra. McDonald and Rhee got in the back. Ramsey, Huston, and Carlson got in the cruiser and we pulled out of the parking lot in tandem. It seemed silly to drive three blocks, but what do you do if you have to engage in pursuit? Or transport three or four cuffed suspects? Call a taxi?

"Good thing we didn't take your Integra," I said to Rhee over my shoulder. "You can hear that thing coming a mile away. Rodriguez would be hanging out his window, wondering who woke him up."

Rhee grinned. "Hey, man. It's my style they sense, not the muffler."

"Fucking thing sounds like a jet," McDonald said. His face was a ruddy pink color and he seemed squeezed into everything: the vest, the jacket, the seat.

"Jerry here is pissed because he has to drive around in an Astro van all the time," Rhee said, still grinning. "What he really wants is a Mustang to hold off that midlife crisis a little longer, but his old lady won't let him."

"Four fucking kids won't let me," McDonald wheezed. "You ever try driving four kids to a soccer game in a Mustang, for Christ's sake?"

"Okay," Bloch said, wanting us to put a lid on it. I always thought banter was good for the nerves, but Bloch seemed to be built different. "We're here."

He pulled over and the cruiser slid in behind us. Landsdowne was a derelict old apartment complex from the sixties or seventies, three stories high with nondescript gray stucco walls. We were about a half block from the leading edge of the apartment building. A scrubby courtyard with three park benches separated the street from the front of the building. External stairs leading to street level separated every ten apartments or so. Busted-out lights and dim "EXIT" signs capped each stairwell. Most of the apartment lights were dark, though here and there a flickering blue light in the window proved that someone was up too late—or too early—watching the tube. We watched for a full minute, wondering if Rhee's buddy had tipped anyone off. But no one ran screaming from the building or fired shots out a window, yelling, "You'll never take me alive, copper," or anything else. Bloch glanced at me.

"Looks good," I said.

We got out and formed a loose circle, looking husky and awkward, inflated by the bulletproof vests and paramilitary outfits. Hands were shoved in pockets or hooked into belts except for Carlson, who had the wicked-looking M4 at a low ready position. Faces were serious, alert. Not a first dance for anyone. Not so routine they were complacent. Bloch had picked well.

"This is it, folks," Bloch said. "Cell phones, beepers off? Radios down? Okay, time check?"

Rhee tilted his wrist to squint at his watch in the lamplight. "4:57."

Bloch pointed to a corner of the building. "Unit 206 is second in from the corner. Second floor, obviously. Ramsey, can you make it from the back?"

"I can count."

"We'll give you five to get in position. Give me two clicks on the radio when you're set."

"I'm gone," she said, and started off toward the rear of the complex at a brisk walk.

"Who's on the ram?"

Huston raised a hand. "I got it."

"Okay, stack order is Huston, Rhee, McDonald, Carlson, Bloch, Singer. McDonald, sit on the women and kids. Rhee, you're translator in case someone wants to play dumb. First priority, though, is Felix Rodriguez or Chillo. Any questions?"

No one answered. We stood there, quiet and keeping our own thoughts. I was chilled in the early-morning air and stamped my feet. I rubbed my fingertips together, trying to get the feeling back into them that chemo had robbed. Huston and Carlson checked their belts and weapons. Rhee did some stretches. I could hear his neck popping from where I stood.

Bloch suddenly glanced down at his belt, checking his radio. "Ramsey's set." He turned to Huston. "Okay, Detective. Take us in."

We got in our stack order and broke into a jog-trot toward the building. At this point, guns were holstered, but most of us kept our hands on the butt anyway. It made moving awkward, but was worth it for the peace of mind. Huston must've been stronger than he looked, because he made carrying the thirty-pound battering ram seem easy. We crossed the courtyard and scuffed our way up the concrete steps closest to 206. I was a little out of breath as we pulled up outside the door and made a mental promise to get back to the gym. If I didn't get shot in the raid and survived cancer, of course.

Everyone drew their weapon. I heard a faint *snick* as Carlson unlatched the safety on the M4. We gathered ourselves mentally and physically in the stark pause before entry. My heart was beating fast and not because of the run up the steps. I heard Carlson swallow. Bloch's eyes were wide as if in mild surprise, but I knew this was how he translated the tension. Huston readied the ram and glanced back. Rhee made quick eye contact with each of us, then made a chopping movement with his hand. Huston started swinging the ram, building momentum. On the third swing, he smashed the ram into the apartment door and the world exploded.

Huston stepped to the side and dropped the ram while the rest of us in the stack burst into the apartment at a run. We spread out, trying to get clear of the doorway where ninety-nine out of a hundred people will shoot when defending themselves from a break-in. Bloch yelled, "Police! On the floor!" while Rhee shouted the same in Spanish. I was fumbling for a light switch when Huston bull-rushed in.

Somewhere in the room a woman started screaming. A male voice, panicky, shouted in Spanish. I finally found the switch and the room flooded with light from an overhead lamp. There was a skinny, half-naked guy and an all-naked girl, their eyes big as eggs, sitting up on a pullout couch, looking terrified. Beer cans and ashtrays littered a coffee table sitting to one side and the place reeked of pizza and pot smoke. Sliding glass doors opened onto the balcony. Bloch and Huston dragged the two lovers off the bed and put them facedown on the rug. Huston pulled the sheet off the bed and covered the girl, who was squirming, trying unsuccessfully to cover herself while keeping her hands glued to the back of her head.

Rhee, his gun out, ran down a hallway leading off the living room with Carlson right behind him. McDonald followed and I trailed last, throwing lights on as I went. More screaming erupted from a bedroom down the hall, followed immediately by the rising wail of a baby. Rhee pointed at the room and yelled, "McDonald!" then headed for the last room off the hallway. McDonald peeled off to try to contain the mother and the baby, while I followed Carlson and Rhee into the last bedroom. The early-morning chill was long gone and sweat rolled into my eyes. I swallowed over and over, trying to get rid of a metallic tang in my mouth.

The three of us burst into the bedroom. Based on the picture we had, Rodriguez was there, trying to pull a pair of jeans on over his boxers, incongruously obsessed with getting it buckled right even as we swarmed into the room, shouting. He was shirtless, showing the dozens of tattoos Bloch had told us about. A girl with dark, tousled hair was sitting up in the bed with the sheet pulled up to her neck. Tears streamed down her face and her heavy makeup, which probably looked fine six hours ago, was paying the price now.

Rhee tackled Rodriguez while Carlson covered the room with his elephant gun. I moved to the girl and firmly coaxed her out from under the linens. It didn't do much for her modesty, but if she had a 9mm under there, it wouldn't be the first time a cop got shot for being gallant. I pushed her down to the carpet like Bloch had done to the two in the living room, then covered her with the sheet when I was sure she was clean. Rhee was yelling at Rodriguez, "*Dónde está Chillo? Dónde está Chillo*, motherfucker?" even as he cuffed him, but the little man was silent, hardly even registering what was happening to him. Then again, maybe he couldn't: we'd kicked the door to the apartment down less than thirty seconds before.

Carlson did a quick check of the single closet in the room. "Anything?" Rhee asked. Carlson shook his head.

Bloch came in and scanned the room. "Chillo?"

"No sign," Rhee said, then shoved Rodriguez's face into the carpet. "This piece of shit isn't talking."

"Dammit," Bloch said. His radio squawked. He put a hand down to it and turned the volume up so we could all hear.

It was Ramsey. "Bloch, lights on in unit 208, next to you. I can see some activity through the windows."

"Bodies?" Bloch yelled into the radio, heading out of the room at a run. I sprinted after him with Carlson close behind.

I didn't hear the answer as he tore through the living room and out the door. McDonald had brought the mother and baby to the living room. He and Huston looked at us from where he was covering the couple, still lying on the rug. I was halfway out the door when I thought of something and stopped dead in my tracks. Carlson plowed into me from behind, nearly knocking me off my feet.

"Jesus, Singer," he said, shooting me a look and running after Bloch.

I turned back to the living room.

"What the hell is going on?" McDonald said.

"Chillo isn't here," I said, hustling to the glass doors. "Ramsey said she saw action from the next unit over."

"Does Bloch think he's dumb enough to come out the front door?"

"That's what I was wondering," I said and unlatched the sliding door. I did a quick peekaboo out and back, then stepped onto the balcony, gun ready. There were more beer cans and a turned-over bistro table with a cracked glass top. I glanced to my right, toward 208. I could hear muffled thumps, maybe as Bloch and Carlson kicked the door down. Light spilled out from the windows and I could see the shadow of frantic movement translated for me on the floor of the balcony.

I squinted, searching for Ramsey, and spotted her two floors down in the parking lot of the complex. Her gun, like mine, was trained on the balcony of the unit next door.

"Bloch and Carlson are on it," I yelled down. "Anything on your end?"

As she opened her mouth to answer, I heard a small, almost tinny *clack-clack* sound behind me. Ramsey screamed my name at the same time I threw myself flat. There was the briefest instant of deep silence and then the insane chatter of automatic rounds stitched the air. The sliding glass doors next to me shattered like they had been hit by a grenade. Thick chunks of glass rained down on my head and neck, getting stuck in my hair and finding their way down my collar. Dozens of bullets hit the thin balcony railing, making pinging noises as they dented the cheap metal. I heard four rapid, singular shots as Ramsey returned fire to the balcony, not to the right of 206, but the left, the corner unit. Inside the apartment, McDonald swore and Huston yelled.

I risked a glance from my position facedown on the concrete. A shadow had separated from the darkness of the balcony and was now jumping over the far side railing, risking the fifteen-foot drop to the ground. I scrambled to my feet and hauled myself over the balcony, holding on to the deformed metal railing before letting go and dropping the remaining eight feet. A shoulder roll took some of the impact of the fall away, but I was as graceful as a rhino on skates and felt something in my ankle go funny, like a rubber band being stretched too far, then *twanged*. Ramsey sprinted past, yelling "Foot pursuit!" into her radio as I struggled to my feet. There was pain, but it was being shoved down by the adrenaline that had my pulse up around 200. It would be ice bags and elevation later but, for now, I limped after Ramsey as fast as I could.

The shadow that had to be Chillo was fast, weaving in and out of the cars in the lot. He turned twice to fire a wild spray of bullets in our direction. Ramsey and I ducked behind cars and trucks as windshield glass shattered around us. I crabbed to the right, trying to cut him off or at least herd him toward Ramsey. If we got lucky, Carlson and Bloch might catch up to us. As long as we could keep pace with the shadow, we'd outlast him, since he was spitting bullets faster than he could replace them. The trick was to not get caught in the last half-dozen bullets he had left.

I was trailing Ramsey by fifteen or twenty feet when Chillo—it was him, I could see the tattoos now in the weak light of a streetlamp, crowding the space on his neck and back—ran out of cars and made a break for it across Landsdowne Avenue. The pale skin of his lower back looked like a sheet running into the night. Ramsey settled into the classic shooter's stance, calling out for him to stop. Chillo twisted his upper body awkwardly as he ran and brought his arm up, trying to get a bead on us. Ramsey's gun kicked once. Chillo was hit before he'd managed to turn even halfway around. Forward momentum took him two more steps, but it was borrowed time, and he pitched to the ground like he'd been swatted by an invisible bat.

Ramsey raced up to him, covering him with her pistol while I limped in second. The black MAC-10 he'd used to put holes in all the neighborhood cars was lying inches out of reach. He stretched his arm out for it, his fingers grasping, his legs swimming ineffectually. I kicked it, sending the gun skittering twenty feet away while Ramsey grabbed Chillo's wrist and pinned it to the other one, ignoring the blood pooling around his legs. He hissed and groaned, eyes bugging out, as she swept both wrists into cuffs.

"Is it serious?" I asked, huffing and puffing like a steam engine, fighting the urge to lean over and put my hands on my knees. I might be retired, but I didn't have to look geriatric.

"I don't think so," she said. "I thought about taking him center mass, then decided, hell, he's almost out of bullets anyway. Let's shoot him in the leg."

"Good Lord," I said, gulping air. "I like confidence in a woman, but for Christ's sake, just shoot him."

She smiled. "US Marshals always get their man." She leaned over and patted Chillo—writhing on the bloodstained ground, covered in ink, looking like something out of Dante's Hell—on the cheek. "Ain't that right, sweetie?"

CHAPTER THIRTY

Twelve hours after the raid, I was at HIDTA's headquarters. I would've given half my pension to have stayed in bed. The office was in Greenbelt, Maryland, not the quickest or easiest drive for someone living in Northern Virginia. And the raid, as thrilling as it was, had given me a twisted ankle and two dozen itching cuts on the neck and hands from the glass of shattered windows. I was tired and sore and felt like I'd done my part. I wanted to sleep. I wanted to be done. I wanted to make good on plans to hang up a hammock in the backyard and lie in it until July.

But Bloch needed to move quickly on the case and I guess I didn't blame him. He and I had cut a lot of corners in our investigation. The smartest thing to do to get the best conviction would be to hurry the case to trial while the raid was still in everyone's minds and local newspapers were running headlines like "Gang Leader Orders Killing of DC Cops." I knew Bloch had gone right to work after the arrest, grilling both Rodriguez and Chillo since they'd been brought in, trying his hardest in the first twenty-four hours to get them to flip and send the other one up the creek. Most crooks with any brains crossed over right away. Others, the hard cases, had to be told what lay in store. It was an education for many of them, since they'd been busted a dozen times at the state and local level and viewed the arraignment and indictment process with derision. They didn't realize that federal charges were a whole new animal. Once you explained that they were looking at twenty to life with no chance of parole, though, they sprinted into the light. The problem was getting that through to them.

Bloch was at his desk, looking down at some papers, his thirty-six-hour day showing in his frown. His eyes were pouched and his five-o'clock shadow had just struck six. He looked like death warmed over. Even more, I thought cheerfully, than me. I'd brought two large cups of coffee in a paper bag. I gave him one and his face brightened, then went dim when he saw there wasn't anything but coffee in it. "No doughnuts?"

"I told you before, Healthy Marty doesn't eat doughnuts," I said. "Sorry."

He grumbled something, but cracked open the plastic lid and took a cautious sip anyway.

"You're welcome," I said.

He read a little more, then sat back and sighed, rubbing his face. "These guys are killing me, Singer."

"Yeah?"

"I have worked them, man. Ten, twelve hours now."

"They standing tall for each other?"

He shot me a look. "That's funny. Gang loyalty? Death before dishonor? Not here. They're both flipping so fast that I can't keep up."

"That's great. What's the problem?"

"They're both saying, in their own special way, that, yeah, they killed these cops. I mean, they don't come out and say they did them. Chillo says Rodriguez is a criminal mastermind and he was just following orders. Rodriguez is saying Chillo is a psychopath killer, put him away for the good of humanity."

"Okay," I said.

"Problem is, neither one is copping to all of the murders."

"Which ones are mysteries for them?"

"Clay Johnson," he said, "and Isaac Okonjo."

"The same one, essentially."

"Yep."

I leaned back in my chair. "What are they saying?"

"That they don't know who the hell we're talking about. It took me eight hours to get them to spill more than their name. Once I started outlining the charges, spinning some bull about a bargain, playing them against each other, then all of a sudden the names make sense. 'Oh, yes, that was one of them. Yes, I remember.'"

"All of them except Johnson and Okonjo," I said.

"It's like I named two dead presidents. They don't have a freaking clue. Chillo was so confused he thought I was talking about two informants. It took me half an hour to get him to understand that I was charging him with their murders."

"No denial, no shift of blame to our boy Felix?"

"Denial, sure. Once he realized he was going to the block for them. But, before that, I could tell he didn't know what I was talking about. It was that magic minute, you know, before they come up with a story. When their eyes look all over the place, trying to find something you'll believe in. With these two names, Chillo just stared back at me."

I put my hands behind my head and laced my fingers together. "Is it possible Rodriguez just used somebody else? Maybe he figured he couldn't trust Chillo all the way and farmed it out to some up-and-comer in the *mara*?"

"Maybe, but he seemed as lost as Chillo. He covered up better. He's used to talking his way out of these things. But I got the same thousand-yard stare when I asked him about Johnson."

"How's that affect the case?"

Bloch made a face, gave a half shrug. "I'm still going to hang Johnson and Okonjo on them. Rodriguez for conspiracy, Chillo for pulling the trigger. I don't care if they won't admit to them or can't get their story straight."

"And if it's not them?"

"I won't lose any sleep over it," he said. "They can rot for all I care."

"No, I mean, if they didn't do it, who did?"

He waved a hand. "Look, it bothers me, but one thing at a time. We have to put these two away just on general principles. Aside from the murders we know they did, they could probably be on the hook for twenty more. When the dust settles, we'll make the case airtight."

"Why do you need me, then?"

"Your buddy Rhee came through again. Said he had a good relationship with Rodriguez's girlfriend, Maria. We were going to have to let her and the other girls go; they're little fish anyway, but she doesn't know that. He talked to her, hinted around that this was a clean sweep, that I was going to lower the boom on her and her friends as much as Chillo and the boys."

"And if she didn't want to end up in prison and her baby go up for adoption . . ."

"That she'd talk to us," Bloch finished. "Makes you feel great to be a cop, doesn't it?"

"You want me to talk to her," I said, figuring out where he was going. "New face, new chance for her."

"Yep."

"Am I good cop or bad?"

"Good. I've already had a crack at her and she thinks I'm a complete asshole."

"No comment," I said.

"You go in there, get on her side. See if you can pry anything out of her to link them up with Johnson or Okonjo."

"Not that I want to shirk my duty, but why me? Why not call Rhee, send him in there?"

"You're the one that scared up the evidence in the first place. You know the time line. Maybe if she lets something slip, you'll pick up on it when I wouldn't."

"I can't find something that isn't there, Bloch," I said.

"I know. Just give it a shot. If you come up empty, we're no worse off than we were before. Even if you strike out, I brought both Chillo and Rodriguez in, stewing in one of the other rooms. If Maria coughs something juicy up, I'll show it to them and try to get them to crack."

"The Illustrated Man's over his gunshot wound?"

"Not really."

"Harsh," I said.

"Fuck him. That's what wheelchairs are for."

"You're an evil man, Bloch," I said.

He glanced at me, looking tired. "We're talking about a serial killer and his boss. Evil's a relative term."

I had a few minutes before I went onstage, so we took our time finishing our coffee, going over the raid like it was a battle in the distant past, reliving the moments and moves and decisions in the slow-motion judgment that memory gives us. He laughed when I told him how Ramsey had actually patted Chillo's cheek like he was a third-grader who hadn't flushed the toilet. We grimaced when we thought more about the collateral damage the gangbanger could've caused swinging the MAC-10 around like it was a fire hose, spraying shots into the cars and apartments. We finished about the same time and tossed our cups into the wastebasket.

He checked his watch. "I'll give you ten to get your thoughts together. Come grab me when you're ready."

I found an empty desk and jotted down some notes. It had been a while since I'd grilled someone, but it wasn't rocket science. Every time, it came down to the two questions at the heart of the process: What did you want to know and what were they trying to hide?

I found Bloch before the ten minutes were up and he led me down to the interrogation room.

The dark-haired girl I remembered from the night of the raid was sitting on one side of a Formica table. She no longer had on makeup— even smeared makeup—and her hair was pulled back into a bun. Tight skinny jeans forced a roll of fat off her hips that a tight, purple stretch top helped highlight rather than hide. Her arms were on the table in front of her, her hands clasped. Her head snapped up when I came in, her eyes a little frightened, a little defiant.

I went through the preamble, telling her who I was and how I was involved in the case.

"I remember you," she said, her voice soft. "You covered me with a sheet."

I nodded. "At least, not after we knew you weren't going to shoot one of us."

"I never shot nobody."

"I know you haven't, Maria," I said. "The problem is, your baby's daddy has. Or he ordered it done."

"That other man said he gonna send my baby to adoption," she said, her face screwing up, tears threatening to spill.

"Los Asesinos is responsible for a lot of deaths, Maria. If you knew about some of them, it makes you guilty, too."

"But I didn't kill nobody," she said. On cue, the tears welled up and slipped down her cheeks.

"You don't have to pull the trigger to go to jail," I said, quiet but firm. "Sometimes knowing is enough. And you knew some things, didn't you?"

"I didn't know nothing," she said.

"Maria. You were around Felix all the time. You're a smart girl. His baby's mother. He probably trusted you, counted on you for advice sometimes, right?"

It was her turn to shrug. Her head went down and the tears fell in her lap.

"The thing is, Maria, we need help. We know the MLA and Chillo killed a lot of people, but we don't know the whole story. Now, we can't make any promises, but you help us, and we'll do our best to help you. We know you and your baby aren't guilty of anything. But a judge might not see it that way. Help us and we can tell the judge how much we needed your information. Things go better for people who help us."

She was quiet, crying in little hiccupy jerks. I waited her out, keeping what I hoped was a kind, neutral expression on my face, though inside I felt like a creep. There was nothing quite like holding a mother's love for her baby over her head to make you feel like a class-A shit. I kept the pictures of the mutilated bodies Bloch had shown me on the first day fresh in my mind. It helped a little.

Finally, she sniffed and rubbed her nose. "What you want to know?"

I tried not to sigh in relief. "There was a police officer named Danny Garcia who dealt with MLA undercover."

She was quiet for a moment, then nodded. Her face was blotchy. "Felix said that the Chicano had robbed him several times, but he didn't know it was him at first."

"Had robbed him? How?"

"He said the Chicano had known about many drug deals and had robbed them and shot some of the *mara*."

"Why didn't he do something about Garcia before this?"

She shrugged. "He didn't know. He thought the Chicano was just a buyer."

"So, how did he find out that Garcia was doing the raids?"

"He didn't, not on his own. He asked for Chillo to come in from San Antonio and help," she said. "Chillo come up with a fake deal. A trap, you know? Then they told a bunch of people."

"And Garcia was one of them?"

She nodded.

"Then what happened?"

"Felix told me that the Chicano showed up like always, but Chillo spotted some friends that had come along with him. That's when they know that they were going to try and rob them."

I felt my scalp tingle. "Who were the friends, Maria?"

She shrugged. "He never found out. Felix grabbed the Chicano, and tried to stop the other two, but they got away. Felix was very mad. He wanted all three, bad."

"Two of them got away?"

"Yes."

"Black? White? Young or old?"

She shrugged. "I don't know. Chillo shot at them, but they got away."

"So his friends left him, but Chillo didn't know who they were?"

She shook her head.

"But they had Garcia."

"Yes," she said, her voice small.

"And they made him pay for robbing the *mara*."

She didn't answer. I heard my own heartbeat drum in my ears.

"Maria?"

"Yes," she said, sadly. "It take a long time."

CHAPTER
THIRTY-ONE

"That was a fucking waste of time," Bloch said in disgust, sitting down with a grunt.

I raised my head from the case file I'd been reading. It wasn't my favorite thing to do—really—but Bloch had left me on my own while he'd spent the last ninety minutes trying to hammer away at first Felix Rodriguez, then a wheelchair-bound Chillo, showing them the tape of Maria's talk with me, trying to get them to say something, anything, more than they'd already let go.

"No dice?"

"Opposite effect," he said, tossing a pen onto the desk. It skittered off the edge and across the floor. "They both clammed up tighter than before."

I looked at him for a second, putting it together. "They think they can get to her and it'll solve all their problems."

He nodded. "I told them I've got the gun, some dope we found in the apartment, other testimony. Doesn't matter. They both think they can have her killed and the case falls apart."

"You putting her in protection?"

He nodded. "For whatever good that'll do. These kids are dumb."

"What do you mean?"

He sighed, scrubbing his face with his hands. "We've done it before. They talk to us, give us some intel we can use, so we send them to a safe house in Ohio or Wisconsin or upstate New York to keep them alive. A week goes by, they get bored, and they grab a bus back to DC. They figure their homies will understand they didn't mean to talk, they didn't say anything important, right? Next thing you know, we're fishing them out of the Potomac or some hiker finds what's left of them on the bike path to Mount Vernon."

"It wasn't time wasted," I said. "You can get her to testify. Maybe she'll open up a little if you keep working on her."

He ran his hands through his hair. "I know. This just seemed really airtight, you know? Get either Rodriguez or Chillo to serve up the other guy on a plate and we're done."

We were both quiet for a minute. Then I said, "Bloch, I don't want to upset your apple cart. But we've still got a problem—"

"I know, I know," he said, sour. "Johnson and Okonjo. You know I don't have any more info than I did two hours ago."

"Not true," I said. "Maria said Rodriguez and Chillo knew there were two friends helping Garcia. The moonlighters. We thought there was someone helping Danny, but we didn't know for sure before."

He opened his mouth as if to say something, then shut it, thinking. After a moment, his fingers started to drum lightly on the desk. I kept going.

"So, we've got a few possibilities. First, Maria was kept in the dark. Maybe Felix didn't tell her everything. Maybe he knew all about Johnson and had Chillo take him out."

"What about Okonjo?"

"We already know it was probably a mistake," I said. "Chillo mistook Okonjo for Johnson. He shoots him, realizes he screwed up, and leaves him."

Bloch thought about it. "Makes sense. But you said Johnson knew whoever killed him, right? That he'd let the killer into the apartment? That doesn't describe Chillo. I mean, if I'm Johnson and I look through my peephole and see that freak show on the other side, I'm not opening the door."

I nodded, conceding the point was weak. "Second possibility. Maria's right and Rodriguez didn't know who they were. He would've given his left nut to know, sure. If he had, he would've told Chillo to take all three of them out. He wanted them bad. But . . . he didn't know."

"Which leaves us back at the beginning. Who killed them? Are they even connected to Rodriguez, and the *mara* and this whole mess?"

"Right," I said. "The key is there were *two* friends. I already know Danny was buds with Johnson from way back. The Garcias don't want to admit it, but he was."

"Friend number one."

"Yes," I said. "And friend number two, assuming Maria is right, is alive. From a crew of cops that made a practice out of busting up drug dealers and gangs on the side. 'Robbing' them, as Maria put it."

"You think they were jacking these crews and pocketing the money?"

I shrugged. "Maybe they were just playing Robin Hood. But two out of three are dead, one of whom was set up. Maria never said how they got word out to Danny. Maybe he was set up by his own guy."

"Garcia, Johnson . . . who's the third?"

I didn't get to finish my thought. There was a knock and a short uniformed officer shaped like a rain barrel took a step into the office. "Sorry, sir. You said you wanted the two prisoners taken back to lockup?"

"Yeah," Bloch said with a sigh, then stood. "Let's get some fresh air. We can keep talking this out while we watch our fish go back to the tank."

He got up from his desk and I followed him out of the room. I wanted to test my theory on him as we walked, but three different cops ran up needing his signature on this, his okay for that. He motioned me along and we headed down two halls and out double glass doors on the side of the building. The day was clear, but the heat fell on us like a brick. May was leaving and summer was closing in.

From a short porch we watched as deputies opened another set of doors and led first Rodriguez, then Chillo out. In the neon orange of a prison inmate, handcuffed and leg-shackled, Rodriguez appeared small and unremarkable. He'd been processed enough to have that steady con look about him: taking no shit, but with an indefinable ducking of the shoulders, trying to fly under everyone's radar. His eyes were a dead brown, like worn leather. A thin mustache gave him a mousy look and he was small, which would probably lead plenty of guys on the inside to underestimate him. It would be their mistake. He'd ordered the deaths of five cops and was probably responsible for dozens of other murders in the last two years.

Chillo was pushed out in a wheelchair. His wrists were cuffed in front of him, a small concession to his medical situation. His tattooed face was impassive, blank as a standing stone, and his eyes, if possible, were deader than Rodriguez's. They flicked over the two of us, then to the security van that had been pulled up at the end of the driveway to take them back to the federal holding building in Alexandria. There was almost no one else around. It was a scene lacking in drama or pathos.

A fat fly moved ponderously through the air and landed on Bloch's shoulder. The stink of gasoline clouded the air from the prison van, kept idling so as not to waste a minute whisking the prisoners away. Bloch reached up to brush the fly away, his chin tucked to his shoulder like a violinist. I turned from Bloch to look at Chillo.

We locked eyes.

I blinked.

And Chillo's head erupted in an explosion of red, white, and gray.

The guard who had been pushing the wheelchair grunted and staggered two steps back, bent over at the waist as though being tugged off stage by a hook. My mouth opened and I knew without thinking that I was throwing myself to the ground, reaching for a gun I hadn't brought. Bloch looked up, frowning, as though he'd heard an off-color joke or just learned about a downturn in the stock market. People began to scatter. I heard my first recognizable sound: the sharp, flat report of a big gun. But it was the second shot fired.

Rodriguez levitated, his feet kicking toward the sky as though he had suddenly decided to throw himself on his back. A pink cloud sprayed the wall behind him and he fell to the ground, convulsed once, then stayed still. The slow-motion progress of the scene disappeared and suddenly everyone was released, free to add to the chaos. I scampered to the far side of the concrete porch, trying to make myself flat behind the scant cover. Bloch dashed to the side of the van and crouched behind the engine, his handgun out. About a half-dozen deputies were scattered across the small courtyard, looking lost, as though someone had dropped them here from out of the sky. All had their guns drawn. The guard who had been pushing Chillo's wheelchair was on his back, writhing, holding his belly. The muscles in his neck stood out like ropes as he kicked his legs, scuffing himself across the concrete sidewalk by his heels.

A few cops had their radios out, others were yelling at the top of their lungs. Bloch screamed at some of his men—stunned at the sudden violence—to get to cover. An alarm wailed throughout the HIDTA compound. It was a strange tableau, with six or eight of us crouching and looking in the same direction, waiting for the next bullet to rip through the air. I stole a glance at Chillo and then Rodriguez. The spreading pool of blood beneath both of them told me they were gone, even if I hadn't seen half of Chillo's skull taken off. His body slumped in the wheelchair where it had been shot, propped in place like a mannequin by the handcuffs and shackles. Rodriguez was a pile of laundry dumped on the sidewalk.

Things couldn't stay frozen forever. After a minute, deputies made a break for the glass doors and rushed inside. Two rushed over to the guard on the ground. I stayed where I was, watching Bloch, who had been taking quick looks in the general direction of the shots. I followed his line of sight and didn't like what I saw. I took a deep breath, then sprinted to Bloch's side.

"See what I see?" he asked, wiping the sweat off his face.

"Yeah. Not good." There were several apartment buildings and a hotel that could've easily hidden the shooter's location. Worse, though, was that HIDTA HQ was near two major four-lane roads and a group of cloverleaf on-ramps and exits for 495, the major highway loop around DC. A quick glance showed a half-dozen spots next to the highway with head-on views of the courtyard. "The overpass."

"Easy in, easy out," he said. His voice was steady, but he wiped a hand across his mustache and his eyes flicked back and forth, trying to pin down the location of the sniper. If he was still there. "Take the shot from the highway, get in the car, drive away."

"Hell of a shot," I said. My voice was hoarse and my throat felt tight, like I'd been flexing all the muscles in my neck. "Four, five hundred yards?"

"Two shots," he said, throwing a glance back at the two bodies. "One per. What the fuck is going on? All of a sudden, we've got a world-class sniper involved in this? What a goddamn clusterfuck."

Sirens pealed from the far side of the building. Ambulances. A little late for Chillo and Rodriguez, maybe, but hopefully in time to help the guard who had been pushing the wheelchair. Bloch's radio squawked and he spoke into it.

"Units are on the way to check the buildings out."

"That's a waste," I said. "Get someone on the Beltway."

"I know, but it's got to be done. I'll have a team on the overpass in a minute. Think we're clear here?"

"Whoever it is, he's gone," I said, casting another glance at the carnage in the courtyard. "He got what he wanted."

Still, we sprinted to the glass doors. The skin across my back was tight as a drum and I fought the urge to crawl on my belly. Rationally, I knew whoever had taken the shots was long gone, or should be. But when you see two guys next to you get potted like plastic ducks at a carnival, your animal brain tends to take over.

When we got inside, a half-dozen cops ran up to Bloch, looking for answers and orders. He took control of the situation as best he could. All the men he spoke to seemed stable, but shaken up, everyone wondering if the bullets had been misses and they'd been the real targets. Bloch got everyone busy doing something, yelling out orders like a drill sergeant. He finally had time to turn to me as cops ran back and forth, shouting and splitting into teams.

"You were about to tell me who you thought was Danny's number three. Whoever put bullets into Chillo and Rodriguez is the same guy. If he thinks Danny spilled the beans to Chillo and Rodriguez before he was killed, then he thinks they know who he is. He didn't want them to talk. Or take a run at him later."

I took a deep breath. The noise and chaos made it hard to concentrate and guesses—even educated ones—seemed out of place next to the battlefield outside. "Three cops, taking dealers out at nights and on weekends. They're righteous, like the Three Musketeers. But one day, one of them thinks, 'Why not clean the streets and put some money away, too?' He starts pocketing the cash they're finding. Johnson goes for it. Danny doesn't."

"Who do you think, Singer?" Bloch said, impatient.

"Caldwell," I said. "He retires this year. He's got a boat and a plan. I don't have a clue about his financial situation, but he's got motive and the connection to Danny."

"You think he set him up?"

"Yes. He and Johnson catch wind of Rodriguez's honeypot deal so he can catch whoever's robbing him. They talk Danny into targeting the deal, like they'd done a dozen times before. Then they back out on him when he needs them the most. Rodriguez and Chillo do their dirty work for them and Danny's out of the picture."

"Doesn't even have to be that complicated," Bloch said, getting into it. "Maybe it was just one of their regular side jobs. When things got a little hot, Caldwell and Johnson said to each other, this is our chance. They skedaddle and hang Danny out to dry."

"That works," I said.

"Then Johnson gets greedy or starts feeling guilty and Caldwell takes him out, too," Bloch said.

"Evidence says Johnson knew whoever killed him," I said. "Caldwell fits the bill."

He jerked a thumb toward the courtyard. "What about this?"

"Just like you said. I told Caldwell the other day that we had fingered Rodriguez for ordering the killings. He's got to assume Danny talked while he was getting worked over, so it stands to reason Rodriguez knows Caldwell's name. Then Caldwell hears about last night's raid and knows if you get Rodriguez to talk—"

"—then we'll know about Caldwell, too," Bloch finished.

"Right. Solution? Take Chillo and Rodriguez out and there's literally no one left."

Bloch glanced toward the direction of the courtyard. "Caldwell strike you as a long-range sniper?"

I shrugged. "He plays the lame baby boomer with a beer gut, but he could also be a crack shot. And he's DEA. For all we know, he got to train with Navy SEALs. We'll find out when we pick him up."

"You bring a gun?"

"No. Didn't think I'd need it."

"C'mon," Bloch said, motioning me to follow. We jogged through the building to his office. Bloch had his radio out, giving orders and telling somebody, his number two probably, to take over. When we got to his desk, he yanked open the bottom drawer and pulled out a leather gun case. He slid it across the desk toward me.

"My Glock. Sorry, no holster. You'll have to go commando. Grab it and load in the car."

We raced back the way we came and out the front entrance of the building to the parking lot. Bloch's Elantra had primo parking near the doors. We hopped in and Bloch punched the gas, racing from the chaos of one scene directly into another.

III.

Two targets, two shots, two kills. Just like they'd taught him.

It wasn't something to celebrate or even smile about, but he allowed himself some satisfaction in the perfect accuracy of the shots, the quick and clean exit from the area, the justice that had been dealt. He basked a little in the glow of a successful mission, replaying the scene in his head . . . until he remembered the cop who had been pushing the wheelchair, staggering backwards, hit by the .308 that had gone through-and-through the piece of shit sitting in the chair. Collateral damage hadn't occurred to him as a possibility until it was right there, centered in his scope. Panic had stopped his heart for a second; he wasn't in this to see more cops go down. But the training had taken over, he forgot about the cop, and then he'd put the second bullet right where he wanted. Casualties were bound to happen, he told himself. That was just reality. Though a voice inside his head reminded him that it wasn't the first.

It would be the last, he promised, squeezing the steering wheel until his hands were bloodless. Traffic on the Beltway zipped past him as he chugged along, keeping the needle right on 55 miles per hour to stay inconspicuous.

He couldn't afford to be stopped now. Events were wrapping up. The last act was ready to be played out.

One more stop and the miserable, fucking tragedy that had started with Detective Danny Garcia's death would be over.

CHAPTER
THIRTY-TWO

Bloch bumped his car up onto the sidewalk at the end of I Street and parked. We got out and headed toward the waterfront. I had Bloch's gun, a Glock 19 Compact, slipped into a back pocket and had untucked my shirt to cover it. I'd spent the better part of thirty years carrying a gun, but always in a holster, and the unfamiliar weight resting like a metal wallet felt completely wrong.

We hurried, taking three jogging steps for every two walking, to eat up the ground. We both had a sense of urgency. Caldwell might be casting off right now or heading for an airport. A shared anxiety also pushed us along. A lot of blood had been spilled so far and we knew we were in dangerous territory. That tight feeling between my shoulder blades was back, as though Caldwell had his gun reticle centered on my spine even now.

The wind was dead calm and the harsh smells of dock life lay heavily in the air. Fish, dirty water, diesel gas. A few people strolled along the wide sidewalk that paralleled the pier, already wiping sweat off their forehead and slowing down into a summer rhythm. Bloch and I eased our pace, trying to hide our nerves, acting like any other two Washingtonians out on an early lunch break.

"Caldwell's boat is just past the midpoint of the marina," I said, pretending I was talking about Senate hearings or the price of corn oil.

"Remind me of the name?"

"*The Loophole*," I said. "Sailboat. Big forty footer."

We made room for a young mother and her three kids. One had an ice cream cone and the top ball of ice cream fell off onto the ground. The girl's crying faded as we walked. Bloch said, "Chances that Caldwell is still here?"

"Slim to none," I said. "If he's good enough to plan all this, has been putting drug dealer cash in a Swiss bank account, and is willing to snipe two witnesses to stay clean, then he's smart enough to get the hell out. Even if he has to leave his boat behind."

Bloch made a face. "So we're just cleaning up."

"He can't be more than twenty minutes ahead of us," I said. "And he's bound to have left something on the boat that'll help us find him. Don't sweat it."

He grimaced and we walked on. Over the masts and bone-white hulls of yachts, I made out the mast of Caldwell's boat peeking over the others. I reached out a hand and slowed Bloch down, pointed. He nodded and we moved closer cautiously, watching the deck and the cabin windows. After a minute, I tugged Bloch's sleeve and motioned for him to fall back.

"What?"

"The boat's lashed to the pier pretty tight, but if we're not careful, he'll feel us climb aboard."

"If he's there," Bloch said.

"If he's there," I agreed. "I'm just saying, do it carefully. Don't leap aboard like a pirate."

He nodded and we headed down the dock once more, guns drawn. Some luck was with us, as *The Loophole* was moored stern-in, so we approached the back of the boat and its pleasant lack of portholes or windows. I crept forward, heel-to-toe, my eye on the lower cabin door. Nothing jumped out at me, nobody fired a cannon. Gingerly, I grabbed the gunwale and eased myself aboard, thinking weightless thoughts and trying to tell whether I'd set the boat rocking. Bloch followed, pulling himself aboard next to me without a sound. I motioned toward the cabin door. We could see all of the deck and the upper cabin, so it was the only place left. He nodded and moved to the right of it.

I crept closer and went down the three short steps to the miniature door. It was open a few inches. I stopped and listened. All I heard was the lapping of wake against the hull and the distant, deep-throated rumblings of inboard engines down the line. I swallowed, readjusted my grip, and pushed the door open with one hand, gun aimed into space with the other.

And stopped.

Bob Caldwell, staring at me with eyes wide and white, was sitting on the bed with his legs splayed out in front of him like a little boy playing jacks. Kneeling on the bed with a thick forearm wrapped around Caldwell's neck and holding a gun to his head was Paul Garcia. He was bareheaded and dressed in the tan and sage camouflage BDUs of an infantry soldier. His eyes, small black dots like raisins in his face, drilled into me. The hand holding the gun was steady.

"Stop right there, Mr. Singer," Paul said. His voice—calm and flat—sounded loud in the tiny cabin. His face and voice were uncolored by emotion, as though he were talking about tide tables or bus schedules. Small windows ringed the sleeping cabin, backlighting both of them and making it difficult to see details.

"Paul," I said, just for something to say. "This isn't what I was expecting."

A thin smile danced on his lips, then disappeared. "No, sir. I imagine it isn't."

"But," I said, slowly, piecing things together, "I guess I should've."

"I was hoping you wouldn't figure any of it out, Mr. Singer."

I nodded. "You knew about the moonlighting your dad was doing?"

"I knew."

"Everything?"

"Yes," Paul said. "My father wanted me to know before I went through the academy."

"And you figured Caldwell sold your dad out?"

"No sell—" Caldwell said, his words choked off as Paul tightened his arm.

"That's not how it looks from here, Bob," I said. It was time to talk about anything to keep Paul from pulling the trigger. I had a bead drawn—ineffectively—on the middle distance between Caldwell's head and Paul's. I'd been too surprised to bring my gun all the way onto the small target that was Paul's head. And if I did it now, I was asking him to pull the trigger. This wasn't some amateur who'd never fired a gun before. This was a trained soldier who had served time in battle. If he saw my gun start to move, he was going to respond. And probably not in a way that would make me feel good.

"Paul," I said. "I'm going to lower my gun. Partly because I'm old and can't hold my arm up anymore. But mostly because this is where we talk it out and keep you from doing anything you'll regret."

"Like quadruple homicide, sir?" he said. "I don't want to sound flippant, but what the hell's one more?"

"Rodriguez and Chillo make two," I said, confused. "I guess I should've seen the Marine Corps training in the shot placement. But the deputy you shot was wearing a vest. He'll have a bruise and some broken ribs, but he's still alive. And you don't have to shoot Caldwell to prove anything."

"With all due respect, sir," Paul said, "you don't know what the fuck you're talking about. It's not about proving anything. It's about exacting a price."

Caldwell tried to speak, but Paul cut it off. The DEA agent blinked slowly, trying to get a breath. My gun was by my side and slowly, intentionally, I relaxed my body, trying to communicate my own calm to the young man.

"I'm working at a deficit, Paul," I said. "I thought I had this figured out. I know your dad was freelancing, taking out the scum he knew the system would never touch. I'm pretty sure Johnson and Caldwell here were his gun buddies. At some point they didn't want to do the vigilante thing for free and decided to help themselves to all that money that was floating around. And your dad didn't like where it was going, so Caldwell hopped in bed with the Salvadoran *mara* to have your dad taken out."

"It would be nice if it were all that neat and tidy," Paul said, staring at me. "If it were just greed, you could almost understand it."

"What else is there?"

"Something so much more basic," he said. For the first time I saw emotion in his face, a glimpse of despair and anger that made his eyes squint. "Cowardice."

"Tell me," I said.

"None of them knew the *mara* was setting them up. They'd been knocking off drug dealers for years and thought they were too careful, too good, to get caught. They took money, all of them. It was dirty, but you start to question what's clean after a while. That wasn't the problem. The problem was that the two of them never believed as deeply as my father. And when things got too hot for them, that lack of belief, that lack of loyalty, that *cowardice*"—he tightened his grip on Caldwell's head until the man's face started to purple—"cost my father his life."

I glanced at Caldwell's face and back. "They didn't set him up. They just . . ."

"Left him," Paul finished. "As simple as that. They left him."

The cabin was very close, uncomfortably warm. My mind raced, fitting things together. "You killed Johnson."

"He invited me over. He wanted to tell me about it, try to get me to understand. How hard it was for him to just drive off, knowing my father was probably being beaten, being tortured. How it *killed* him, knowing my father was counting on his buddies to bail him out."

"He didn't know you'd already taken a run at him," I said. Paul flinched.

"Okonjo was a mistake," he said. He blinked rapidly and readjusted his grip on the gun, his fingers opening and closing on the butt. "I didn't even know what I was doing. Or even if I was going to do it. It was nothing like Iraq or Afghanistan, where they told you who the hell to kill. This was all on me. And I screwed up."

"So don't screw up again," I said. I nodded toward Caldwell, who sat inert, looking back at me. "He's going up the river for all kinds of things. You don't have to put a bullet in his head to exact justice."

Paul smiled and his face relaxed. "That's exactly what they told my dad the first time he watched a gangbanger walk out of the courtroom. And that's when he vowed that he'd see justice done, no matter what the price. Whatever else I am, I am my father's son. *Esto es para Él.*"

Quick, so quick. Caldwell sensed it and his hands started to come up, but there were two loud *flacks* and Caldwell's head exploded, red matter striking the cabin wall. I raised my gun, dropping into a kneeling position, but Paul reversed the pistol and put the end of the barrel in his mouth. At the same time he pulled the trigger, the glass from one of the small windows shattered and Bloch's shot took him high in the left shoulder, knocking him flat onto the bed. I leapt forward, but I was too late for Caldwell, too late for Paul. Bloch's shot would've stopped him, but it had come too late, as well. The two bodies slumped, coming to rest side by side on the cabin bed, like characters from a Greek trag-edy. Footsteps pounded on the deck above, then Bloch appeared in the doorway a second later, his face distraught. He looked at the bed, then at me, a question forming.

With the stink of the shots filling my nose, the sound of the shots still ringing in my ears, I shook my head and put the gun away.

CHAPTER
THIRTY-THREE

Paul's funeral was held at Quantico National Cemetery. I didn't know all the intricacies of whether a felony murder compromised an honorable discharge. But Bloch talked to someone who talked to someone else and by the Friday following the shoot-out at Caldwell's boat, I was standing a few rows back from a casket with a flag draped across it. I had skipped the church service, not wanting to intrude, but felt compelled to go to the grave site. Libney Garcia was near the edge of the grave, leaning on the arm of an older woman, as they lowered the casket into the hole. She was a husk of a person, looking stunned and uncomprehending. I could only imagine how inconceivable it must seem that her son should survive four years in combat yet die at home within a few months of her husband.

Amanda was to my left, Bloch to my right. I caught sight of Chuck Rhee standing toward the back, looking slick and modern in a designer suit and wraparound shades. I nodded to him, he nodded back. About ten or twelve guys from Paul's former Marine outfit were there, some in uniform, others dressed as civilians. They were somber, straight-backed, standing close together in solidarity. Besides Bloch and Rhee, there were no police officers, no reps from MPDC. An honor guard stood well off to one side, staring into the distance, their rifles held at their sides.

The service finished quickly. The guns were fired, the tri-corner flag was given to the mother, and a bugler played "Taps" from beyond the honor guard. The small crowd began to break apart. Bloch hurried over to speak to Libney, but her face was blank and she shrugged off his condolences. The elderly woman put an arm around her shoulders and turned her away from Bloch. He returned to where I was standing, his expression pinched.

"I tried," he said.

"You did. But you can't really blame her. A husband, a son, two friends. Or former friends. All gone."

He watched them walk away. "I didn't predict a happy ending, but this . . . this has been horrific."

I grabbed his arm. There was a note in his voice I didn't like. "This isn't on you, okay? You did the best you could when no one else was doing anything. Maybe it ended up in the can, but we didn't put it there."

"Yeah," he said, but sounded unconvinced. He shook his head, then turned to look at us. "You heading back?"

I nodded. "Maybe a stopover for a drink or a coffee. Want to join us?"

"No, thanks," he said. "I have to think about this some more."

He shook my hand, nodded to Amanda, and walked toward the entrance to the cemetery. Rhee was already gone. I gave Bloch a head start, then went the same way, Amanda next to me. We picked our path around wilting flowers and headstones.

"I'm sorry about all this, Marty," she said after a moment.

"Me, too," I said. "I'd call it a waste, but that wouldn't even begin to cover it."

"What happens now? Legally, I mean."

"Who knows. There's no one left to prosecute," I said. "A bunch of cases, old and new, get closed. Arlington PD won't be too happy to have Torres's dirty laundry aired in public, but they'll be able to balance that out with the fact that two members of a notorious gang are off the streets."

"While avoiding any mention that they were shot and killed in the process."

"Well, sure," I said. "It just wasn't *their* process."

"What will happen to Bloch?"

I snorted. "He should be promoted. And he'll get public claps on the back, but internally he'll be a black sheep. Independent thinkers make the higher-ups nervous. They like the results, just not the methods."

"Like pulling in former cops to do all the legwork?"

"Something like that."

She nodded and we walked along a little further. The late May sun was hidden behind a raft of clouds, limning everything in dull gray. A cool, ugly day for a funeral. It matched my mood.

Amanda cleared her throat and said, "I got a funny phone call the other day."

"Yeah?"

"I guess your oncologist's office had kept my number as a backup contact. Someone must've mixed up the primary contact with me."

"Oh," I said, swallowing.

I could feel her eyes on me. "And they asked me what time they thought they could schedule your surgical procedure."

We took a few steps. "Yeah, well. I'm sorry about that. I didn't want you to get worried with everything that's going on, with your job hunt and all. Plus this thing with Bloch."

"Uh-huh," she said. "Want to tell me now?"

So I did. It felt good to talk it out and I realized that, if I'd been half as smart as I thought I was, I would've told her about the surgery as soon as I'd known. She asked sharp questions and said just the right things. We reached the cemetery parking lot and got in my car.

"When's the surgery?" she asked.

"As soon as I can schedule it."

"And who's going to feed Pierre while you're in the hospital?"

I opened my mouth, closed it. In typical Marty Singer fashion, I hadn't thought that far ahead. I realized I would've asked Amanda, but there was a good chance she wouldn't be here. "I . . . don't know. I guess I'll have to find someone."

She smiled. "No, you won't."

"What do you mean?"

"Austin and Chicago called back with offers, but the money was insanely bad. I mean, I never expected to get rich, but I have to eat. Baltimore was a bust all around."

"And?"

"And the clinic in DC came through. The money is enough to live on. They do wonderful work. Oh, and I hear there's a cat that needs to be fed while his owner is recovering from a successful surgery."

A grin split my face. A tight band across my chest that I didn't know was there melted away. "I don't think Pierre really has an *owner*."

"We'll see about that," she said with a grin of her own, then put her hand out. I reached over, wrapped my hand around hers, and squeezed. We drove out of the cemetery and into the day.

PLEASE CONTINUE READING TO
SAMPLE THE NEXT MARTY SINGER
MYSTERY, *ONE RIGHT THING.*

CHAPTER ONE

The billboard was colossal and would've gotten my attention, if only for a brief second, no matter what had been on it. The verdant hills and bucolic horse farms lining southern Virginia's Route 29 are cute enough for a postcard, but they go on and on and on in a mind-numbing mosaic of pastoral beauty. Anything that breaks up the monotony will catch the eye, and a sign fifty feet wide and twenty feet high, in the middle of nowhere—a nowhere called Cain's Crossing, according to the last road sign I'd passed—qualified.

But it was what I saw on the sign that caused me to glance back once, twice, and swear out loud. Unable to look away, my head swiveled, following the billboard as I passed. The semi next to me let me know that I'd drifted into his lane by laying on his air horn and I twitched the wheel to the right to keep from getting flattened, my heart in my throat. We zipped down the road at seventy, though my mind was churning faster than that. A mile passed in a blur before I found a good place for a U-turn. I raced back to the billboard, crossed at one of those turnarounds that says "Authorized Vehicles Only," and pulled off the highway at the base of the enormous metal pillar. I hunched forward in the driver's seat, my chin almost resting on the steering wheel, in order to see the whole sign.

A white man—slim, forty-something, with messy blond hair and a beard going gray—gazed out over the highway. Deep crow's-feet around dark brown eyes made him appear older than I knew he was and the beard was patchy in places, like he'd trimmed it in the dark. His mouth was open and his eyebrows slightly raised in mild surprise, as though the photo had been snapped just as he'd turned around. Next to the picture was some text. It said:

J. D. HOPE WAS MURDERED ON MAY 6TH. DO YOU KNOW WHY?

Underneath it was a phone number. Nothing else. Without taking my eyes off the sign, I pawed open my glove compartment and fumbled for my notebook and a pen. I jotted down the number, then scribbled "J. D. HOPE" beneath it and underlined the name twice. I stared at it, barely aware of the traffic hurtling past me, buffeting my car, rocking it from side to side.

I peered at the face on the billboard again. Given time, I would've recognized him, I think, but he hadn't worn a beard when I'd known him and the lines around his eyes hadn't been so deep that they gave him a permanent squint. Aggressively white teeth that I knew had to be dentures or prosthetics peeked out from the open mouth. I thought about the last time I'd seen him and a jumble of emotions welled up from some hidden place I thought I'd tucked away.

I pulled out my phone and stared at it.

Options, choices, decisions. I was a retired homicide cop with time on my hands. No job to return to, no pressing deadlines. Connections, maybe, but no real family obligations tugging me home. The journey to the heartland of south-central Virginia to visit a friend was one of the few pleasure trips I'd taken in the last year, but I was on my way back, not down; I was tired and ready to be home. I could, in good conscience, put the car in drive, point it toward Arlington, and forget

I'd ever seen the billboard. I didn't owe J. D. Hope or the people who cared for him a thing. Theoretically.

I glanced at the sign a third time. J. D. Hope continued to look back at me with the same expression of mild surprise. Perhaps at the fact that he'd been murdered. The car rocked again from a passing truck. I sat there for maybe another five minutes until, in a daze, like my fingers were working on their own, I turned on my phone and punched in the number. I raised the phone to my ear, but looked up at the billboard while it rang, as though I were calling J. D. himself. But it was a woman's voice that answered.

"Mrs. Hope?" I asked.

"No, this is Mary Beth Able," she said. "I am—I . . . was J. D.'s sister. Are you calling about the sign?"

I took a deep breath and said, "Yes, ma'am. My name is Marty Singer. Twenty years ago, I arrested your brother for murder."

Please visit www.matthew-iden.com to find out more about *One Right Thing* and the other books in the Marty Singer Mystery series.

AUTHOR'S NOTE

DC residents will recognize that I took liberties in describing some of the geography of the Metro area. Marty's oddball discovery of the buried boundary stone marking the border of Washington, DC, however, is true—though my description of the Blue Plains impoundment lot is entirely fabricated. Read about the extraordinary journey of the SE8 boundary stone at www.boundarystones.org.

The theories behind Jake Valenti's extemporaneous criminology lecture on the steps of the Seventh Street Portrait Gallery in chapter 22 are my own creation.

The National Law Enforcement Officers Memorial is a very real place of serenity and power. Located at the center of the 400 block of E Street, NW, Washington, DC, it is well worth your time to visit. Learn more at www.nleomf.org.

ACKNOWLEDGMENTS

I found many sources of inspiration, help, and education along the way to finishing *Blueblood*.

The continued love and support from my wife, Renee, makes the whole writing endeavor possible. *Blueblood*, as does all my writing, owes its existence to her.

Friends and family have been my unflagging cheerleaders and helpers. Sally Iden, Gary Iden, Kris Iden, Frank Gallivan, Carie Rothenbacher, Jeff Ziskind, Amy and Pete Talbot, David Jacobstein, and Eleonora Ibrani were all sounding boards, unstinting supporters, and readers throughout the birth of *Blueblood*. Karen Cantwell has been a wonderful colleague to work with throughout my nascent self-publishing career, never failing to give advice, pitch in on tough issues, or lend her experience.

Many thanks to Chip Cochran for sharing with me his expertise in law enforcement. His knowledge was critical in finishing the book. Any inaccuracies in a legal or law enforcement context are mine—though sometimes truth is stranger than fiction.

Officer Chuck Gallagher of the Foxboro, Massachusetts, Police Department was kind enough to give his permission to use the wonderful photograph of the inaugural MPDC badge that graces the cover of *Blueblood*. Chuck is also an encyclopedic font of knowledge on all things about the history of the MPDC. Learn more—and view his stunning collection of MPDC memorabilia—at his site, www.dcmetropolicecollector.com.

My editors Alison Dasho (née Janssen) and Michael Mandarano cleaned up what I *thought* was a brilliant first draft and have been invaluable in the process of making me a better writer. Alison and Michael, thank you.

Ambush Alley: The Most Extraordinary Battle of the Iraq War by Tim Pritchard was of great help in filling out Paul Garcia's battle experience, though the names and places have been altered. Samuel Logan's *This Is for the Mara Salvatrucha: Inside the MS-13, America's Most Violent Gang* was of enormous aid in dissecting Salvadoran gang violence in the United States and the circumstances that lead to it.

To my editor Kjersti Egerdahl and the team at Thomas & Mercer—thank you for giving me the opportunity to pursue my dream.

Finally, thank you to all the men and women who serve in law enforcement and in our military. In valor there is hope.

ABOUT THE AUTHOR

Photo © 2014 Sally Iden

Matthew Iden writes hard-boiled detective fiction, fantasy, science fiction, horror, thrillers, and contemporary literary fiction with a psychological twist. He is the author of the Marty Singer detective series:

A Reason to Live
Blueblood
One Right Thing
The Spike
The Wicked Flee

Visit www.matthew-iden.com for information on upcoming appearances, new releases, and to receive a free copy of *The Guardian: A Marty Singer Short Story*—not available anywhere else.

IF YOU LIKED *BLUEBLOOD* . . .

Writers can only survive and flourish with the help of readers. If you like what you've read, please consider reviewing *Blueblood* on Amazon. com or your favorite readers' website. Just three or four short sentences are all it takes to make a huge difference! Thank you.

STAY IN TOUCH

Please say hello via email, matt.iden@matthew-iden.com, through Facebook (www.facebook.com/matthew.iden), or Twitter (@CrimeRighter). I also enjoy connecting with readers and writers at my website, www.matthew-iden.com.